OUT OF PLACE

OUT OF PLACE
stories and poems

Edited by Ven Begamudré
and Judith Krause

Coteau Books

Book design by Shelley Sopher, Coteau Books.

Cover art © 1990 Adobe Systems Incorporated. All rights reserved. Used with permission.

Typeset by Lines and Letters.

Printed and bound in Canada.

The publisher gratefully acknowledges the financial assistance of the Saskatchewan Arts Board, the Canada Council and Multiculturalism and Citizenship Canada.

Canadian Cataloguing in Publication Data

Main entry under title:

Out of place

   (Carlyle King series ; 3)
   ISBN 1-55050-019-8

1. Canadian literature (English) – 20th century.*
2. Multiculturalism – Canada – Literary collections.*
I. Begamudré, Ven, 1956-. II. Krause, Judith, 1952-.
III. Series: The Carlyle King anthology series ; 3.

PS8251.O88 1991   C810/.8/0054   C91-097025-4
PR9194.9.O88 1991

C O T E A U   B O O K S
401– 2206 Dewdney Avenue
Regina, Saskatchewan
S4R 1H3

for Pat Krause

Contents

VEN BEGAMUDRÉ AND JUDITH KRAUSE

Preface

In revising a work of literature, it often helps to break the word *revision* into its components. RE-VISION thus means "to see again." If such works are to be enjoyable and meaningful, their creators must see them again before presenting them to an audience.

When we taught together at the Saskatchewan School of the Arts in 1987, we were impressed with the quality of work being done by younger writers, the risks they were taking, and the range of material they were exploring. Our initial idea for *Out of Place* focused on providing a forum for these new writers. But as the book evolved, its concept underwent numerous RE-VISIONS. Many of the writers whose work we had in mind chose, for whatever reason, not to submit work. We decided to concentrate on the idea of dislocation and our changing sense of place and not to restrict ourselves to any group of writers other than those who had some connection with the Prairies. We were overwhelmed by the quantity and delighted by the quality of the work we received.

In many of these stories and poems, there is a sophistication and wariness that may surprise some readers. As the world shrinks, problems often associated with other places are transplanted to become our own, and the question of who we are looms larger. But beyond the social and political implications of these stories and poems, we hope you will continue responding to them as we did: that by enjoying them, you will see again; that while seeing again—and reading again—you will enjoy.

ALBERTO MANGUEL

Introduction: Homecoming

Of all of Ulysses' adventures, none is as moving as his home-coming. The sirens, the Cyclops, the sorceress and her spells, are prodigious wonders, but the old man who weeps at the sight of the remembered shore and the dog who dies of a broken heart at the feet of his remembered master seem truer and more compelling than the marvels. Nine-tenths of the poem consists of surprise; the end is mere recognition.

We perceive the world in one of two ways: as a foreign land or as home. We are either astounded by the differences or com-forted by the similitudes between places. Wherever it is we make our home we behave either as wanderers or as travellers returned.

Until recently, my experience had always been that of the wanderer. I never lived long enough in one place to call it home—that is to say, no one landscape became the setting of my imagination. Argentina and its vicissitudes, Europe and its elephantine traditions, the South Pacific and its idyllic geo-graphy—all these places I had lived in, but they were not my place. I believe that this sense of displacement is in direct rela-tion to the sense these places have of being the navel of the world, if not the world itself. They demand full and blind allegiance, in heart and mind, and those who don't comply are, and will always be, foreigners. As in ancient Greece, the foreigner is he whose blood has not fallen on the nation's field.

In 1982 I arrived in Canada and was struck almost imme-diately by a different perception of place. Perhaps because this country was born out of a negative desire—the desire not to be an independant nation, not to be the United States of America—it has always put forward a shadowy image of itself, vast and imprecise. No lifelong requirements are needed to be Canadian; travellers passing by—Malcolm Lowry for instance—are amicably recruited, and even those who spend most of their life within its frontiers are encouraged to retain their mythical pasts. What appealed to me, however, was the fact that everything seemed to be beginning, that history had not solidified itself around everyday things, that traditions were still in the making and authority could be contested.

From abroad Canada has been perceived as a land of good savages (mainly among French novelists), as a place of redemp-tion (countless are the books in which fallen sinners find a new life in the Frozen North), as utopia (the setting for many fantastic stories; for instance, Frankenstein's monster disappears into our icy wasteland). Also as Cloudcuckooland: for the prisoners at Auschwitz, the tent in which their goods were kept was called "Canada."

Most places are, like the adventure-stops in Ulysses' travels, worlds of wonder in which we are invited to marvel at the inventiveness, the uniqueness, the power and prestige of its illustrious citizens. Invited as onlookers, not performers. In Canada, perhaps because it is considered bad form to brag, exclusivity is not exclusive. It does have, of course, as one soon discovers, its private clubs and cosy ghettoes, its undercurrents of prejudice and its own species of hatred. But overall, it appears as a welcoming place, a place to which you return even though you may never have been here before. Even to a stranger, it becomes in no time at all, as familiar as Ithaca.

The worst aspect of exile is that distance, in time and space, drains a place from our memory. That which remains in our thoughts no longer exists on firm ground: it grows, it changes without us. There is no escape from this, except to construct, like Robinson Crusoe, an icon of that place elsewhere. In Canada such constructions are easy—or easier than in much of the rest of the world in which the task is merely impossible. My Canadian exile smacks of homecoming.

BRENDA BAKER

This Is Exactly the Kind of Thing
Her Parents Have Been Warning Her About
Since She Was a Child

This is exactly the kind of thing
her parents have been warning her about
since she was a child.

Riding with a stranger
on a motorcycle.

And if he should slip right now, leave their bodies scraped over
one another on the highway, it would be quite a mystery

> how she came to be in his company in the first place

> what she was doing without her luggage halfway between
> Cannes and Antibes at 4:30 in the morning

> why she was seen late the night before on the bow of a filthy
> rich Arab's yacht in the port of Antibes

She has always believed her death would be a logical conclusion,
and now the possibility of its mystery exhilarates her. Even
terrifies her, a little.

He likes his women a little terrified and goes faster, sliding the
wheels side to side, riding the back of some enormous snake. He
gets the desired response. Tighter. Closer.

She believes she would never sleep with a man like this one, yet
holding him this way is a oneness much like orgasm's melting
clutch.
 The sun below the horizon is white, whitens the sky. As they
drive toward Antibes she takes in the ocean, eyes blink and water
in the wind. *There* she yells. *Look. That's what my home looks like.*
Mediterranean prairie.

God, he loves this but he can never go fast enough. He will
probably die of speed either now or one day. He feels her arms
strapped around his chest tighten, her thighs press harder against
him. Faster. He hears her yell something like *That's what my home
looks like.* Flat as the ocean. Really.

He remembers the rose he bought her last night. She had reminded him of the girl he once lived with in Belfast, and now he knows that this girl's grandparents on both sides were originally from Ireland and that, other than her looks, she is not one bit like his former lover. But what the hell. He thinks about taking her to his tent. The logistics. Timing. He's got a job in Nice at three. With his luck she'll be the kind to keep him awake with talk or rolling in her sleep.

Her heart is slower. Now she is accustomed to the wind buzzing against her skin. She thinks about

> the muscles in his young, strong arms, his shoulders
>
> how easily she is sucked in by charm (the adorable accent, the yellow rose)
>
> how much he looks like her uncle (the familiar Irish nose, mischievous eyes)
>
> his absolute gentleness when he finally kissed her, slow-dancing on the boat
>
> how at that moment it came into her head to ask him if he had ever killed anyone during his service, but it seemed in-appropriate to discuss anti-terrorist tactics while kissing, so she didn't ask

They swerve out to pass a car. Their legs almost touch the tarmac. Her heart reaches into her wrists and knees.

Antibes is just in sight. Which exit should he take when he gets there? Should he ask her first or just arrive at the trailer park? He reviews his situation:

> she looks like someone he once loved, which is to say he likes the way she looks
>
> she hasn't tried anything, but then neither has he
>
> she must be adventurous, else why would she travel alone, and why would she have gone to the yacht with him and his friends
>
> she's a nice girl but a smart ass who plays (or maybe is) hard to get,
>
> > gave him a hard time at the pub in front of his buddies by sending the flower girl back to return the rose with a note

saying *If you really want to impress me send over a dozen. Red please. And a bottle of wine. Same colour.*

and when he told her he was a bodyguard she said *Oh yeah, so'd you go to university for that or what?* and he told her *No, spent six years with the RUC* and she'd never heard of it so he explained *The Royal Ulster Constabulary, the anti-IRA police* and she still didn't believe him and said *So just who do you bodyguard then?* and he replied *Sammy Davis Junior, Roger Moore, did Madonna in Rome a few weeks ago and yesterday some oil tycoon from Egypt* and she just laughed so he showed her his card and the tip from the Egyptian (five crisp American hundred dollar bills) and she stopped laughing

she'll probably want to ask him more about the Troubles and he isn't in the mood for it

he doesn't like the way she says things like *What's going on in Ireland seems so silly. Where I live Catholics and Protestants get along just fine* and these words from a girl who had to ask *Would being an anti-terrorist make you a Catholic or a Protestant?* a question which immediately irritated him, though at the same time he found her naivety refreshing. She went on *I mean it doesn't matter to me what you are, although I have to admit the Pope's attitude to women and birth control really bugs me.* Then he'd said *So you're Protestant, too* and asked her more about her Irish roots, about which she appeared to know little. *My grandfathers were both farmers and I remember my mom saying something about her dad being an Orange guy or whatever* and he raised his eyebrows and said with a slight smile *You don't even know what an Orangeman is, do you?*

The exits are still a ways off. He can't make up his mind. He sees her breasts in his hands. Flicks the accelerator. Sparks fly through the motorcycle.

The bike's sudden surge creates a mildly pleasurable pressure on her tailbone. She feels small and weightless flying behind him. An image comes to mind, something she'd forgotten till now. Two young men standing outside the Turkish Embassy in Amsterdam. She'd seen them last week when she was lost on a sidestreet. They appeared out of nowhere and stood just yards away. Large, handsome Caucasians in expensive-looking suits. Brandishing what appeared to be machine guns. Their sunglasses glinted while they surveyed the quiet neighbourhood with guns erect. Two limos (one black, one white) pulled up to the embassy door, four men got into the black one, and the gunmen backed themselves into the other while looking in all directions and pulling their guns into the car last before speeding away. Aside from cop shows, she'd never seen anything like it. At home, the closest she'd come was walking by a dumpy-looking Brinks truck guy, outside a bank, his hand resting gently on a little hip holster.

Now it strikes her the man she's holding onto must occasionally do the same kind of work as the men she'd seen in Amsterdam. She wants to know what it feels like to be poised to kill like that. How it feels to be a target. Whether a five hundred dollar tip covers it.

She can just make out the big hotel near the boat. Perhaps the sailor who invited half the Brits in the pub to party on his boss's yacht is still passed out, with every speaker from one end to the other still blaring "Born in the USA." When they get to the boat she'll ask him about pointing guns at people. Maybe. Maybe not. But she's curious. She's never met anyone, at least not of her own generation, who's been in any kind of war. Or maybe she'll provoke him and say *What if I lied to you about my religion? What if it turned out I was Catholic? What then?* and just see what happens.

He's going as fast as even he dares go. He can feel she has released her grip. He jerks the machine suddenly to the left and her fingers dig under his rib cage. He feels her heart pound against his back.

She almost wets her pants. She feels him laughing, the creep. She squeezes him tighter than ever and closes her eyes. She imagines home. Sees her mother and father sitting on the couch watching "Hockey Night in Canada." On the floor in front of them is a toddler, herself. She is playing with something, a pair of scissors. She puts them in her mouth and her father shouts *Don't do that. You'll hurt yourself.* Her mother slaps her hand and takes them away. The child cries.

It would be about noonhour in Saskatoon right now. Her father, home after a busy morning at the store, will be at the kitchen table going through the mail, probably looking for her letter. Her mother is serving the soup. Suddenly she wants to phone them, to tell them she's safe. Perhaps even tell them she's met an interesting man.

She envisions returning home with her bodyguard in tow, a suitcase in his one hand, machine gun in the other. How would they compare him to her ex-boyfriends: the med student, the accountant, the engineer, the high school principal?

He wishes she was his old girlfriend. He didn't own a bike back then, and now he wants to feel her around him. Not this one. He conjures his favourite memory of her, naked in the dark, bending over to turn up the fire, face and breasts outlined by its pink light. The last time he missed her like this was Rome, at the reception. It was a small one. They could relax while Madonna was chatted up by the Italian elite. He and the other guys ordered virgin drinks and watched the millionaires and billionaires waltz around them, sometimes giving them polite smiles. The tuxedos made the bodyguards acceptable, but it didn't camouflage their real status. For a moment he wanted her to be with him to see the spectacle, witness who he rubs shoulders with now. And then he just wanted to be back in their flat, the kettle whistling at them to make the tea.

She makes a mental note to herself: when she sees her parents she'll ask about her grandfather the Orangeman. She wants to understand why he seemed to be amused by that bit of her history. She hates looking ignorant. Then she remembers how he insisted Canada was just another US state. She is consoled by his own blatant ignorance.

He steers with one hand and places his other on hers, clasped at his belly. Rubs her cold fingers with his warm palm, then lifts his jacket just enough to allow her hands to slide underneath. He's thinking about how she got so upset with him when he teased her about being a Yank. *After all* he said *you talk like one. Dress like one.* He refrained from saying she was as aggressive as any American girl he'd ever met, a quality he found entertaining but disconcerting.
   He knows he has a knack for picking up the ardent ones, the ones impressed by the glamour that goes along with his work. And he has a lot of them to choose from. Girls, and women too, from all over the world. Although it's discouraged by the agency, he meets some of them through his job, since most VIPs bring an entourage which might include a secretary, or two, a manager, maybe a hairdresser, or even, with any luck, a fitness coach. Some he meets because the agency is based in Nice and the Riviera is always thick with girls who are more than a little willing to parade their smooth ochre legs and bare breasts along the beach. On first meeting, he is most attracted to the flamboyant types, those with

a sense of humour. In the long run they're also the ones who satisfy him least. He'd made a sincere effort to stay with one of these women, a fashion boutique owner in Nice, for more than a month. But she soon became critical of the fact that he frequently carried a gun. And she began to make biting comments about his having to occasionally "discourage" the odd individual from being a nuisance to the person he was guarding. The relationship ended when he called her a two-faced bitch, because she always seemed to forget how he earned his money whenever he bought her a beautiful gift or took her to Nice's most exclusive restaurants.

He looks out at the sea. The sky is so clear. Compared to the oppressive sky of Belfast, this one offers him such infinite space. Possibilities are limitless. That's what he remembers thinking the first time he saw the Mediterranean almost a year ago. The possibilities are limitless. When the woman who owns his agency came to Belfast to scout out new talent, as she called it, she promised he wouldn't want to return to Ulster if he came to work for her. She was bang on.

By that time he was pretty sure his lover had left him for good. But still, every so often, he replays their last conversation

how he was so afraid to ring her and waited for months, hoping she would change her mind on her own and call him

the way he worded his opening lines when he finally phoned her: *I got a great job in France. A very prestigious company. They say it's so gorgeous there I won't ever want to come back.*

how he waited for her to sound even mildly interested before asking *Will you come over? Join me there?*

The disdain in her voice when she refused, saying *Your being a bodyguard instead of working for the police won't make things much better for us.*

the anger when he shouted back at her *For Christ's sake, it's what I do. It's what they trained me for. It's what I'm good at. And what's more, I like it. Even the shitty stuff that happens. It's okay.*

how when he hung up he could not believe he'd just been talking to the same little girl he'd brought to Belfast six years earlier. The same one who'd attached herself to his side from the first day they met at a party in their hometown. The one who loved him so well, looked after him so well, in whose eyes he could do no wrong.

A flesh coloured veil has dropped across the sky. The sun pokes up from behind the sea. She draws a grain elevator on the horizon. It almost works, the sea as field. It reminds her of a mural in the campus bar at home. A simplified Saskatchewan landscape. The bar is filled with young men and women whose eyes scan the room every thirty seconds. Most of the women are well-dressed, attractive and laugh boisterously. Most of the men are cocky, self-assured, flirtatious. Over Top Forty tunes, everyone talks loudly about

> how hard they studied that night
>
> the newest computer programs
>
> the waitress whose clothes are painted on
>
> the NHL, NFL, WHL, etc.
>
> beer and parties
>
> where the best Masters programs are
>
> fashion
>
> who got interviews with which firms
>
> what they will buy once the loans are paid off
>
> moving out of their parents' homes
>
> and occasionally sex, politics or religion

It's a Friday night, and she's nineteen. She and her friends are into the Schloss again, past the point of worrying about how she's going to explain her hangover this time, and hoping if she throws up it will be before she gets home. If she's discovered she'll be grounded forever. For her own good.

He can't get the snap at the neck of his jacket fastened. He just bought it a few days ago, and it doesn't work for him yet. Can't find the pockets easily. Has to look down to do it up. It cost nearly four hundred quid but now he's glad he opted for leather. Besides, he looks good in it. He thinks about the next trip home. He'll wear it to the pub. He'll walk around town. Maybe he'll run into her. Maybe he'll ring her up, go for a pint. She'll see how good he's looking. How well he's doing.

Yes, he would take the jacket with him if it weren't for his dad being on the dole again. Ever since they were both let go from the factory, his father has been unable to find a full-time job. When he joined the RUC, he began sending his father generous cheques. And his dad boasted to the neighbours: not only was his lad protecting the rights of good Protestants, he was making more money in a few months than most people see at the factories in a year. Despite leaving school at sixteen. His dad was embarrassingly proud of him, but the last time he arrived home, dressed in a chic Italian suit, with posh gifts and photos of himself and his bodyguard friends posed with movie stars, there was a distinct tension between him and his father. And he changed the subject whenever his father asked *When are you coming home?*

When are you coming home? She hears the words as clearly as the day she told them she'd be in Europe for the whole summer. Not *That'll be a good experience* or *You need the break;* just *When are you coming home?* She shouldn't have been surprised by it. They never had any desire to travel anywhere but Banff to see the Rockies, or Toronto to see her aunt and uncle. Once when they left Toronto for home, they took a detour to Niagara Falls, but otherwise they drove straight through to Saskatoon and only stopped to rest at motels.

She wants them to get used to the idea of her not living in the same city. She applied for jobs in Alberta and Manitoba. She figures she'll be able to move by next spring.

She used to hate her parents. There was

the night one of the most popular boys at school took her out to a movie. She was seventeen, he was eighteen. And she got home three hours after curfew, so they phoned his parents the next day, her mother at first politely expressing concern, her father taking the phone and eventually blasting *I am not over-reacting. I just happen to care what people think of my daughter's behaviour. Necking in some young fellow's car in front of our house at three in the morning is simply unacceptable. Your son should be reprimanded too.*

the time they grounded her in first-year university because she failed two mid-terms, and how she just let her friends think she was buckling down on her studies when they saw her only during classes

the day they helped her move into her first apartment, a ratty little basement suite. The look of disapproval on their faces when they walked in and said *Why don't you wait until you find a job, get a nicer place. We'll pay your first month's rent.*

the autumn morning when she left for campus in the car they'd bought for her and, instead of turning left on College, she turned right and drove until she ran out of gas on a gravel road in the middle of some field three hours from town, stripped down to her undies, stretched out in the sun and stared up at a clear blue sky for most of the afternoon (plotting her escape, imagining a life without them) until a farmer noticed her car and stopped to see what was going on

And now, six years since she lay in that field, she sometimes thinks she loves her parents too much. She sees her mother's body changing shape, her spine growing more rounded, while her father's skin becomes translucent, hair and beard silvery white.

In recent years she has not been able to find it in herself to say *No*. She's lost her strength to rebel. She still disagrees with them on just about everything, and would rather they not write her into their plans without consulting her, but she cannot tell them so. She wants some days to scream *No, no, no, no, NO* but she understands now how much power she has over them, how easily she could cut open the delicate membrane that contains who they really are. She loves them too much.

He regrets the way he lied to her last night. *I'd live there again. Sure. I'll be going back* and then almost too adamantly *I love Ulster. It's a beautiful country.* Perhaps he was simply hurt by her comment about what she'd seen of Ulster on TV: *To me it seems like such a depressing way to live.* And he could not admit she was right. That living there is like having some kind of sickness, a bug that gets into the water source and you have no choice, everybody's got to drink it down and live with the consequences, and most don't even know they're sick because they don't know what the water is supposed to taste like. Maybe he'll tell her this when they get there. Maybe it'll feel good to say it out loud. *I'm not going back. I am one of the lucky ones, the escapees, and I never have to live there again.* He pictures the girl he loves, feels his arms around her waist and, for the first time, he is certain not even she could pull him back to his home.

Once she moves, that'll be it. She'll visit them on holidays. Occasional weekends. She'll work at letting go of the guilt. She's already forgotten how the argument started. She only remembers it began over something small, and it happened shortly after she moved out. She wants to forget

what she said to them

how the words colour everything she says to them now

the looks on their faces

the nausea she felt when it was out: *Stop telling me what to do. Just stop it. What the hell does it matter what you think. You keep telling me what's right and what's wrong and now I want to know what makes you think you know what's best for me. Based on what? What? All that stuff you learned reading purchase orders? Playing bridge? Or maybe it was the church. We went at least once a year. Or maybe you're wise from all that international travel you did. Stop telling me what to do. Why should I listen to such dull, ignorant people?*

the way her mother cried

the sound of her father's voice, yelling over her own *Stop it. Just stop it.*

She wants to forget she discovered the sword children may choose to wield over their parents.

He throws his head back. Closes his eyes. Lets the wind rush up his nostrils. Fills his lungs with cool air. Now he wants her. He wants to cover her with his body. She is so small he could hide her completely under him, as he could with his old girlfriend. That's how he used to have to comfort her. Make her snug, warm under him and say *Look, look, I'm home now, I'm sorry I didn't call, you know there's no way I could have and it wasn't as bad as the news reported.* He thought she'd get used to it. But over the years she grew more and more distraught whenever he was late getting home. The night he made the mistake of taking a short-cut through a Catholic area, took a beating and didn't get home at all, the only thing he wanted was for her not to see him in the hospital. The last straw came a year later when he announced he'd be getting a substantial raise. He'd been assigned to the E4A. *We'll put the extra toward that fancy wedding you want,* he told her.

They pass the exit sign for Grasse. The one for the trailer park is seven or eight minutes away. He turns his head to her. *How are you doing?*

Okay she yells. *Do we have to go so fast?* She waits for an answer. The bike slows down for a few seconds, then revs up to speed again, slows down, speeds up, down, up, down, up. *Stop it* and she pinches him. She decides he is definitely immature and scolds herself for having hooked up with a younger man in the first place. What is she doing here anyway? Why does she do these things? What if she did die right now? What then?

She can see them all at her funeral, shaking their heads and saying

what's a thirty-year-old woman doing behaving like a teenager?

such a waste of life

I hear she was with an Irish man she met in a bar

she should have known better, riding a motorcycle like that, with a stranger

She dismisses the comments at her funeral. They were not here last night, she thinks. They don't know anything. They didn't see

how he looked at her the first time their eyes met

how he continued to observe her, as if he was searching for something

the way he reached out to run a finger along her eyebrow, down her cheek to her lips, to hear him say *You are so beautiful*

his giving her his jacket in the chilly night and wrapping himself around her till she was warm

her laughing at him leaping around the huge master bedroom on the yacht, with him excited as a kid with a new toy, saying *Isn't this great? Can you believe the bathroom's got gold taps? Look at this* as he knocked on the headboard of the bed *I would bet this is mahogany. Fuckin' unbelievable. I've been on a few yachts but this one beats all.*

how he jumped onto the bed beside her and said *Let's run off together. Let's just get on my bike and drive. You don't really want to go back to Canada anyway. Teaching must be so boring. You can stay and I'll get rich on tips from oil tycoons and movie stars. I'll buy us a yacht just like this one.* And they laughed and played out roles of rich and famous people until he said *Would you marry a poor man?* and when she asked *Why?* he said *Just curious.*

But there are her parents, in black, and they're saying *We told her about taking rides with strangers, about motorcycles* and they begin to blame themselves forever for the death of their only child. For not getting through to her. For not making her understand how just one indiscretion can lead to such horror.

Stop. This is stupid. Nothing's going to happen. If it ends this way it will be somewhere else, some other time, when she least expects it. Perhaps this is how it feels to be a target. Continually telling yourself if you're going to die it will be some other day. To walk in a uniform through Belfast streets and know there are people out there who see you with an X drawn between your eyes, another one over your heart. Or standing outside some embassy and you know one day you're actually going to fire that gun and you can't even tell yourself not to worry, It'll happen when you least expect it 'cause you've got to expect it all the time. And you don't even consider what'll happen if you're just wounded, 'cause you know they're going to shoot at you more than once if they get the chance to shoot at all. The trick must be to see them before they see you, with that X between your eyes.

He feels her lay her head, her cheek, against his spine, then her hands slipping under his T-shirt. A sudden warmth spreads through him. No arousal, just a warm sense of déjà-vu. He racks his brain. What is this? When has he felt this before?

She slides her hands over the small smooth fold of skin where his waist creases, then up to his chest. Her hands are almost too hot now. The image of her parents dressed in black will not go away. They tumble into an old picture, the three of them in the kitchen. Everyone is yelling. She is twenty-four and in love. Last night she took a chance and stayed at her boyfriend's. *How could you not let us know you were okay? You could have been lying dead in a ditch for all we knew* and later they're all in tears and her dad says so quietly *We just ask that you understand: our greatest fear is that you could die before we do.*

Now it strikes her this guy's parents must share the same fear. But, in his case, they will have so many other things to blame besides themselves.

It has come to him. He fights back the images his déjà-vu has triggered. They appear in the same order as always, without sound

a grey figure moves in the window of a small shed in a field

the figure moves into his sight, then crumples somewhere beneath the window ledge

splinters, popping from the surface of the shed door, match the rhythm of the gun banging against his gut two bodies strewn on the shed floor

the back of the boy's head, a piece of his skull blown off, hair dripping blood

the boy's face: soft, dark hairs over his lip clearly defined by the sunlight streaming through the window

the three useless, rusty old rifles, unabashedly set along the wall

the faces of the rest of the E4A once they realized what they had done

And that night in bed he turned away from her to cry, but she pressed herself, the side of her face, tight against his back. Stroked his body. Tried to push the trembling out of his muscles. And even though they had known for some time she would be leaving him, she still said *It'll be all right. You'll be okay. I love you. I love you.*

A man, a woman, and a dog are running on the beach. She lifts her head to check where they're at. The boat masts seem a tangled mess in the harbour. They come to the first stop light. She's surprised at the number of cars on the street at this hour. In a minute or so they'll be at the yacht.

For the last while he has been driving slowly and now she is quite comfortable cuddled up to him like this. She wonders what would have happened if she hadn't insisted they turn back at Cannes. How far would he have taken her? Maybe she'll suggest they find a place on the boat and lay down in each other's arms. Just get some sleep. As they approach the piers, she wonders what he's thinking. What he's expecting.

She can't believe that next Monday she'll be standing in front of a new class of grade twelves, trying to explain to them why they need to learn geo-trig. She'll look across the room at indifferent faces, the girls with their first-day-back outfits and strategically applied make-up, the boys, in their casual but usually trendy attire, beginning to look more like men than boys. Some students are just back from Californian vacations, or trips to visit their relatives. Some have been working at the golf course, or at MacDonald's, or some department store. Others spent the days lying in the sun, the nights cruising Eighth Street.

She'll give the usual introductory spiel about how it may seem like a useless class at first, but in the end they'll thank her for it. She'll tell them to look at her not as a teacher, but as a guardian angel who wants to prepare them for life in the real world of job markets and pay cheques. Then she'll pick up the chalk and begin writing out rudimentary definitions

> geometry: science of properties and relations of lines, surfaces and solids

> trigonometry: branch of mathematics dealing with relations of sides and angles of triangles, and with relevant functions of any angles

> logarithm: one of a series of arithmetic exponents tabulated to simplify computation by making it possible to use addition and subtraction instead of multiplication and division

And under the soft scrape of the chalk, the humming of a motor will grow and fill her head. She'll feel her heartbeat quicken with each dip and turn of the bike. She'll feel his lips brush against her neck. She'll be in his arms again, inventing questions she will not ask.

ANNE SZUMIGALSKI

The Margin

One morning in late spring a young woman wakens alone on a strange shore. When she sits up and looks about her she sees that she has been sleeping in the sheltered hollow between two sandhills. All around her the low dunes are spread with patches of seaholly and spike grass. Because it is not yet summer the grass is still sharply green and the holly's glaucous leaves are still pliant in their papery bracts.

She gets to her feet and looks eastward. At first all she can see is endless quilted sand, but when she shades her eyes and looks into the sun she can just make out a narrow strip of ocean glittering in the brilliant light. It is as though the sea were a snail which has felt the land's thrust as the prod of a finger, and has shrunk back immediately into its shell of pearly sky and distance.

The woman has no idea where she has come from. All she knows is that the journey took many days, weeks perhaps, even a month. She has travelled from a great city in another country but has forgotten the name of that place, the names of her companions, even her own name. She is ragged and travel-weary, but happier than she has ever dreamt of being.

> *My hands are fishes*
> *Loosed from the angler's barb,*

she sings clearly in a language she has never heard before,

> *My feet are otters*
> *Sprung from the trap.*

Sometime later, she tells herself, she may bring to mind that other place, those other people, that other language. But for now she is content to wander on the beach foraging for food and naming everything she sees in the new words which come so freely to her tongue.

ARCHIBALD J. CRAIL

The New Man

In my ninth year he came. We never saw him arriving, though. One morning he was just there, the young man of the twenty-odd summers with his laughing blue eyes and the blond hair of the Hongkoiqua, the smooth-haired ones, who walked as if he had no cares. With the early morning sun behind him, his body cast a long, thin shadow over the whitewashed farmhouse. Only when he turned to answer our greetings did I see that he was of average height. For a very brief instant, the sunlight gleamed and sparkled on his boots and coat buttons. Perhaps it was his military past which gave him his air of purpose. These were my first impressions of Jean du Plessis.

When he arrived on this farm, his presence held so much promise. In this land where the Hongkoiqua rule as absolute masters and our existence depends on their benevolence, he gave us a different view of life. Maybe he should have been a stronger man and perhaps then his compassion would not have been his weakness. But if he had been stronger, maybe there would have been no difference between him and the other white men.

There had been many other white men with blue eyes and blond hair who had come this way. Some worked for six months and others a year or so in the vineyards. Ultimately they always left for the interior. The promise of wealth inland was too strong an attraction, so they left this place for the gold fields and diamond mines. The temporary sojourn on this wine farm was only a chance to raise enough money for that journey inland. Most of them had arrived penniless at Cape Town.

These white men would, in their broken Dutch and attempts at the Khoikhoi language, speak of war and rumours of war. That seemed to be the sum total of their lives in countries called Prussia, Luxembourg, Flanders and so on. To me these places were merely names, but from the light in their eyes, I could see that to the Hongkoiqua they were places of much suffering and death. Until Jean du Plessis came, I never knew what white men thought; only what they remembered and what work needed to be done. But Jean took the time to explain that farm-workers in his home country were no better off than us in South Africa. When I told him I always thought white men were bred in Europe to be bosses in my land, he said it wasn't so. "There are rich and poor everywhere," he answered, "but that is no reason for people to suffer. Things can be changed."

16

He himself didn't come here to be a boss. He came to work and was made a boss.

Sometimes the Dutch East India Company would send young white girls from an orphanage in Europe. They never lasted very long either. Indentured to become wives of the colonists, their job was to learn the elements of housekeeping. Jasmina, the cook, had the job of training these youngsters. She never got much training done, because at these times the old baas would always hang around the kitchen and wait for a chance to rape the girls. I suppose a second white woman, even a child of twelve, was too much for him to resist. Needless to say, it was always his wife, the old nooi, who chased the girls off the farm afterwards.

After a week of working under Jean, I started getting comfortable with his presence. I learnt he was a man of few words, not because he couldn't speak our tongue but that this was his nature. Instead of overseeing our work, he'd more often join us in cutting and pruning the vines.

The oubaas didn't like this at all.

"Well, Jean," the oubaas said one day. "You sure have a knack for these pruning shears. Which part of France are you from again?"

"Alsace, Monsieur. My family, they lost all in the war."

"And how did you escape?"

"I, Monsieur, I just ran and walked until I came to the mer at Marseilles."

There was a moment's silence between them. I collected a bundle of cuttings and took it to the end of the row of vines. When I got back, the oubaas was just getting ready to leave.

"Life is hard, Jean, and you're a very good worker. But I want you to be firm with my workers. Be friendly, but be firm. A white man will not survive in this country if he doesn't show strength and character. You understand me?"

"Oui, Monsieur."

I suppose in any society where there is peace and justice, Jean would have had no problem adapting himself to fit the ways of the people. At peace with himself and those around him, he seemed content with merely being alive. Ours was a society of neither peace nor justice, and he should never have come here.

One day, after the second daily wine rations had been dished out, Jean followed us to the labourers' compound. From a few chimneys, thin wisps of blue-white smoke were already spiralling toward the pale blue heavens while a few women were still chopping kindling in preparation for supper. In an attempt at friendliness, small baas Jean started sharing his tobacco with the men scattered about the yard. I left the company of the men to do my chores but couldn't help overhearing part of a conversation between Piet and Willem.

"Why is this white man always hanging around us?" Piet asked.

"Don't you like his tobacco?" Willem replied.

"That's not the point. I can't look at the face of my baas for so long in the day."

"Well, the man seems honest enough. But you know the honkey from overseas. They always start out this way. Soon enough he'll change his ways and know his place."

But things didn't change. After a month, we noticed Jean's eyes kept following Lena wherever she went.

My sister was not the most beautiful of women. At fifteen years of age, she was so angular and thin you could tie a shoe-string around her waist. But in her walk and movement there was a catlike, easy grace which reflected an air of freedom. Everything she did had a musical quality to it. When picking potatoes, her long fingers would move swiftly from one potato to the other while her back remained bent, and she never raised her head until she had to move her feet. Then there was the liquid-smooth movement of foot, leg, thigh and hip to the next row. All this came as unconsciously as her breathing.

Of all the workers on this farm, the kitchen helpers seemed to think they had a monopoly on the white man's language. In the company of the white woman and her children for most of the day, they'd afterward in the labourers' compound mimic every accent and tone and think themselves better than other blacks. My sister Lena also used to work in the kitchen, but she never changed her ways. Although, like us, she spoke Afrikaans with the rhythm, idiom and accent of our own Khoikhoi language, her voice had a soft, melodious quality like a rippling brook in the forest. None of this Boer Afrikaans, affected by the kitchen help, would ever come from her mouth. Even when she cursed and swore, there was a sweet quality to her voice. Of course the men went crazy for her. Then she behaved as if none of them were good enough. I was often bribed with a lump of sugar, a bit of beef jerky or some toy just to carry messages to her.

Well, Jean wouldn't have had any difficulty in getting a pretty woman from his own race. At first he merely looked at Lena. Later he reserved the easiest work for her in the barn. Then he always went in with her to count crates, sweep the floor, or do one of the many small jobs nobody else had time for.

I once sneaked up on them. Through a crack in the woodwork, I saw Lena counting hessian bags and deftly piling them in neat bundles. Farther on my left, the small baas repaired some piece of machinery. Every now and then he'd take a peek in her direction. She seemed to ignore him completely. A few times he cleared his throat as if to say something, looked in her direction and, receiving no response, resumed his tinkering. I left the peephole feeling sorry for the shy man.

One evening I overheard Ma and Lena discussing him.

"Ma, I don't like the way this white man is looking at me."

"Yes, my child. Just stay out of his way and do your work."

"I am doing my work, Ma. But he's always sending me to the barn and then he follows me."

"Yes, my child."

"Ma, he's not like other men. What I mean to say is that he says nothing but just hangs around. And then there's Willem, Ma."

"Yes, my child."

"Ma, what I'm trying to say is that Willem has asked for homerights to come and visit and I don't know what the white man has in mind. I don't want a child from a white man, Ma. They all just up and leave you."

"Just leave it to me, Leentjie."

The following afternoon, I went with Ma to the small baas's room in the oubaas's backyard. Ma stopped a little distance from his door and sent me to call Jean. He emerged with a happy look on his face and gave me a farthing for my efforts. Ma was wringing her hands when we got to her.

"Small baas, I only want to speak padlangs straight. My child does not know how she has it with the small baas. It has now been a considerable time that my child has been so uneasy."

"I hear you, Toekoe."

"Small baas, my child is still very young and if things cannot improve, I will have to send her to another relative on some other farm."

He straightened his shoulders and took both of Ma's hands in his own. "I did not mean any harm, Toekoe. How can the child think such things of me? Why didn't she speak to me herself? She's such a sweet and kind-hearted person and I was only trying to be helpful. She seems a fragile person and I didn't want to overburden her. Please tell her that I'd like to speak to her myself."

I could almost see his mind at work. This occasion had given him the chance to say to Lena all the things he had so long carried inside himself. Besides, it wasn't as if he was forcing her into anything. Ma would be sending Lena to him. In parting, he went to get a pail of rice and some sugar from his room and gave it to Ma. She was pleased.

"Now you see what I have to put up with for you two?" she said to me on the way home. "I have to be both mother and father. Hopefully you'll appreciate it one day."

"Yes, Ma," I replied.

Whatever ill feeling she might have had against the white man was now absolved by the gifts. When Lena came home from work, Ma told her to return the empty pail and hear what baas Jean had to say.

Lena refused. "But Ma, surely Jonah can take it back? I don't want to talk to that man."

I immediately protested that I still had to feed the chickens. Seeing this man twice in one day was too much for me. He always gave me something and I had nothing with which to reciprocate. Once I took him two gold-spotted finch eggs and he angrily told me to replace them in the nest. I learnt then that he had a great reverence for life and also that, as a poor person, I could give him only my friendship. I refused to listen to Lena's excuses and went off to do my chores.

When I returned I found that she had gone after all. Later in the evening she returned. She was very quiet and answered Ma in a subdued voice.

"Did you see the white man?"

"Yes'm."

"What did he say?"

"Oh, nothing really."

"And what took you so long?"

"Oh he just wanted to talk."

Ma was getting ready for bed. "Well, I hope that has put an end to your fretting and worries. Goodnight."

"Night, Ma."

Afterward Lena sat at the kitchen table for a long time, drawing lines with her thumbnail in the open grain pine top.

In the weeks and months that followed, my sister grew plumper and stronger. There was a noticeable swelling in her stomach and the other girls started teasing her about "carrying a white man's child." At first she denied she had anything to do with small baas

20

Jean. As her stomach became bigger, she told them it was none of their business.

Now there was meat in the house every day. Ma accepted the meat, flour, coffee and sugar gratefully from small baas Jean. To Lena she was alternately abusive and consoling. "How could you allow yourself this? My own child pregnant with the seed of the Hongkoiqua. The honkey will flee like all the others."

"No, Ma," Lena pleaded. "The man promised he will marry me."

"Marry you? No way will he marry you. Just you mark my words."

In the evenings, she spread buchu powder over Lena's feet and in the old language prayed for a safe delivery.

Lunchtimes and evenings, my sister and her lover became inseparable. Sometimes I'd catch them sitting quietly side by side in the shade of an oak tree. Not a word would pass between them. Being in love was enough.

There was great joy in our house when the child was born. All the women came to see the blue-eyed child whose father had not deserted him. When finally Jean came, it took much prodding and insistence from Ma to get him to bury the afterbirth in the backyard as is the custom with our people. They don't have such customs with the Hongkoiqua but, since he stayed, Ma said he must learn to share the responsibility with the pleasure.

It was just before harvest, when the child was about one year old, that his father asked the oubaas for a special request. I remember the morning very well. The air was crisp and clean and a light frost covered every blade of grass in a silvery white sheet. If the frost came too early, a whole crop of grapes could be destroyed. Now that the grapes were already ripe, the frost merely increased the sugar content. This made the oubaas very happy. When he was happy, all of us were overjoyed.

On this morning small baas Jean asked the oubaas if Lena could move into his living quarters with him. He explained self-consciously that they had been going out for such a long time that they wanted nothing else but to be together. It sounded such a beautiful request that I stopped loading the wine wagon and watched him talking with much gesturing where the words failed to come.

Of course I had already seen this coming for a long time. It was almost as if he was part of our family now. Except on rare occasions, I hardly called him "small baas." He was more like an older brother to me and I called him by his first name. This upset quite a few people but he didn't care. I was his "mon ami." At home, Lena washed and mended his clothes like a married woman would. On Sundays he'd even eat over at our house.

Most of his free time was spent at our place playing with the child or telling Ma stories from the old country. At other times he'd tell us about the wonderful plans he had for Lena and his child. How he was going to build a house with many windows, a house which would be bigger than any of us had ever seen. There'd be separate bedrooms for him and Lena, special rooms for eating and dancing, and a parlour where she'd be able to receive her guests just like the rich people in his country. I wanted to ask him what a "parlour" was but Ma cut me short with a hard stare. Quite obviously she enjoyed hearing Jean speak as much as I did and wanted no interruptions. Lena, on the other hand, had no time for idle talk. She'd invariably be busy puttering around the kitchen and, if there wasn't any work to do inside the house, she'd keep herself busy in the garden. Once he mentioned wistfully that he'd like to show his child to his relatives overseas. However, he never once said how he was going to make the money for all these fanciful plans.

This question of their living together seemed such an innocent, small thing that I thought the oubaas would readily agree. After all, Jean was a model overseer. There were hardly any problems with any of the farm-workers. All the work was done on time and there was nothing the old baas could complain about. His ferocious attack came as a total surprise.

"I've been watching you for the past year, Frenchman!" he shouted in his hoarse, wheezy little voice. "I've been watching you! All around people are talking about you and this Hotnot meid."

"But, Monsieur . . ." Jean answered. He looked so embarrassed, he did not know what to do with his dexterous, capable hands. "Please, Monsieur."

"Don't Monsieur me!" the oubaas retorted. "And be quiet while I'm speaking!"

"Oui, Monsieur," Jean answered meekly. He clasped and unclasped his hands behind his back.

"Now listen to me. You're a good and honest worker." The oubaas suddenly became aware of my presence. Totally engrossed in this verbal assault, I stood as if rooted to the ground. I felt so much for Jean that it seemed as if the old baas were attacking me personally. He turned his old, grizzled face toward me. "Stop staring at me, Hotnot! Go get some work done!"

I turned my back on them, mumbled, "Yes, baas," and started unpacking the crates from the wine wagon.

"Like I said you're a good worker," the hoarse, wheezy little voice continued behind me. "But what you want to do now is totally against church rules. It's even against my own principles. You can have as many of the black bitches as you want, but I won't allow you to sink so low as to live with one of them. It's totally immoral!" He screamed, "Totally immoral! You hear me, Frenchman? Here you'll do as I say!"

"Oui, Monsieur," came the trembling reply.

"It's either that or you fuck off from my farm."

I wondered for a minute whether Jean was going to stand up to him. Give him some rude reply or even fight him. Jean was, after all, a white man. I wanted him to fight the oubaas. Either through words or by using his fists. How could he betray my sister by letting another man call her a black bitch?

The quick footfalls of Jean's shoes on the gravel made me glance over my shoulder. A feeling of utter contempt took hold of me. Instead of fighting it out, the man was running away from his problems.

Halfway to the farmgate Jean stopped in his tracks and turned around. A new resolve seemed to have taken hold of him while he approached the oubaas again. "Monsieur," he begged. "Will you let me stay on as an ordinary worker? I promise I will work harder than before."

Jean and Lena moved into a two-room structure in the compound. Lena did her best to keep the place neat and tidy. However, the flowers she planted were always trampled by jealous neighbours and once somebody defecated just outside her front door. In the fields, Jean worked harder than the rest of us. The new overseer was a brutal man and always taunted Jean about his "Hotnot wife." To all this Jean was deaf. He now had a wife and two children to care for, and with his reduced income he had a hard time feeding his family.

Although Jean was now regarded as less than a white man, we workers still had a measure of deference for him. Even in his reduced state we learnt from him that a man could forgo tobacco and wine so his children could eat a good meal. Besides, he never complained to anybody. I suppose he must have thought his condition was of his own choice, ultimately, and not to be blamed on anybody else. With such goodness, perhaps he should have been a missionary. Yet with all that suffering he still remained proud of his origins and his culture. In his free time I'd see him laboriously teaching his eldest blue-eyed daughter the language of the French people.

And one day it happened. His attempts at keeping a vegetable patch and a few chickens and sheep were destroyed when the oubaas came to tell him he had no right to raise anything on this farm without permission. The chickens and sheep were slaughtered and the meat distributed among the rest of us. The vegetables were dug up and fed to the oubaas's pigs. Ma felt too broken-hearted to return the meat to Lena and Jean. Instead she fed it to the dogs.

When finally he was reduced to a state of absolute dependence like the rest of us, the drinking started. The oubaas saw this and exploited it. Jean was given a double portion of wine in the morning and evening because he was "still a white man." Like most of the desperately poor, Jean became a bully. He beat up my sister after his drinking bouts. She'd tell Ma how he'd afterward possess her with the ferocity of a lion. Perhaps in his embraces he wanted to rid himself of his own weakness and pour it into Lena.

I was about eighteen years old when I couldn't stand his behaviour any longer.

"Jean du Plessis!" I confronted him one afternoon. "I'm sick and tired of you beating up my sister."

"Mind your own business," he answered. His breath stank of stale liquor. "I'll do as I please." He stared at me contemptuously through puffed-up, red-rimmed eyelids.

I tried to be conciliatory. "Don't you see that the way you're carrying on isn't doing anybody any good?"

"Tell your sister that. You go tell her to be a good wife and I'll change. She's the cause of all this!" He shrieked, "You're all ganging up against me. So just fuck off, I've got no time for you!" He made a wild lunge at me.

From a few doorways there were curious stares. I hated this encounter with the man. He was part of my family. Besides, at his age men on this farm do not behave like fools.

"Jean," I implored him. "I don't want to fight you. I just want to talk."

He was crying in his drunken fury. "All these years I've sacrificed for your sister and she hasn't given me an ounce of thanks. Not you, not she, not anybody! I could've been a rich man but she kept me in this bloody place."

I wasn't really angry now. I felt only a deep embarrassment. Before he could go any further and tell the whole world how he'd fed us in meagre times, I gave him two quick slaps across the face. A look of utter surprise showed in his eyes and he grabbed for a stick lying nearby. This time I gave him two solid punches in the jaw followed by a blow in the ribs. Then I beat him till I was tired.

I suppose that under any other circumstances I would have been in serious trouble for beating up a white man. But nobody cared any more for this shell of a man. Not one of the workers went to report to the old baas that I was beating up his erstwhile overseer. A small crowd had gathered to watch the spectacle and from the teenaged boys came a few sniggers. I felt no sense of victory; only a deep and profound shame as he cringed before me in the dirt.

Lena struggled to get through the throng but I shoved her angrily away. What more did she want from this loathsome drunkard?

Another growl came from the broken figure. He shouted at me through broken teeth, "You're just a bully and a beater of old men!"

This time I could have killed him if Ma hadn't come in between us. I turned my back and walked away. Behind me sudden peals of raucous laughter broke the tension. Jean struggled to his feet and ran to escape the jeers from the onlookers. The next morning he was gone. Nobody could tell me where he'd gone or when he had left. I felt so much remorse afterward. How could I have beaten the man knowing full well that he was already a broken reed?

Two years after his departure, Jean du Plessis made a sudden reappearance. He came back wearing a flowing white robe. He looked a lot like Moses with his long hair and golden beard. I asked him what had brought him back, and he said he came to bring me Jesus.

ELIZABETH ALLEN

Playing the Odds

Does it always
come to this in the end?
This shuffling of cards
this way and that looking
for the aces, the full house,
the perfect pair? Of course
the odds against it are
light years out of reach.

Playing the "Pokies" in Dungog, NSW,
taking a chance on fortune
in the parlour of the flashing lights
the bump and grind of wheels
machines swallowing coins
one after another. But in the end
I win, just as I have with you,
realizing the only way out
is to quit while I'm ahead
go home alone, happy
with my pockets full
of unspent coins.

MICHELENE ADAMS

Pañols an Caribs

Nate an Hully swingin in de trees near de edge a de fores behin de church. Hully drop onto de muddy groun an stretch out on his back lookin up at Nate. "Mih hans tired," Hully say. "Lehs play someting else—cowboy an Indians," an he jump to his feet. Nate say no sense playin cowboy an Indians when dey never even had no cowboys in de country. He say dey should play Pañols an Caribs instead. Hully say if das wha dey playin den he fen to be a Pañol, cause de Caribs never even own no guns an if he's a Carib he boun to die off quick, an he ain see no point in dat. Nate say da suit him jus fine cause de Caribs have tricks up dey sleeve de Pañols never even dream bout. "Ever hear bout poison darts?" Nate ask, an he run off leavin Hully wid his mout open.

Nate run till he get to a thick stan a trees. De branches meetin overhead an hardly any light comin through. He crouch down in de mud quiet quiet to wait. "Ah loadin up mih musket!" Hully shout, an Nate could tell he still far away. An from how quiet he stay when he finish say it, he know Hully ain sure where to fin him. He rub his hans in de mud, smear it on his face. He squeeze it between his fingers, slide it over his arms up to where de shirt sleeves reach. He get down on all fours so he could leap if he get ketch buh he know dat ain go happen. He could hear de smalles soun: birds in de branches; insecs eatin smaller insecs; he could hear de river windin through de trees at his back. He ketch a flash a grey shirt an pants. Move backwards till he hidden between tree trunks. His skin same colour as de bark a de tree. Nobody could spot him. Especially not no sof-hide-musket-carryin Pañol who doh even know where to fin de waterfalls, doh know why de mountains have de names dey have, doh know de difference between one sea an de nex, one islan an de nex. He could smell him comin, smell de open space on him. He crouchin, his fingers danglin loose off his knees, eyes wide open. Pañol stannin inches away, not seein him. Lookin roun an not seein nuttin, not hearin.

He pounce. Head connec wid ches, knock de Pañol into de mud, pin his legs to de groun, hol down his arms. Pañol writhin like some animal, gaspin, strugglin to get free, sayin someting buh not words dat have any meanin, not any language he know. Till he scream in pain. Nate roll off him. He on his knees in de mud

27

watchin Hully. "Wha de hell, Nate! Is only a game!" Hully shout. "Yuh like a savage. Yuh come jus like one a dem savage Carib Indians! I goin home."

Nate watch Hully get up slow from de mud an he open his mout to say someting, but he ain bother. He follow Hully, walkin a few yards behin him all de way home.

DAVE MARGOSHES

Angela Davis in Regina

Sixteen years after those shots rang out
their echoes clatter in this classroom,
oaths chalked across the blackboard.
You're late, missed your plane because
of a traffic jam, we hear, and should be
just arriving at the airport now. We
mill in the lobby, eyeing each other,
comparing. "I'm surprised to see
so many," a plump pink woman in fur says,
approvingly. "She has her loyal fans." I'm one
of them, I know, but the words rub across me
like those gunshots and I turn away. Chalk
in the mouth, whitening the teeth.

Three hundred people, a third
of them black, every black in town
must be here—
but I turn away
from the word, even in the privacy
of my mind, replacing it with *Africans*,
thinking "African in the sense that
I am *European*"—
even children, a whole family,
three boys in squirming ironed shirts,
a wafer-thin girl in painful braids
in front of me, trying to make
sense of words like those the talking
head on TV uses for the news, but
more of them, and spoken
with a drawl, Eartha Kitt style,
syllables dragged like prisoners
across a killing ground,
"nineteen-forty-fiiive . . . we have
to luuurn a lesson agaaaain."

How light you are, reddish brown
hair in what I take to be
loose curls down to the shoulders
but turn out, when I get closer later,
to be dreadlocks,
dirty yellow blonde,
what they used to call high yellow
crinkled papery skin like that of an old woman
who has spent more time in it
than she had meant to,
eyes tired, almost pale,
a gap between your upper front teeth
some force tearing you apart
focusing in on you where
it will hurt the most,
like sly white men squinting strategy
outside the church, their ears
already filled with the deafening,
not hearing the cries.

After your talk, there are polite questions
and the one I want to ask is avoided:
Not, did you do it—the jury said
you didn't, after all, after all
the long time running, in jail,
in the courtroom under the eye
of history and the evening news—
not, did you do it
but, how could you not have?
Shuffling past as people gather
you seem smaller than I had thought,
prettier, your skin yellower,
not *black* at all, cheated even of that.

JIM MCLEAN

a black man looks like Bob Davey

on North Michigan
just across the river
from the Wrigley Building
a black man looks like my cousin
the same grumpy aggressiveness
masking that nervous apprehension
he and I and Zena know about
that same skin-tight
high cheek-bone skull
a few shades darker
that's all

I want to stop
ask if he remembers
the collection of *Classics Illustrated* comics
a galvanized washtub at the centre of the kitchen
the coyote hounds, Blue Boy and Sandy,
catcher and killer

in the time it takes
to pass by on the sidewalk
I picture him
riding a good two or three miles
from his house to mine
on his tricycle
to mark the first day of summer holidays
and the white teeth
laughing in his dark face
as I try, clumsy as a bear
to climb the snow-fence

MICK BURRS

No More Babushka Plowing Demonstrations

in this invasion of grandmothers
how many of you
looked like mine

the same solemn Slavic features
the same orthodox Jewish faces
the same strong Polish Ukrainian hands
the same weathered skin and stout bodies

I had never seen
a holy army of babas before

you, the old women
were wearing
your heavy black workshoes
your long plain dresses
and your babushka scarves
wrapped around your chins and ears

you were pulling together as a team
an old wooden plow
      over soil & weeds & stones
      digging hard furrows in the field

but especially you, the woman in the lead
straining in your harness
diminutive as an angel
      your delicate bones
      not yet broken

we were told this is how it was
in Old Mother Russia
this is how it was
in the pioneering days
on the Canadian prairies

yes, it was only a demonstration
but I witnessed it yesterday
in Yorkton, Saskatchewan

and I saw you, the eighty-year-old leader
your white socks falling from your ankles
as you stamped your shoes upon the earth
    the globes of salty sweat
    pouring down your reddened face

and I thought
she's going to have a heart attack
    and I wanted to shout
                Stop

but no one would hear me
in the cheering, neck-craning, awe-struck crowd

maybe I was mistaken

maybe this plowing demonstration
is a neglected form of exercise
to be recommended
for all octogenarians
    (of both sexes)

or maybe it is a necessary ritual
of suffering and endurance
preparing us each
for the blessings of heaven

or maybe it is merely
another chunk of evidence
    this crazy world
    is crazy for eternity

O babushkas
O grandmothers
O workhorse angels
O serene old women serving as substitutes for oxen

tell us the truth

if we never see you again on earth
will this also mark the end
of all babushka plowing demonstrations
in the fields of heaven

DONNA CARUSO

Palumello

On her dresser, the vigil light flickered in front of the picture of
Mother Cabrini. I stood on tip toe and inhaled the holy scent of
the beeswax candle carefully, so as not to disturb the flame with
my breath. I dipped my finger into the warm, melted wax and
lifted it up into the cool air to watch it cloud over and harden into
a perfect veil—not unlike the one Mother Cabrini wore in her
picture, not unlike what women wore in church.

It was long ago, when I was only a girl, and my grandmother,
Michelina, was living in my parents' house. I heard her call:

"Dona Maria, veni ca."

Donna Marie, come here.

"Va dormi, va dormi, Dona Marie!"

Go to sleep, go to sleep.

My grandmother would sit on the couch in the afternoon, and
I would lie next to her with my head on her lap. I was three. I
myself spoke no Italian, her only tongue. But somehow I could
understand her every word. She told me of Mother Cabrini's
miracles, ones she had witnessed herself.

Like the time an overpowering smell of roses filled the house
all day long, when there was in fact only one rose in the house. A
blood red one, in front of Mother Cabrini's picture. It was the
middle of winter. The same day the letter from Italy came telling
my grandma of her mother's death. She knew from the smell of
the roses that her mother was with Mother Cabrini in heaven. It
was a sign. It kept her heart from breaking.

"Nona, nona," she sang, "filia mia va dormi."

Her lullaby for me. She would ever so gently rock her legs
back and forth, singing and singing, until the world fell away and
I was sound asleep.

Outdoor sounds, breeze.

Outdoors in summer, she would sit in the sunshine, in her
hand a glass sugar jar, an inch of sugar in the bottom. I would be
over on the grass watching the bees dancing on the flower tops.

"Dona Maria, veni ca."

A butterfly would light on the sugar, and she would slip the
lid onto the jar, then hold it in the sunlight for me to see. We
would look at the creature in awe, see it shimmering and happy,
then free again, fluttering off, like a houseguest after Sunday
dinner warm with love and food.

"Palumello . . . "
"Butterfly," she would sing . . .
"Semper vole . . ."
Always flying . . .
"Gope bracha de nina mia . . ."
Now on the arms of my baby . . .
"A ciell' achendere . . ."
Up into the sky . . .
"Quandi mauro . . ."
When I die . . .
"Paluma mia, paluma mia, Io 'scende con te."
My butterfly, my butterfly, I'll fly with you.
The sound of "Santa Lucia" on a concertina.

There was an old photograph she had, formal and posed. In it, she stood next to a small man. She was straighter than he; taller. They looked ahead, separate, unsmiling. It was taken on their wedding anniversary.

She held the photograph for me to see as we sat on the couch, the streams of afternoon sunlight making my eyelids heavy with sleep. Again and again she would look from the photo off into space, to the world of her memories, then back again. The story was there in the photo, and there in her sighs. It was a private story, full of love and hope, of disappointment and pain. Full of too many things for a little girl to understand.

Back in my actual time with her, when she gently stroked my hair and coaxed me to sleep, all I understood was, "This was your grandpa. He died before you were born." But later, many years later, after she too was gone, I was haunted by her story, silent yet indelible, written on the walls of my memory.

The sound of a boxing match on TV.

In the evening every Friday, she watched the fights on TV as religiously as she tended the vigil light before Mother Cabrini's picture in her room.

I sat beside her on the couch.

The TV picture was black and white in those days, the men black and white as well. Such fascinating men, in their fancy underwear, hitting each other week after week. Spitting in their corners, sweating, bleeding—their large feet danced as they circled each other, then charged. Fists connected so squarely, I could feel the pain myself.

As we sat together quietly on the couch, never cheering lest we disturb someone, we spent the hour wide-eyed, captivated by the shirtless men in the box. She may have spoken no English, but she understood the language of the fights, as did I. Grandma and I spoke fluent "Friday Night Fights."

Saturday afternoon there was wrestling. Grandma and I watched that, too. But it was my nap time, so I drifted off to sleep as Wild Man was about to pounce on Red Devil, the midget tag-team about to attack the Giant.

I would eventually go to school, the Catholic school, run by nuns who obviously were as enamoured of the Friday Night Fights and wrestling as my grandmother and I. Anything but shirtless and sweaty, they nonetheless knew the power of a quick right to the jaw and the righteousness of a solid headlock.

My grandmother carried her rosary with her always, just as the nuns did. She would sit for hours fingering the beads, petitioning heaven for who knew what.

"Baggi la groce."

"Kiss the cross," she would entreat me in Italian. "Kiss the cross." I would kiss the metal crucifix, warm with the heat of my grandmother's hands. It was Jesus, the Son of God, she said. I remember wondering if Jesus, Son of God, was ever on the Friday Night Fights.

In the other photograph she had, she sat with her four living children, unbelievably young, standing around her. My own mother barely two. It was taken long ago in the days before candid photography, back when every photo was serious and painfully posed, with the children in unfamiliar, stiff clothing and shoes that pinched. No wonder everyone was unsmiling.

There was no man in the picture. It would have been taken in Italy to be sent to Grandpa across the ocean. For he had left his wife and babies in Italy while he worked in the new world, where there was opportunity unlike any other. For twenty years he went back and forth and back and forth across the ocean like a migrating bird, while she was free to raise her children alone.

But she was never angry, not when I knew her.

Each morning she would braid up her waist-length hair into a bun and fasten it with long, dark pins. I would stand by her side as, unhurried, she brushed, then braided. The vigil light before Mother Cabrini's picture felt warm on my face as I watched the ritual. The smell of my grandma's hair cream, mixing with the smell of the wax, created the special aroma of my shrine of my grandmother.

She rarely spoke, so each word became a blessing.

"Io te ho cucinato un po di pastina. Mange! Mange!"

"I made you some pastina," she would say as she put the bowl, filled with pasta stars laced with olive oil, before me. My mother fed me Cheerios. Grandma fed me stars. Surely the woman came from heaven if this is what she gave small children for breakfast.

She herself never ate, except for the occasional broiled lamb chop or bowl of homemade soup or piece of fresh fruit. While I ate my pastina, she would stand looking out the window. We were on the second floor, over my parents' grocery store. The kitchen faced the backyard, where there were large fruit trees and rows of my father's lush rosebushes. Birds rested on the telephone wires and paused in their flight across the huge, blue sky. Bees danced on the yellow heads of the dandelions.

We would go out onto the small, second-storey back porch to hang out the wash after breakfast, and I would smell the clean white sheets as she hung them on the line in the breeze. They would billow, once released, like a ship's sail on the ocean. She had crossed an ocean as blue and as vast as the sky to live here with that small dark man in the photograph. The journey had taken nine long days. She must have wondered if the sails that brought her here would ever take her home.

My grandmother and I would sit together on that small back porch enjoying the morning sunshine, high above the yard, and look out over the neighbourhood. Our laundry sailed above that of the neighbours and made us feel we were far in the lead in an important regatta. Ours was the highest clothesline, the longest clothesline, and easily the most spirited. Where we were headed was less important than that we were sailing.

For when it was hot, I wore nothing but the cast which covered me from my waist to my ankles. It had the colour of the white sheets on the line but nothing of the spirit. My shell for a full year, it was the reason my grandmother spent so much time with me. Unlike the others, who were free to go when they liked, I stayed with her, and she stayed with me. For years. She was the old and foreign one; I, a crippled toddler. We didn't matter to anyone and nobody listened to us but, for one another, day by day, we made life wonderful and mysterious.

Sometimes, the other family members would bring the wild western culture home with a bang. From our usual station, the couch, she and I would watch whatever we could not or would not take part in.

Mambo lessons come to mind.

The music was as hot as the Latin countries from which it had sprung. My parents, my aunts and uncles, and seemingly all of their friends wanted to learn this and other exuberant dances.

The living-room, which usually seemed large enough in the quiet afternoons when just my grandmother and I were there, seemed dangerously inadequate to hold the teeming throng of enthusiastic dancers invading the house every Sunday night with their loud and pulsating music.

The instructor made them pair off and learn new steps for an hour, then left them to practise on their own. These practices were what really cemented the relationship between my grandmother and me.

"Setta ca."

"Sit here," she would entreat me as the dancing began. I was only too happy to oblige her by climbing on the couch beside her and snuggling close.

Neither of us could move too quickly: I because of the heavy, unwieldy plaster cast, and she because of the age in her joints. If it became apparent we were no longer safe on the couch—which usually was clear after someone's circle skirt had spun in our faces, or someone had landed in our laps—then it was no easy task to make it past the dancers. We would tightly hold the other's hand, each of us staggering in our own way. As plodding as the dancers were graceful.

In the safety of my grandmother's room, we would lie down on the bed and watch the flickering of the vigil light. Mother Cabrini's face was always serene no matter what the circumstances. The vigil light a soft, flickering glow contrasting with the fire of music and dance consuming the living-room. Grandma would sing to me:

"Palumello . . ."

Butterfly . . .

"Semper vole . . ."

Always flying . . .

"Gope bracha de nina mia . . ."

Now on the arms of my baby . . .

"A ciell' achendere . . ."

Up into the sky . . .

"Quandi mauro . . ."

When I die . . .

"Paluma mia, paluma mia, Io 'scende con te . . ."

My butterfly, my butterfly, I'll fly with you.

I was thirteen when she died, the day of her burial in late December most bitterly cold. We lined up, dozens of us, her descendants, her family, and one by one we were handed a cool long-stemmed, blood-red rose to throw into her grave, atop her coffin.

As I approached the open pit, too cold a place for anything but death, as I was about to throw in my rose, the smell of roses wafted through the frigid air. A smell of roses so strong, I knew it was a sign, a sign she had joined all the other daughters of roses in heaven.

Now, as my own life unfolds, I find I decipher more of hers—the cryptic pictures and sighs rubbed clean and intelligible. Her language, my own.

GEORGE AMABILE

Basilico

1

Three basil plants
in one styrofoam cup.
A gift from a friend.

Their smell dissolves
the afternoon. Revives
my grandfather's garden, Sunday

and *pomidoro* sauce in a cast iron pot,
guests arriving in old cars from the city
soft nights, mandolins and laughter

under the window where I fought
off sleep, only to ride
my mother's clear soprano into dreams.

2

Something's wrong. Flooded
with sun on the windowsill, their leaves
go brown at the edges.

I drench them with mist
and sing to them in southern Italian
but it does no good. They suffer

as we do from too much
togetherness. I pull away
the puffed-rice cup, crumble the earth ball

and tug their nest of roots
apart. It sounds like thin
stitches ripping.

3

In their new pots, they have the look
of radical exiles, resentful
and sullen. I put them out

in the spring sun to heal. All evening
at the concert hall, *Le Ballet Jazz*
erases their claim on my heart

until I wake in the dark and feel them
wilting under an unpredictable frost.
I go out on bare feet and retrieve them.

4

All day I set them in different windows
following the sun, learning how light
and shadow arrange new moods

for the house. When evening comes
I spray their limp
dishevelled leaves and give

them up to the dark. Awake
with the first light, I'm surprised
and happy to see their pumped up leaves

drinking the dawn. I decide
to celebrate, pour a cold beer
into the tall green glass

I found in my mother's cupboard
after she died. I hold it up
to the window, watch

the bubbles rise and bolt
it back. A warm jolt spreads
from my stomach up to my brain

and it's only then that I notice
how their stems are leaning
over, trying to sleep. So I twist

a pair of old chopsticks
into the soil and tie their heads
up straight. But when I step back

to admire my artfulness, the edge
of my hand brushes the glass
and it falls to the floor. The sound

it makes as it shatters
triggers the same stab of panic
I had to control as a child whenever she left

the room. I see her perched on a stool
at the stove in her small house, drained
by cancer, cooking the last

meals of her life. I bend
and sweep up the delicate shards, green
as my birthstone, brokenly

musical as they slide
from the dustpan into the trash.
The room fills with more and more light.

And it all comes close again: Her wisdom.
Her temper. Her cuisine. No one
has ever got her tomato sauce right

though she gave us her secret freely:
Five or more leaves of fresh Basilico.
Half an afternoon at moderate heat.

GERALD HILL

Welcome in Edmonton

1

Oh it must be exciting she says
to move to a new place
                    and it is
to enter the empty space and stand there
hollow in the hall and naked
as a brand new key

Oh it must be exciting she says
                         and it is
the Utility company demands
confirmation of my birth
                      my shoe size
the surnames of my uncles
                oh it *is*
the backyard needs
just three more days of drought
to qualify as scrap earth
                   oh it already is
there's an airport half a block away
the 737s rise like bug-seeking missles
from bungalows across the street
neighbours whom I've never seen
are busy with the countdown
                    oh it *is* exciting
other neighbours born again are sure
my daughter will burn in hell
if she mentions her vagina
they hide tomatoes
                build their fence so high
the pickets cross above their house
and their yard resembles an echidna
hiding from its neighbours' eyes
                    oh
it is

2

The only movement
normal these quiet afternoons
is the drifting of branches
magpies or cats

I have spread to this silence like a migratory bird
dodging extinction
                    settling again
in a meadow between rows of empty bungalows
delivery vans idle and go
like insects in grass
Page Boy Cleaners
                    Chuck's Electric
otherwise just the cats
and magpies drifting over fields
of vision
            timeless as bugs

3

The principal is straight
as a lapel at recess
                    he says
I like to show my face out here
so I'm not just an ogre behind a desk

Standing there he resembles a bird
more than an ogre
                    a junior bird
assigned to the head of the flock
although not yet fully mature

Then he speeds inside to practise
the language of newsletters
and phonecalls to central office
unsure of rules about snacks
rubber boots and field trips

His beak like his brain
is tiny
        but he knows
how to keep his feathers clean

4

In the arc of a door's closing
just before winter I see
the sunrise
               feel its cold

I speak to the landlord
(a musician in Phoenix)
of warm air lost to grey
skies through the attic

The landlord speaks to me
of cash flows and how
he just can't afford insulation right now
he's had to re-string
one of his harpsichords

Last night I had a dream (I say)
of entrapment in the Arctic Circle
I pounded on the tundra
doors closed
               that dream I had last night
was so cold

Isn't the furnace working?

But the house passes heat
like a cup of hot tea
                   pigeons
nudge against the gables
                       gurgle and preen
content
        the yard's an oasis
in a desert of frost

Well how cold can it be?

Cold enough to snap
the glass on your diplomas upstairs
my daughter wears gloves to play her xylophone
the guest room is closed until break-up
when hot air rises it dies

Oh yes I used to keep my tools up there

So what do you say
you sell a clarinet
or up the fees for your clavier gigs
and get this job done

I'll call you back he says
the phone
                will sound bells
frozen air

5

The chill brings out the berries
in the front yard
                        magpies occupy the trees
a single jay

Quiet as geraniums bending
this is the new world
all motion is event

This afternoon silence
breaks like the window
I hammer to get in

Blizzard

This is the real danger of our distance:
when we meet again—voices emptied
and dried on pages that crease
the back of our minds—we face the ungainly
hope of two people who just don't know
each other well enough to say
what we've already written.

I worry too much. I said so in a letter
and you carry the knowledge with more
certainty than you could trace my spine
with one finger now. I laugh
at your jokes, smile at your broken
English. Every curve of your letters
is part of me now: I can utter
each word you've sent, but I've lost
your voice. All I have is what I hear
at the end of another transatlantic call.

Three months only, you say, and I nod
with verbal punctuation. How will we speak
when our faces' shifting contours are real,
are trap lines or blind, blind alleys?

My calendar shows me its wide
surprise, its arms that open, open
all that way before the hands curl
round to join us. How can I live
in its slippery grip, its oh
so slowly closing arms? Your
last year's face above my telephone
only smiles. When we meet
will our greetings freeze
in each other's changed
and changing faces? We've yet to find
our way through the features
concealed in these flat companions
whose smiles were trapped in someone else's eye
long before we met.

The radio tells me a blizzard is coming.
Winter begins, the clock slips another notch
toward you, and I stand at the window
which faces you, as ultimately they all do
if I could only see far enough, and I look
into evening as the view to the river
shrinks toward me, puckered with cold,
and the air fills with the shattered white horizon
blowing in on a wind from the south, or
somewhere, blowing in, from
you.

KRISTJANA GUNNARS

Mass and a Dance

The ground crackled when she walked. It was frozen snow, not ice. Minus thirty-three. Smoke from all the chimneys filled the town of St. Norbert. The air was white. The sky was white. The sun was white. She had learned to like this place from constant use. The corner store, the little post office, the crude statue of Mother Mary across from the Catholic church. All the dedications in this tiny French Manitoba village to the battles of the Metis. History invaded by Winnipeg suburban developments: brand new single storey homes erected in droves over the summer. When the wind blew, whole walls of the unfinished constructions collapsed. It was not a pretty village but it had that edge of ruined history about it. An old village cradled by a bend in the Red River that insinuated: you may have lost but you're still here.

That's the whole point right there, she thought as she walked along the suburban street on her way home. To be *still here*. The thought stung her. She was placid enough yet maddened by a sense of inescapable grief: a grief like the atmosphere of the earth. Something so fundamental she knew she could not come out of it. A grief that comes to people when they know something that had life is irretrievably lost. It was not a person: it was a history. Is this how the native Indians feel, she asked herself, when they have lost territories to encroaching civilization? Or people who have lived in tiny railroad hamlets out on the prairie, when the railroad cuts service to them and the hamlet dies for lack of use? Do they feel like this?

She came to Canada because it was somehow no longer feasible to live in the town she came from. It was territory now laid waste. Since she could not stay there, she decided to quit the country altogether, refusing the daily reminders of loss: the cold rain, the northern wind, the midnight sun. She grew up in the Vestfjords of Iceland, a desolate region far in the north-west of a desolate island in the North Atlantic. Life was never easy there but, when modernity invaded the island, new urban centres sucked people out of little hard-won villages and emptied them. She thought of modern civilization as a trashcan into which everything gets thrown.

What is still called Sléttuhreppur, "Plains District," was once the northernmost inhabited region of the Vestfirdings. In nineteen forty nearly five hundred people lived there. Ten years later it was a ghost fjord. The sun rose over Hornbjarg mountain, illuminated the water in the bay, and no one saw. The church in Stadur was a ghost church. Small, wooden, white, four windows on each side and a tiny bell tower facing the sea. No one rang the bell. The Vestfirdings were gone.

She looked around her in the St. Norbert winter. It was so silent, she seemed to have lost her hearing. All she could see were bi-level houses squarely facing the sun. The crunch of her footsteps seemed to come from inside a tunnel. A bird screeched. When she looked, there were only barren branches and the bird was gone.

She still did not know why all the Vestfirdings deserted Sléttuhreppur. Most of them went to the capital city in the south. Some went abroad: Greece, America, Spain. When they were gone, thinking they had improved their lot in life, they discovered they missed their northern Arctic environment. Services were cut so there was little hope of re-establishing a community. Instead they staged a *reunion*. The previous summer. She came along with all the others. There would be a dance and a mass in the church. There was a chartered coach to Stadur in Adalvík and on the way they picked up Jakob, the priest from Isafjördur, to bless them at the end of the weekend.

The last time she was in the little church was at her confirmation. They were several very young angels draped in white from neck to toe. They made a holy procession down the aisle, their black psalters clutched to their chests. They knelt before the altar, hands folded, looking up. The priest placed his hand on her head. Her elaborate hairdo went down. She forgot about the blessing: her only thought was that the priest did not understand the matter of hairdos.

On Advent Sunday they always lit the candles and then they were angels holding candles. Now Hákon the composer brought a choir to sing for them. They sang a choral work he had composed: *The Gravestone Suite*. Hákon had gone to the graveyard and written chants of the inscriptions on all the tombstones. When he conducted his choir, he stood on a table so they could all see him. After Advent mass there was coffee in the community room. Hákon again got up on the table. He stood among the coffee cups and the choir sang a chant for the food.

For the reunion mass in Stadur, all the old relics were brought back and put in their former places. There must have been eighty people. No one could bring the organ on the coach, so Reynir the organist played the accordion instead. In the evening, Reynir the organist played his accordion for the dance.

50

At the dance many women wore the national costume. Black skirts, black vests, white aprons and black caps with long tassels. By midnight they were all tipsy. By two in the morning these black swans all had to be taken to the coach. They were smiling obliviously. She left the dance at seven next morning. Dawn had long passed. The coach driver was waiting. Passengers were impatient. Some were draped over their seats, others curled into balls. An elderly Sléttuhreppur farmer had imprisoned her in conversation in the community kitchen on the topic of education. Everyone thought they were doing something else. When she came out and realized the communal mistake, she was too embarrassed to correct it.

She crawled into her coach seat and went to sleep. The elderly farmer's son, whom she had a crush on as a teenager, had disappeared. He had long, dark blond locks and an athletic body. She used to frequent soccer matches just to look at his body. She went to men's swimming competitions for the same reason. He had not shown up for the reunion: they said he was somewhere in South Africa. After gymnasium in the city he went to college in America where he met an education student from South Africa, married her and went into the South African bush while she did research on the education of native tribes.

Meanwhile she found herself in the dead of winter in the Canadian prairie. Manitoba. Stalled cars with their hoods up littered the highway in this cold. They stood abandoned, collecting a coating of ice. Schoolchildren rolled like balls out of the yellow schoolbus and trundled home, packed in snowsuits, scarves and moonboots. They had trouble walking straight bundled up as they were.

She wondered whether her *bitterness*, that must be the word, over the *dissolution* of her birth community had something to do with the young farmer's son who had seemed to her the ideal of northern beauty. That they were *forced* to part company: forced to be the captives of *distance*?

There were moments when she appreciated the scattered clouds as they conspired with the frost to block out the sun. Every cloud over the prairie had a south-eastern lining, in gold. On days like this, all seemed to her discontinuity. No single train of thought remained steady. Stories were broken into flakes: of memory, of history, of ice. Sometimes it snowed. She had never been able to relate a story from beginning to end in this place. Not even to herself. Yet life seemed to fall into patterns: obvious patterns, sometimes so startling she wondered who designed them.

The place she now lived in seemed to her a place without beginning. Without end. Without rise and fall. It was something else. She did not understand the ground she walked on, the air she breathed. Was this what they meant by the word *alien?* Alien: a person who does not understand the place she is in. Snow was falling on the St. Norbert streets. Snow is a story that breaks off from heaven and falls down at random, she thought. Snow longs to be whole again. It longs for its origins and cannot remember when it was together. It has fallen on an unknown country. If there is a little wind, the snowflakes dance during their descent.

She recalled walking home from school, across the mountain. She was fifteen. There was a blizzard. Thick snowflakes filled the entire air, rushing from one mountain to another. She could not see. The road was no longer visible. She did not know whether she was walking into the desert tundra, forever to perish, or home. There was fear. Wanderers had been lost in these mountains since time immemorial. Their bones had been found in the spring, lying among the sheep. Suddenly headlights appeared behind her out of the snow. A car door opened and she was pulled in. Saved. She looked to see who her rescuer was: it was Fleming, the Danish fellow. Once again, bad luck.

The church in Stadur was cold the afternoon mass was again sung in Adalvík, after twenty years of standing empty. The day everyone arrived together in a coach for a reunion. People wore skin-lined jackets in the pews because there was no heat. A small kerosene camp heater stood on the floor in front of the altar. Jakob the priest prayed from behind the small communion railing. On the walls, the oil lamps tried to compete with the sun that never sets in the Arctic.

The wooden walls of the church had become attuned to silence. They echoed the silence of desertion. People could tell there were ghosts: and the curious sensation that *they themselves were the ghosts come to haunt the place where they once lived.* Reynir sat in the first pew, against the wall by the window. He had his accordion in his lap. People sang from little black hymnals with woollen sweaters draped around their shoulders. On the lectern a frayed guestbook lay open and blank. No names were written in the pages for twenty years. The stairs up to the choir loft creaked.

She sat in the second pew on the eastern side. Next to her sat a man who had become her lover when they met in Greece: the writer who had settled in Athens. Hákon the choir director looked back over his shoulder. He was a friend of the writer's other lover, the violinist who had moved to Austria. There would be talk of triangles and quadrangles. She played dumb, for lack of a better idea. Halldór the red cheeked schoolteacher sat behind them. He had taught them geometry when they were children.

She liked the way the snow fell in Canada. It did not come straight down but meandered in the air for a long time before settling. She watched one snowflake float in spirals, then up a bit, to the left, up again, down. This could go on for ten minutes before the flake joined the others on the white bundle below. At night scrapers in St. Norbert amused themselves by scraping the streets. They scraped down to the pavement and left mountains of packed snow cakes in front of the houses for the inhabitants to rid aside in the morning with useless tin shovels that folded under the impact of hard ice.

At the Adalvík reunion, after the mass people hung about outside the church. Wild angelica flowers reached up to their knees. A number of people were standing looking at the water in the bay. One by one the riplets gently licked the stones on the shore. Around the church, old gravestones leaned with the weather into the mountains.

The first time a rumour came that she would go to America occurred when she was eight. She told her friend Sjöfn. They had a game of exchanging all their clothes, including underwear and socks. Sjöfn pulled her into the street and pushed her in front of all passers-by crying out: *she's going to America*. Sjöfn pushed her into Jói's grocery store and announced: *she's going to America*. The customers turned and looked at her. She was standing in her white jacket, embarrassed, playing imbecile for lack of a better idea. Many years later she got a letter from Sjöfn, posted in Ohio. She looked for a return address but found none. Evidently Sjöfn herself had gone to America.

It was said that Reynir the organist was a lucky piece of driftwood on the beach of the Vestfirdings. He was handy with several musical instruments and could, at one go, play for both the mass and the dance. The dance that night was held in the schoolhouse at Saebólsgrundir. Reynir pumped the accordion without pause all night. Like the midnight sun, he would not set.

They got their dance partners by matching halves of verses. The man who had the last two lines to go with her first two lines turned out to be Halldór the schoolteacher. Once again, bad luck. He was fond of the Polka and they danced the Polka for an hour. Then she sat down in the hall among the smiling black swans: the elderly women in their national costumes, seldom worn any more. She felt out of place in her white dress, purchased in Toronto.

She went outside during a lull in the dancing. A number of Adalvíkings had gathered on the grass tufts where the mountains began to rise a short distance away. It was the middle of the night but still as bright as day. A feeling of dusk pervaded the silent air. Reynir had taken his accordion out and Baldur, the priest's grandson, had brought a guitar. They were singing. Their mis-matched voices sounded clearly in the stillness and echoed across the valley below.

It was a little chilly. She made her way across the tufts slowly, savouring the fresh air. Adalvík: where she liked to be alone among the singing of the ghosts. They did not see her. Many were busy covering up the left ear, the one facing the wind.

Those were the tufts of grass she ran across one day when she was eleven, very fast. She had the sudden notion she wanted to be on the next Olympic swimming team and started training the same day. She ran the six kilometers from home to the sulphuric swimming pool and swam for two hours without stopping, racing from one end to the other. Then she ran the six kilometers back. She did not get as far as the Olympic team: she got sick instead and lay in bed all next day. That was her at eleven.

How the snow in St. Norbert was floundering, undecided whether to go back up or come down for good. The flakes blew in swirls and patterns in the gentle gusts of wind. Oblivious to the cold, they swam about in the air.

The streetkeepers came and broke the peaceful quiet of this French-Canadian town. Clamorous machines lumbered up and down the road with scathing noise. Those monsters left moun-tains of brown snow cakes behind them. Children in moonboots who came out of yellow schoolbuses could barely climb over the ice mountains to get home. They wiggled up on their tummies, thick arms and legs clinging to protruding ice shelves. She stood on the other side watching. In case one of these little balls missed its footing. But they all made it over, like diligent winter ants.

As she stood the singing of the Adalvíkings swirled in her head. It was still the middle of the night and the Adalvíkings were singing under the open sky. The sun, which had been sleeping on top of Hornbjarg mountain for a while, began to rise. Suddenly the eastern sky, the sea, the stones, the hair of the singers became drenched in gold. It was for this moment every-one had come back, she thought. *For this moment when the sun begins to ascend and the earth becomes a stone garden drenched in gold.*

The Adalvíkings were singing fatherland songs. They started up on something from Hákon's *Graveyard Suite*:

Sun sinks in the sea
Showers the mountain peaks with gold
Swans fly full of song
South toward the warm wind
Blossoms gently sway
Smile in tender oblivion
When this evening peace descends
The most beautiful of all is Adalvík.

That was from the tombstone of Einar the poet.

ANNE SZUMIGALSKI

Jerusalem

that city of glass these words are printed in the book that lies open
before you   I'm reading over your shoulder and cannot see your
face but I know that your slightly bulging eyes blue as glass are
staring at the page I know that from between those eyes the
thought darts out and hits the print with its point that never again
will you enter jerusalem

send me I want to tell you but you hush me with the warmth of
your hand which is resting on my hand am I cooling your fingers
or are you warming mine this question occurs at the same time as
conjectures about my journey to that place of iron doors and
minarets lighted against the sky whose gates are closed until
morning

whose walls are huge blocks of traprock says the book where men in
black homburgs weep and wail their tears run down their faces,
run down the stones leaving long ribbons of rust

soon I shall scale these walls and enter the city and search up and
down the streets for those whose names were once known to you
will they put on a false front of flesh will they come shaved and
powdered to greet me

or when at last I see them face to face will they turn quickly away
and hurry down a sidestreet while one explains to the other a new
process for adding gold to the glass of an office building *it's true*
he admits that the windows shine rather dully in the sun but then
the people inside never have to pull down the blinds for in that
place there is neither glitter nor glare but always just enough light
to read by

NANCY MATTSON

Kanadalainen

To have left behind the language
that flowed like spring water
the easy seepage
of fresh words every hour

To have come to a land
of thorough drought
with a dry tongue

To have to pump the handle
like a child again
lifted off the platform
by every upstroke
the pump so stiff
the well so dark
you doubt the alkali earth
will ever release its sour water

To hang a new pail
from the knuckle
on the pump mouth
watching the water trickle
slowly at first
   then slowly faster
   until the pail is overflowing
only to stumble on a root
on the path to the house

To watch the pumped water
settle and seep
into insatiable
Canadian earth

To have believed the words
would ever flow together
into sentences

SARAH KLASSEN

Geography

Ladies in my childhood are women who speak only English. They come afternoons, gloved and curled, their fresh red lips brilliant wounds in my mother's kitchen. She serves tea nervously with cream in good chipped cups on a worn tablecloth. Her fear commands me in from summer dreams under blue sky or the cool shade of poplars.

"Wie sagt mann *Dorf Obstgarten hintergeblieben Krieg* auf englisch?" my mother whispers.

I suffer her clumsy answers to their curious presence, the apron of bleached flour sack, her terrible need of my tongue. "You should speak English to your daughter," the ladies say. These ladies suffer, if they suffer, in a different geography. They can't imagine watermelon fields, a white picket fence outlining the village street, blossoming apricot orchards that float like pink clouds around my mother's longing. They can't hear the choir singing *Grosser Gott*, they are deaf to the wind that won't stop moaning in the corners of her torn heart.

KIM MORRISSEY

Grandmother

you were born
into poplar and sand
dark dapples salt tears
in sweet autumn nights

your young girls are flushed
with the mark of spring mushrooms
rolled finger to thumb
darkening

their young men move to town
and they follow:

they learn to tell new friends they're French
bring their children at Christmas
high cheek-boned fair-haired

when you are old great-grandchildren
meet you on sidewalks
step aside pass
without speaking

ALICE LEE

Café Talk

Grandfather sleeps his final sleep on freshly cut pine. His house a small frame box. "A box within a box," Kookum says as grandfather is fit through doorways. Sweet smells of pine and death are strong in my nostrils.

Kookum sits in the silence of her kitchen. I move to her side. She reaches for my hands and puts them on her face. My fingers trace the empty hollows where her eyes should be.

She is my other mother. A medicine woman. Born without eyes. She sliced me from my mother's womb with a cutting stone. In my dreams I see inside her medicine bundle.

"My girl, I need salt. You go for me to Old Man Toy's."

Old Man Toy's is just past the railway tracks and grain elevators. Elevators. Tall white boxes reach from the ground to steal space from the sky. A house for giants. I think I see white faces through high glass windows. Watching me.

Old Man Toy. Brown curtain eyes. People in town call him a china man. Kookum drinks her tea from a china cup. The matching saucer is broken. Kookum said you have to be careful how you handle china. It breaks easy.

Old Man Toy's café. He is hunched over Chinese newspapers. Jukebox music playing. High backed booths. Red cushioned counter stools. Behind the counter, canned ham and salmon. Silver tinned sardines. And the candy. The candy.

Town people talking to town people. Reserve people talking with Indian words I don't understand. Between their words, silence. They watch the town people. Words become English. "We will get the vote. It will be better."

Footsteps behind me. White hands pull brown braids. "Stay away from the town toilet. It's not meant for you people."

Old Man Toy's eyes. "Leave her. The grandfather die!" He turns his face away from my own. Leaving me alone with my shame. "Here, free ice cream for you. Your grandfather die. A sad time for you." A small animal in me wants to cry out. I lick the ice cream like a wound.

The reserve people talking again. "Diefenbaker will help. He will get us the vote."

Sometimes I get pictures in my head. I call them my awake dreams. I see this Diefenbaker. Deep asleep on satin. Gold handles on smooth polished wood. He is carried by train.

Outside on the sidewalk, a brown bird with a broken wing. People hurry by. No one sees. I don't understand. The bird is right there in front of their eyes. The bird hops by, dragging its wing. Eyes full of pain. I reach out. Reach out and wring the bird's neck.

JOE WELSH

The 1949 Election

I am 25 dat year
Strong like a horse too
Work ever'day   even in duh winter
Chopping wood en building fence
Stuff like dat

Election time come aroun' dat spring
Politicians was ever'where
Passing out beer en promising ever'body a job
Duh Conservateur he give me five dollar to vote fer him
Duh Liberal he give me a case of beer
En duh CCf guy he don' give me notting
But he say I can go on welfare
In duh hard time he tell me

So me I take duh five dollar en duh beer
But I don' vote fer nobody

I am drunk en on welfare ever since

Goddam Liberal   goddam Conservateur   goddam CCf

Goddam me

JOE WELSH

Janvier Makes a Picnic

Ever'time Janvier make a picnic
Wit Rosalie Boyer
He take Fodder Beaulieu dog wit dem
So one day I tell him
How come you take Fodder Beaulieu dog
When you make a picnic
Wit Rosalie Boyer

So he tell me
Flies
Dey use to bodder me lots
So one day I tink
I like to borrow dat ugly dog
En duh priest he tink I like duh dog
En Rosalie she don' mind
She let him ride in her car

When we get to duh picnic place
I let duh dog out
En he run aroun' fer a while
Pretty soon he have a shit
Den we move duh picnic up out duh wind
En duh flies
Dey don' bodder us no more

Sometime when dey get real bad
I borrow Gilbert LaRoque dog too

LALA HEINE-KOEHN

Praca Jest Najlepszym Lekarstwem*

She washes the windows before
and after it rains.
She wipes the dust before it
settles, attacks all fingermarks
savagely. Perhaps they remind her
of someone's touch.
Kneading the bread dough,
she punches it three times more
than she was taught.

And each time or close to it,
she takes the time to rest.
Wrapping her black quilted coat
around her, the flour still
on her face, she goes outside
to sit in an iron chair. Pushing
the budding vines aside, she hides
her folded hands to warm them
under the apron. Though it is
spring again, the clouds are lead-
heavy; so is the sea. Shivering,
she stares at the sky, wondering
if today the sun will come out.

And sometimes she goes to the attic,
where she keeps her photographs.
She looks at her wedding pictures,
remembers making the stays for the lace
collar of the dress the girl is wearing,
but the girl is a stranger, and standing
beside her, so is the smiling man.
Which is which she wonders, looking
at the baby pictures of her children,
each one flaxen, blue-eyed,
each one wearing a lawn shirt
trimmed with hand-crocheted lace.

At the bottom of the box lies
part of a torn photograph;
a sunray motif, bursting from
under a roof, carved balconies
rambling the upper floors.
*Whatever happened to the other
half* she puzzles *that's where
Father's library and our nursery
were. That's where Mother's ebony
grand piano stood.*

She puts the photographs away,
walks down the attic stairs
to the second floor, stepping
firmly to hear them creak. She closes
the bedroom door behind her.
Her amber beads are strung across
the large mirror, she lifts them up,
holding them above her face.

This is how she used to drink honey
when she was little, tipping the jar,
the golden liquid trickling
down into her mouth . . .

*A very well-known and often-used Polish proverb:
"Work is the best medicine."*

DAVE MARGOSHES

Feathers and Blood

One day in the spring of 1927, a young woman by the name of Rebeccah Kristol sent my father a letter from Cleveland with the message: "Now."

At that time, my father was already firmly established as a reporter on *The Day*, the Yiddish-language daily that sent its messages of the toils and joys of Jewish life in New York from the Lower East Side throughout the city and even into the country-side beyond the rivers, and had begun the career that would carry him for the next forty years and more. But before that, there had been moments, sighs, passions, endless nights, bottles of whiskey, fierce friendships and women who, in the telling later, became blurred, indistinct as buildings viewed through fog, perhaps to spare my mother, perhaps merely so my father, who enjoyed telling stories of his youth, could keep some small pieces of it private, for his own, like good luck coins fingered and shiny in his pocket. He never said so, but I suspect Rebeccah Kristol was one of those coins, not just a friend from the old days in Cleveland, as he described her when he told the story, but one of the women who had been part of his life in those years before my mother, before my sisters and I were given our chance to be.

Rebeccah was a strong woman, my father used to tell us, a determined woman with ideas of her own and the courage to put some, if not all, of them into effect. She was a drinker and a smoker, mildly shocking behaviour for a woman in those days, at least in some stratas of society, even the society my father and Rebeccah inhabited, as well as a freethinker and free-lover, an anarchist follower of Anna Goldman, dabbler in vegetarianism, frequenter of cafés and theatres, friend of artists and writers, which is how my father, who was a writer himself and part of the Bohemian café circle, such as it was in Cleveland, came to know her. He had one photograph of her. One of several brittle, yellow tintypes from his early days, it could be found scattered in among the more abundant family portraits and snapshots—of my mother's childhood, of them as a young couple, of us children— that filled a shoebox my mother kept in a dresser drawer. That one photograph revealed Rebeccah as clearly possessed of those qualities of character he ascribed to her but contained not a hint of her predilections and interests. She is one of only three women in a portrait filled with men, a solemn, formal study of activity suddenly arrested in the newsroom of *The Day*, circa 1930, more than a decade before my birth. He himself is sitting at a desk in the pose I like best to remember him in, hands poised over the keys of an ancient stand-up typewriter, head slightly lowered, moustache bristling, cigarette dangling from a mouth pursed with concentration, his hair only just beginning to thin, still rich and black. The other men and one of the women are captured in similar freezes, at typewriters or bent over teletype machines, reading, one or two on the telephone, a few with their backs to the camera, and there is a sense of busy-ness and purpose to the scene unmarred by the other two women. They stand, stiff and vigilant at either end of the room, like prim bookends. Rebeccah is the one on the right, in a long black skirt and ruffled white blouse with a bow at the throat, her dark hair in a severe bun, her face partially shielded by thick-rimmed glasses. She was, at the time the photograph was taken, less than thirty, but there is a sort of agelessness about her face, her strong, well defined features facing the camera with intelligent interest, neither youthfully beautiful nor showing any of the decay of years. Her eyes seem to sparkle, and her mouth and chin are firm, as if they are being held into the wind. But her clothes, her hairstyle, even the rigid way she holds her arms by her sides, one hand seeming to be smoothing a pleat in her skirt, all point to a manner of conventionality which runs against the way my father described her.

"She was a changed woman when she came to New York," my father said while he showed me the picture, anticipating my thoughts. "Whatever happened to her in that love affair, in that marriage, in that boat ride, it turned her inside out." He carefully deposited the photograph in its protective envelope, along with a few others from the same era, and looked at me. "She never lost her intelligence, of course, or her taste, but her curiosity about the world shrivelled, and she became the sort of person she had always disliked, a closed sort of person. As if she was making up for something."

All of this, my father used to say when he told the story, was so much more perplexing because of the kind of woman she had been, "a woman who"—and here, if they were in the room, my mother and sisters, who were quite a bit older than me, would grimace and my sisters actually groan—"had all the intellectual and creative abilities and instincts of a man." After she'd sent him that note, he'd kept his promise and gotten her a job, as a bookkeeper at *The Day*, the place she would remain all her working life, rising to be chief bookkeeper, the austere, dark-clothinged, slightly plump woman with a wart on her nose who would greet me so cheerily on those infrequent occasions I would visit my father in his office, where even the air in the newsroom was redolent with the smell of printers ink wafting in from the black-walled pressroom downstairs. He'd gotten her the job, helped her settle in, and been as much of a friend to her as he could. But they'd never been really close again, not close enough for her to go beyond telling him *what* had happened, to *why*.

It began, he knew, when she'd met the man, a salesman who had worked his way up to manager of a small haberdashery on Lake Street in downtown Cleveland, then bought out the widow of the man he'd worked for. His name, my father thought, was Greenspan, although that didn't seem to matter. Nothing about him, my father said, seemed to matter, since the problem was within Rebeccah. The first time I can recall hearing the story, when I was six or seven, and for several retellings afterward, my father explained she'd had earlier sweethearts, and her husband-to-be was jealous. This had "caused problems," my father said with a wink, "but nothing that feminine wiles couldn't cope with." Later, when I was twelve or thirteen, the story changed accordingly, and my father explained the "problem" was that Rebeccah was not a virgin, a condition sure to cause displeasure for her husband—"not all husbands," my father added quickly, "but some men care, and this one definitely." And, finally, at some point during the year I went away to college, on one of those short but intense visits home, the story came full cycle and my father related with head-shaking wonder the facts he had come to know in detail some time after she'd come to New York: how, to stave off discovery, she'd planned and carried out the simple subterfuge, as brilliant and easily accomplished as the friend who had coached her had promised: the douche of a mixture of water, alum and vinegar, the feigned cries of pain, the small balloon filled with chicken blood concealed first under the pillow and then in her palm, the jab with one long, sleekly polished nail. It had gone well, my father said, but afterward, while the husband lay sleeping, Rebeccah had walked the deck of their honeymoon cruise ship, stared into the dark impenetrable waves of Lake Erie and come to some, to my father, inexplicable resolve. She'd gone back to their cabin just for a few minutes, to throw a few things into a suitcase, then she'd hidden in a washroom until the ship docked in fog-shrouded Buffalo and disembarked with the first crowds, losing herself amid the noise and crowds on the dock.

It was sometime soon afterward that she'd written the note to my father as a fulfillment of some late-night café pledge he'd made when they'd been close: when she was ready to leave Cleveland, where some family obligation he was never clear about kept her bound, and escape to New York, where he was now headed, she would let him know and he would help her find a job, help her make what, in those days, and for a woman, was still a difficult passage. The note she sent—and he was sorry, my father always said, he hadn't saved it—didn't have to say more than it did, because he knew from that one word, "Now," all he needed, really: that she was ready to come, that she wanted his help and, more, that it was a cry for help, a signal for freedom.

His name, in fact, was Greenspun, Aaron Greenspun, whose family had settled in Akron, where an uncle became the first Jew to serve on a city council in Ohio. He had yellow eyes, like a cat's, and Rebeccah, dreaming of them, thought his name should more truly be *Gold*spun, so did it seem those eyes must have been fashioned. He was tall, well built, like a Greek god, Rebeccah told her best friend Belle and the other women she drank coffee with at the café—women who pursed their mouths in impressed wonder while they gazed at the rumpled, round-shouldered men arguing at the next table, then giggled at the perceived possibilities—and he had only the slightest curved Semitic nose in his otherwise smooth and blandly featured face to betray his origins. He was altogether beautiful, "the most beautiful thing I've ever seen," Rebeccah, conscious of her choice of words, told her friends. Her attraction to him frightened her.

They had absolutely nothing in common and shouldn't have even met except there was a family connection, Rebeccah's one weakness. A Greenspun cousin had married a Williams cousin— Williams being Rebeccah's mother's family name, the Americanized version of Wilchevski the mother's father, Rebeccah's hard-headed, bristly bearded grandfather, had adopted in one of those Ellis Island subterfuges that had smoothed the wrinkles from so many Russian and Polish names. The old man, long dead now, had begun as a peddler but had worked his horse and wagon into a stand, then a small shop, then Williams Brothers, one of Cleveland's better furniture stores, and proved his abilities as a merchant and his sagacity, he always claimed, as a name-picker. That side of the family—the store was now run by Rebeccah's uncles Meyer and Robert—seemed to have much in common with the Greenspuns of Akron and their one Cleveland offshoot, all of them prosperous, right-thinking family people who erected big brick houses near the lakefront and gave work to coloured maids who, as Uncle Meyer once explained to Rebeccah, would be jobless and go hungry otherwise, "which you, I suppose, Miss High and Mighty, would rather see?"

Rebeccah herself was considerably different. She'd had the good fortune, she liked to tell her friends, of "marrying smart," referring not to herself but to her mother. Jacob Kristol was a working man and union organizer with rough hands and an intelligence striving to free itself of an inadequate education— not a trader, by any means, but a man who would smile when he saw children stealing apples from a street vendor. He'd had three years of school in Russia, then another two in New York's Brownsville, enough to give him sufficient English to go to work, at a factory manufacturing umbrella handles, but the bulk of what he knew of the world came from night school, correspondence courses, workshops put on by the union and a voracious appetite for reading that had made him, in his old age, a favourite of the librarians at the stately Carnegie in downtown Cleveland, where he would spend most of his afternoons from the time of his retirement until his death, in the reading room, crumpled over *Crime and Punishment*, which he was reading for the fourth time. He'd come to Cleveland as a young man, on a freight train with a trio of anarchists, to work and help organize the foundry. Then he'd stayed and married, as the Williamses always put it, "above his position," and fathered two children, a son who took after his mother's side of the family but died in the war, and a daughter— Rebeccah—who took after him.

Rebeccah's devotion to him was, in some respects, her un-doing. Jacob Kristol had married late, so he was already an old man through most of the time his daughter knew him, retired before she was through with school and dead before she had barely reached twenty. But his impact on her was powerful. It made her different from most of the girls with whom she went to school, and left her bored and dissatisfied with the few boys willing to penetrate the veil of sarcasm and feigned intellec-tualism with which she clothed herself, and she would have liked to have fled from the small city provincialism of Cleveland when she graduated, but her father's failing health kept her at home. Then, when he died, a pledge to him that she would look after her mother, who was also ailing, continued to keep her bound. By this time, she had a job, an apartment and a life of her own, and had discovered the small society of artists and poets, actors and anarchists who frequented the cluster of cafés and delicatessens along River Avenue on either side of the Rialto Theatre, where touring companies from New York would stage the latest in Yiddish productions.

70

"You're too good for this narrow stage," one of the actors—a handsome man with a cleft in his chin who went on to have a career in Hollywood under a new name—told her after they'd made love on the mattress of straw-filled ticking she'd affected in her small, darkly lit loft. "Why don't you come with me?"

"And you'll make me a star?" Rebeccah asked, batting the long, artificially thickened lashes of her large, luminous eyes.

"Seriously," the actor said. "You're too beautiful, too intelligent to let yourself stifle in this ridiculous city where it's always either too hot or too cold."

"And in your bed, the temperature is better controlled?" Rebeccah asked.

My father tried too. "Come with me to New York," he told her when he was getting ready to leave. He had gone west with the intention of seeing the world and, hopefully, writing about it, but he'd gotten no farther than Chicago before his money ran out and he'd circled back to Cleveland, where he'd heard, from a poet fleeing the place, of a job on a Yiddish newspaper. He spent three years there, learning the craft that would carry him for the rest of his life, before he felt he was ready to go home, and he would have liked to take her with him—this beautiful creature with wild, tangled hair and nicotine and paint stains on her long, delicate fingers—like some sort of souvenir of the great hinterlands across the Hudson River, proof of his passage.

Rebeccah kissed him, gently, like an echo. "You know I can't, Morgenstern," she said. "But I will someday."

"Will you let me know?" my father asked fervently.

"I'll let you know when I'm ready," Rebeccah said.

Before that happened, she met Aaron Greenspun.

Perhaps she'd meant it, always meant to leave, to find a broader world to the east, in New York, on which so much of the nightly café talk centred, or perhaps even in Paris, where she longed to study art at the Sorbonne, but time passed, her mother lingered, then died, freeing Rebeccah from her final bond but, still, somehow, she stayed and, before she could muster her energies for that flight, he appeared, changing everything.

It was at a family gathering, the first one of any real consequence since the marriage of the cousins, and he was there, being led through the gauntlet of Williamses by Aunt Ruth.

"And this is Rebeccah, our darling black sheep."

The black sheep was a tag Rebeccah had smilingly endured for years, even before her father's death, but tonight, with her hair in a woolly, swirling halo around her head and dressed all in black, even to her stockings, the tag seemed exceptionally appropriate, and she was radiantly bewitching, a fact which was hardly lost on the tall, handsome man in Aunt Ruth's tow. Nor was her effect on him lost on Rebeccah. They smiled at each other and a current of sexual tension crackled between them like an electric spark running along a twist of broken copper wire.

"The black sheep? More like a black diamond," Aaron said, in Yiddish almost cultured in its precision.

"Coal, you mean," Rebeccah said. She gave him her most radiant smile, showing all her teeth, and made a noise somewhat like a hiss.

"No, no, a sheep, a poor little lamb," Aunt Ruth said, putting her arm around Rebeccah and rocking her gently against her shoulder. "This child just lost her mother, my darling sister, so treat her gently."

"Aunt Ruth, that was almost two years ago."

"And still unmarried. Just a lamb, a poor lost lamb, but a *black* lost lamb, so what's to do with her?"

Aunt Ruth gave both their hands a squeeze and looked from face to face, then seemed to make a decision. "Be nice to each other, children. Rebeccah is a lost black lamb, Aaron is a stranger, a Jew among Jews, of course, but a stranger nonetheless." She moved on, with no indication he should follow.

Aaron shifted his weight from one lean hip to the other and cleared his throat. If Rebeccah truly was a black sheep, he was a white shepherd, dressed in grey trousers with a sharp crease— just the kind, her father used to say, the bosses use to cut the throat of the working man—and a white linen jacket with an ironed handkerchief in the breast pocket. And his yellow eyes, gazing shyly at her. "A white knight," Rebeccah said.

"Pardon?"

"That's you. I'm the black sheep, you're the white knight."

"A white night," he said, gesturing with his chin toward the window to underline his pun, "That's once a year if you're lucky, don't you agree? A full moon, starry sky, not a cloud."

Rebeccah smiled at him. There was an attraction, of course, and no sense denying it, but she already knew enough about him, from family gossip, to know better. She took the edge of her lower lip gently between her teeth and made a decision.

"That's too dizzying an abstraction for this poor lamb," she said, and began to move away.

His hand on her arm brought her up short. "Wait." He looked embarrassed by his abrupt gesture. "I'd like to see you again."

"Again? I'm just going across the room to have a canapé. My

stomach is growling. Look over there in a moment and you'll see me."

"I mean," Aaron said, twisting his resolve, "again, after this. Some place else. Perhaps we could have a meal."

"I don't like to cook," Rebeccah said with suspicion.

"I mean in a restaurant," he said in sudden English, as if it were a secret he wanted no one overhearing to understand.

She took a step back and looked him over, from the top of his sandy brown hair, neatly parted in the centre of his well-shaped head, down along the smooth contour of brow, nose, cleanly chiselled mouth and chin, the starched white collar, down the perfectly tied necktie, the immaculate linen jacket, pausing for a moment at his crotch, where, despite the loose drape of his trousers, she believed she saw a barely perceptible movement, then down the crease of the trousers to the glimmering black wings of his oxfords, then up again, letting her eyes take their time while he stood motionless, awaiting their verdict. "I want you to know," she said finally, "that you represent just about everything I detest and abhor about this society, capitalism at its most rapacious, mercantilism at its basest, petty bourgeois mentality at its narrowest, dandyism, masculine superiority, class and sexual arrogance . . ." Her hand darted out from her side in a palm-up gesture of dismay, as if she were overwhelmed by the enormity of the list she was prepared to recite, but her voice trailed off.

Aaron observed her with the same aloof detachment she had spent on him, a small smile seeping into his lips, and he shrugged, a shrug coloured with a boldness that made her think she had, perhaps, been wrong. "I may represent those things," he said. "I think you're wrong, but I won't argue with you now, here. I may *represent* them, but that wouldn't necessarily mean I *am* them. You *are* wrong there."

Four days later, resplendent in a blue and white striped gabardine suit and a straw hat, a bouquet of flowers in his freshly manicured hand, he showed up at the department store where she worked as a window dresser. "We're in the same business," he said as he greeted her, in the flow of employees through the staff entrance, at six o'clock.

"Not exactly. You sell, I decorate, though I'll concede there's a connection. More importantly, you own, I toil." But she was pleased to see him, flattered by the flowers he now proffered, making a gallant sort of dip with his head and shoulders, his free hand behind his back.

"The same business just the same. Mercantilism at its basest. And the fact that you're a Williams had nothing to do, I suppose, with your getting a job at Loew's."

"I'm not a Williams," Rebeccah said fiercely. "I'm a Kristol."

"Excuse me, no disrespect meant to the memory of your father, who I'm told was a fine man, I regret I never had the pleasure of meeting him. Working here rather than in the family store eases the conscience, don't you agree?"

Rebeccah let a smile slowly form. "That's a contradiction I'm still grappling with, yes." She observed him coolly, conscious of the slight pressure at the back of her neck caused by having to tilt her head upward to meet his eyes. "I don't know that meeting my father would have been a pleasure for you, though. He was a man who said what he thought."

"Like his daughter?"

"Like his daughter, yes."

"There's no accounting for taste," Aaron said, with a light laugh. "Don't you agree?"

He took her to as good a restaurant as was possible, considering the way she was dressed, and afterward to a place on the lake where they drank wine and danced. He took her home in his automobile, a Packard with shimmering chrome, and on the street gazed thoughtfully up at the dark windows of her loft, on the upper floor of a building that had once been a warehouse and was now honeycombed with small apartments. "You must be lonely there," he said with warmth.

"Not really," Rebeccah answered dryly, considering the options that faced her now. "There are ghosts."

But he didn't ask to come up, didn't make a move to kiss her goodnight. Instead, he offered his hand and shook hers vigorously.

After that, they saw each other often, dining out, dancing, attending the theatre and concerts, going to the museum and galleries. He had little interest in art, he admitted, and a tin ear, but he seemed happy to accompany her wherever she wished to go, and expressed an interest in learning about the things for which she had passions, which were many. He even, on the two or three occasions she took him, after the theatre, to the Royal Café for coffee, endured the thinly veiled insults of her friends. Rebeccah made no attempt to defend him and watched thoughtfully while he gingerly fended off her friend Belle's parries, like a man wearing white gloves suddenly handed something slick and foul smelling.

After two months, she was summoned to her Aunt Ruth's for Friday dinner. "And Aaron?" Aunt Ruth inquired after the dishes had been washed and Uncle Avrom had taken the dog and his pipe for a stroll in the late summer evening. The two women sat in the kitchen, drinking cool tea in the flickering candlelight.

"Aaron? That name sounds familiar. Wasn't he a fellow in the Bible?"

"The Bible! You've heard of that, Miss Fancypants, what a surprise."

"My father mentioned it once or twice, said it was suitable for use as kindling, if dead leaves were not close at hand."

"Your father! God rest his soul. He probably did say that. You like him?"

"My father? Of course I liked him." Aunt Ruth had been her mother's closest sister, and Rebeccah had a special affection for her, visiting often since her mother's death. But this was the first time she'd known her aunt to intrude.

"Aaron! Oh, you *know* who I mean. Aaron Greenspun. The man is crazy about you and you don't know who he is."

"Oh, Mr. Goldspun."

"It's Greenspun, dear."

"I know, Aunt Ruth. That's just a little joke."

"A joke! The man wants to marry you and you make jokes about his name that should be your name soon."

Rebeccah stared at her aunt for a moment, then laughed. "Marry me? Aunt Ruth, the man has only kissed me once, and that so softly it felt like a butterfly batting its wings against my lips. And *that* only because it was my birthday. When he escorts me home after an evening together he shakes my hand like it was the handle of a pump and he was dying of thirst."

"The man is a gentleman," Aunt Ruth said sternly. "You don't appreciate that, but you'll learn to."

"The man is beautiful but hollow," Rebeccah retorted. "He's like that candle, flickering, precious, hypnotic if you let yourself look too long, but of no substance." She leaned over and, as if to demonstrate her point, brushed her hand through the small flame, extinguishing it.

"Candles!" Aunt Ruth snorted through her nose. "You're burning yours at both ends, Miss Fancypants. Are you twenty-six now, or is it twenty-seven?"

Rebeccah wrinkled her nose to show her displeasure, but kept her voice soft. "Twenty-five, thank you, just as of three weeks ago, as you well know, since you sent me that lovely crinoline robe." She paused, tilting her chin slightly up. "You *witch*. I thought that was an odd gift to be coming from you. You're preparing my trousseau, aren't you?"

"Your mother, God rest her soul, isn't here to look after you. You're incapable of doing it yourself, so someone has to. It's a burden, but I take it happily, Bubela."

The two women stared at each other through the growing darkness, which had pounced on the room when the candle went out. Finally, Rebeccah blinked. "What do you mean, he wants to marry me?"

"Just that. Would it be plainer if I spoke in English?"

"You're crazy, Aunt Ruth, forgive me for saying so. How do you dream of such things?"

"There's no dreaming, Miss Fancypants. The man said so himself."

"Said so. To who? You?"

"Not to me, of course, silly," Aunt Ruth said. "To Uncle Meyer. He was a bit flummoxed, the poor man, his nose always in the store's books, he hardly knows there's a real world spinning around him, he asked me to have a word with you, and your Uncle Avrom to look after things. Oh, for goodness sake, Rebeccah, sit back down."

Rebeccah was on her feet, her hands closing into small, tight fists at her side. "He told Uncle Meyer he wanted to marry me? Aaron Greenspun did that?"

"Of course he did, Bubela. Now sit down."

She was speechless, words spinning around in her mind but failing to properly lodge on her tongue—like gears in a machine that won't engage. Worse, she felt, inexplicably, a profound sense of shame, as if she had been caught out in some disgusting betrayal. Blood rushed to her cheeks, making her feel faint. "Who . . . who . . ." she stammered.

"Who does he think he is? A gentleman, that's who." Aunt Ruth put her hand on Rebeccah's wrist and tugged at it until she sat down. "Let me ask you this, Miss Modern Woman, Miss Artist and Literary Type. If your father, God rest his soul, were alive, and if Aaron Greenspun or any other man, I mean any other man of breeding and manners, this isn't your friends like Morgenstern or that actor I'm talking about, but men who still have the old country in their minds and hearts, if such a man wanted to marry you and your father was alive, wouldn't you expect such a man to have the courtesy of talking to your father. *Not*"—she held up a silencing hand—"to ask permission, just to inform. Wouldn't you expect that? Wouldn't you even, maybe, be hurt, just a little, if such a man didn't do that, Miss Head-in-the-Clouds?"

Rebeccah allowed that maybe she would, "if it was that type of man, yes, maybe. Not if Morgenstern didn't do it." And she laughed at that thought, of my father paying a courtesy call.

"Well, what an admission! But Mr. Greenspun *is* that sort of man. He's a gentleman and an old country man. And wait, wait just a second, darling, let me ask you one more thing. Since your father, God rest his soul, *isn't* here, wouldn't it be proper then for Mr. Greenspun to talk to some other member of the Kristol family, if there was one nearby? Your father's brother, Mort, maybe, except that he lives a thousand miles away?"

Rebeccah nodded slowly.

"So, all right. Your father, God rest his soul, isn't alive, nor, God rest her soul, is your mother, my darling Rachel, and your father's brother and other relatives are a thousand miles away. So who should Mr. Greenspun talk to about his intentions but your Uncle Meyer, woolly headed though he is, he *is* the head of the Williams family, your mother's people."

"He could have talked to me, damn it," Rebeccah said in English.

Aunt Ruth smiled and patted Rebeccah's hand, which had grown cold. "He will, Bubela, he will. As soon as I tell him you'd like him to. Oh, come on, come on. He's a gentleman, I keep telling you. And maybe just a little bit shy, too."

Rebeccah went home and, over the next three days, while she brushed her teeth and combed her hair, while she steamed her vegetables for dinner, while she painted, standing nude under the skylights of her loft, she contemplated her life. She was, in fact, twenty-five years old and, as her father had died at sixty-eight, her mother at sixty-three, Rebeccah was well into what was likely the second third of her life. There had been no money left after her mother's illness, so her father's wispy promises that maybe, someday, she would go to art school had entirely evaporated. She had delayed her departure to New York and points farther on so long that, now, the thought of leaving Cleveland terrified her. And, worse yet, the paintings she had done, piled up like neatly stacked picket signs awaiting the next strike in her father's old office at the union hall, even the painting she was working on now, were shit, no other word for it, in Yiddish, English or any other language. She sighed, lit another cigarette and went to stand in front of her one concession to vanity, a full-length mirror she had justified when bought as essential to her study of anatomy. She stood there, in the bright, white northern light streaming down from the ceiling window, for a long time, observing the beginning sag of her breasts, the little puckering of skin along her belly.

On the third day, Monday, when Aaron came to call for her at the store, she found herself looking at him more closely than usual, *examining* him, with her painter's eye, as if looking for defects to match the ones she had found in herself. He had shaven within the hour and there were tiny pinpricks of dried blood clustered along the firm line of his jaw, but his cheeks and neck, when she reached across the table suddenly to stroke them, taking him aback and bringing a pleased, bashful smile to his strong mouth, were smooth as a baby's. His yellow eyes glistened like those of a cat watching the progress of a mouse across the room, and she had to admit he was simply beautiful, as flawless as a baby that had not yet begun to puncture its possibilities. But, at the same time, he was hollow, as she had told her aunt; he was filled with vapid observations about the weather, the people who worked for him in his shop, the politics of the city. Two weeks before, she remembered, after the theatre, an Ibsen play, his only comment had been a vague "What a way to live."

"You don't have an idea in your head, do you?" she asked suddenly, surprising herself that the thought had translated itself into words, slipping out of her mouth before she could stop them. Aaron blinked, looked surprised but not particularly displeased, as if her comment had referred to his new jacket, a grey seersucker he had taken off the rack that afternoon.

"I have an idea I'd like to get to know you better. How's that?"

Rebeccah smiled despite herself. So it was out, the overture that, from almost any other man of her acquaintance, likely would have come on the first night, certainly on the second, but from Aaron Greenspun had taken two months. She wondered if he had spoken with her aunt over the weekend, whether something she had said had emboldened him. Well, it didn't matter. The next step was up to her.

"That would be very nice," she said. "Yes, I'd like that."

That was all there was to it. So simple, that small exchange, but now there was an understanding between them, and that night, for the first time, when he escorted her home, he kissed her goodnight, and she knew the inexorable journey to their marriage had begun.

The engagement was announced within weeks but the marriage itself didn't take place until the following spring, after a suitable period of adjustment to the idea and an opportunity for

Aaron to purchase and, with Rebeccah's guidance, furnish a house, in the growing suburb of Shaker Heights, where streets lay like quiet ribbons beneath tall canopies of leaves. The honeymoon was to include an overnight trip on a paddle wheel schooner that plied Lake Erie and would take them from Cleveland to Buffalo, from where they would go by train to Niagara Falls, there spending several days admiring the scenery. It would be aboard the ship, on its first night out, in their stateroom, that their marriage was to be consummated. It was not a fit topic for conversation between betrothed, but Aaron, always a gentleman, did have this observation to make, three weeks before the wedding, when Rebeccah was still assembling the items for her trousseau: "And as to the rest . . . what will come afterwards . . . well, I just want you to have no concern. I'm not entirely without experience"—here he offered her his shyest smile, while his eyes blazed with boldness—"and I can promise you that I'll be gentle. It will be something wonderful, the two of us, don't you agree?"

Rebeccah awaited that something wonderful with a great deal of concern, in fact, since she was not without some *considerable* experience. The subject of virginity was not discussed, but it became clear to her, both from Aaron's manner and occasional small things he said, that he assumed he would be the first man to share sex with her—although he knew she had many male friends, most of whom he disapproved of—and that it was important to him. Honesty seemed out of the question, and the strategy of deception appeared to be inevitable.

"That will be no trouble at all, don't worry your head about it," Belle told her. She was a woman of indeterminable age but at least beyond forty to judge from the wealth of experience she had crammed into her life; a Romanian who had travelled for several years in France and England on her way to America; a friend, so she said, of Virginia Woolf and Emma Goldman; a painter of note who had benefited Rebeccah with encouragement and gentle criticism; and a Lesbian, though that was not a term then in vogue, who had buried three husbands already, one in each of the previous countries where she'd lived. "Men are such children, it's easy to deceive them. Flatter them and they're only too happy to believe anything, no matter how unlikely." She puffed on one of the slim black cigars she had developed a taste for in Paris and raised her magnificent eyebrows. "When it comes to sex, it's all the easier since, in bed, they are so helpless. So *strong*, they think they are, just because blood rushes to one pathetic portion of their anatomy and makes it stiff. At the same time, the rest of them turns to jelly." She shrugged her shoulders and gestured with a slim, black-gloved hand, as if uncovering some vast expanse. "Men are such children, take it from me, darling Rebeccah. They preen and swagger, they bellow and fight, they spend money like it was water and let compliments flow from their tongues like honey from the rock, they even *marry* you, so desperate are some of them, all to get you in bed, then, a little kiss, a little pat, a jiggle, a thrust, another jiggle, and it's all over. They roll over and lie there like exhausted warriors who have single-handedly defeated great armies, a beatific smile playing about their lips like a butterfly among flowers. No, don't worry your head darling, it will be easy to deceive your Mr. Spun From Gold. We'll devise a plan."

The deception was remarkably simple, consisting of an easily mixed douche of water, vinegar and alum, guaranteed, Belle promised, to give Rebeccah the rasping friction of a thirteen-year-old girl, and a small quantity of chicken blood, concealed in a pink balloon, the sort children blow up at birthday parties. The rest, Belle explained, was merely a sleight of hand, a bit of acting and, she said, "that famous guile we women are supposed to have in such abundance. Let's see if it's true." And, on the couch in Belle's studio, not far from Rebeccah's own loft, they practised the weary motions, with Belle taking Aaron's part.

"Ah, my darling, my sweet *chérie*, don't be frightened, I weeell be gentle," she sing-songed in English rich with French resonance, and the two of them burst into schoolgirl giggles, rolling together on the sofa like young athletes, though it went no further than that. "Ah, my darling," Belle gasped, breathless with laughter, "you are so, how they say? Wonderfully . . . tight."

Rebeccah herself went to the pharmacist for the alum, and prepared the mixture as to Belle's instructions, starting its use two days before the wedding, to be sure. "I feel like the inside of a pickled egg," she reported. "Ah, how wonderfully tasty," Belle retorted, arching her brows.

But Belle, on the day of the wedding itself, attended to the blood, so it would be fresh, by visiting at the slaughterhouse a kosher rabbi she was acquainted with. He provided what she needed, no questions asked.

The wedding was small, by the standards of the community, with only family, from Akron as well as Cleveland, and a few of Rebeccah's and Aaron's closest friends attending. Rebeccah had doubted most of her café friends would be interested, or would approve; besides, she had found herself, in recent months, drifting away from them, with the exception of Belle and a couple of other women. Uncle Meyer, as head of the family, and the wealthiest, hosted the party at his home in the Heights, though Uncle Avrom, as the favourite uncle, played the part of the surrogate father, standing up to give the bride away. Aaron broke the muffled glass with one determined stomp, there was dizzying music, and there were crowded tables of food all seemingly flavoured with honey, and glasses of sweet wine that couldn't be emptied. Then, as her head spun, Rebeccah was led by the hand to a waiting motorcar by Aaron, her husband—her *husband*—and they were off to the docks.

Her head was still filled with spinning wafts of wool when they were shown to their cabin and, as soon as the porter was gone, Aaron had her in his arms, covering her mouth, nose, ears and neck with moist, indistinct kisses. She extricated herself, took her overnight bag and locked herself in the small bathroom, where she made one final application of the douche before putting on her nightgown. Then, with the balloon cupped in her palm, she made her entrance.

"You look wonderful, darling," Aaron said in English, his yellow eyes seeming to dance in the soft glow of the kerosene lamp. "You get into bed, I'll just be a minute."

She did as he said and, as soon as the door softly shut behind him, slipped the balloon under her pillow. Then, with her eyes gradually slipping into a sharp focus on what was either a stain or a shadow on the ceiling, she waited, her breath ragged, her heart pounding, just as if she really were a virgin.

Afterward, while he slept, she put a robe over her gown, slid her feet into slippers and crept from the cabin to walk along the deserted deck. The night was thick and dark, like an old woollen cloak, and cold. She stood against the rail, shivering and clutching her arms, and stared down at where, from the choppy roll of the deck beneath her feet, she could tell the foaming waves of the lake were splattering against the ship's hull. But she could see nothing and even the sound of the waves was absent, drowned out by the whining of the engines, which must have been close to where she stood. She could have just as easily been aboard one of Jules Verne's fantastic ships, sailing through the darkness of space, as on the paddle wheeler *Albany*, somewhere in the middle of Lake Erie, suspended between two countries and two worlds. The deception had been so simple, so absurdly successful, just as Belle had promised. Aaron had been still a little drunk, his shining eyes excited but only half open when he slipped into bed and turned to her, and he'd been hasty, clumsy, needing, despite her pretence of innocence, her discreet hand to guide

him. The alum had done its job almost too well, and there had
been pain, for him as well as her, and then it was over, almost
before it had begun, leaving her barely enough time to reach back
beneath the pillow for the balloon, sliding it down along her
sweaty side, before he rolled away. She clenched it tightly in her
palm, pricking it with the nail of her index finger, and smeared
the tepid blood along her thighs and into the dripping wet hair
covering her aching vulva. She had lain there for a moment,
feeling like the victim of some bizarre religious ritual, waiting for
him to lift the sheet, to seek the evidence for himself, but he was
already drifting off to sleep, one hand tossed lightly across her
breast like a statement of trust and possession, and he never did
look.

Just before he screwed his face closer into the pillow and fell
asleep, as quickly and firmly as a stone being dropped into water,
he half opened his eyes and murmured: "That was wonderful,
darling, don't you agree?"

She hadn't said anything, just watched him, in the flickering
light of the lamp, fall asleep. She'd insisted he leave the lamp
burning, so she could see him, those brilliant cat's eyes, so he
could see her, because he was so beautiful and she wanted to feel
beautiful. But after they had started, he'd closed his eyes, and it
had seemed to her he could have been anyone. Just the same,
there had been a moment even as he'd slid into her, a moment
above the pain even as her nerve endings and skin had responded
on their own, when they had moved together as one, when her
passion had risen with the alacrity all those months of courtship
seemed to have been foreshadowing and their breaths had
merged into one fierce, staccato rhythm. She thought about that
moment while she stood along the railing, her teeth chattering
with cold, her eyes streaming with tears while they stared blankly
into the darkness below. There had been that moment, that was
all. There had even been one moment when, allowing her imagi-
nation to run wild, she had believed she might love him. But it
had just been that one moment, and then it was gone.

82

ANDREW WREGGITT

In Defense of the Burning of Some Letters

You feel it is your right,
that you have been cheated
because I burned those letters from Russia
You think your heritage was lost to you,
that it was I who robbed you of it
What your mother has told you is true
I burned them all, every date and name they contained
and much more
I am not sorry, *mien Grottsehn*

You ask for what was never yours,
accusing me from your modern life
You feel it is your right
to cannibalize the past,
the dry bones of your ancestors
Perhaps it is
But first, listen
I can tell you this now because you are grown,
because there is no one alive from that time
At last, that suffering is over

Listen. The sorrow you would take from those letters
is not yours
It is not something you might find
at the bottom of a closet,
something to dust off and wear on your coat
What you want to know as history,
was to us the world groaning and dying,
was to us the terrible end of all we had known

Your mother could not have told you
that I wept as I burned those letters,
the horses pulling slower and slower
on the road back from town

Past the church, the fields
of our neighbours, wheat murmuring,
meadow larks in the ditches
           Strange to have heard those sweet voices
           as I read those words,
           terrible words . . .
                tou schlemm

The letters were a catalogue of the dead
Our families, our neighbours in Russia
murdered by the Bolsheviks,
tortured or simply taken away,
not seen again . . .
Helen, Martin, Henry,
Sarah, who sang so beautifully,
her voice like an angel's . . .
Isaac and all his brothers,
all their children . . .

These were not detached accounts
in the way you might read them now,
historical texts to be studied, analysed
I lived each event as I read of it
I knew each barn where a man was hung
for the crime of owning a Bible,
how the light fell through
the gapped planks of the stalls,
how the wind bent the crops in the fields where . . .
leva Gott . . . people slaughtered like livestock!
They were the lost of a family
such as you will never know,
Mennonite brethren, shattered seed of God

This is what I read in those letters,
the horror I could not release
           Slow plodding steps of the horses
           finding their own way
           in the dust and deep rutted track,
           the creaking of the harnesses

Each death was my loss,
each blow a wound in me
I looked up into the bright daylight,
beside me the little blonde girl, your mother,
who woke to the smell of burning paper,
who knew not to talk about the letters at home
Little daughter . . .
> *tjlienit Schoptji . . .*

Still, you want to know why
Yes, I remember the little boy with the questions, *Grottsehn*,
Do not be impatient with me
Understand that I burned those letters
because I had to . . .

> *Husband, you were the one who died in 1959*
> > *the lucky one*
> *You could not have imagined*
> *I would live for another thirty years*
> *Thirty years!*

> *At first, there were shock treatments*
> *in places with caged windows, prisons!*
> *The shouting all night . . .*
> *I curled up and stayed so quiet . . .*
> > *little lamb*
> *Later, there were drugs*
> *and then the homes*

> *Who would have thought there would be*
> *so many of us,*
> *crowding into the cafeterias*
> *like sick cattle?*
> *Banging our spoons*
> *on the shiny tables . . .*
> *The lost ones lurching in the hallway . . .*

My wife, Martha, was ill by then,
a disease of the mind
There is a name for it now, I suppose
To us, it was mysterious, unpredictable
She lived on the edge of a personal chaos
so dark . . .
the smallest thing would send her reeling
into that black world
A dusty plate,
a jar of milk gone sour
She would shut herself in her room
for days, her rage uncontrollable,
her depression
The children would whisper to each other
in the kitchen, afraid,
wondering what they had done wrong

How could I show her those letters?

> *I knew I was ill those years,*
> > *at least at times*
> *I pitied you, when I saw you*
> *sitting by the stove in the morning,*
> > *so tired . . . your hands curled that way*
> *There was love too, those*
> *tender moments . . .   nah yoh . . .*
>
> *But it was the girls I pitied most*
> *Like me, they had no choice,*
> > *they were born to it . . . this sadness*
>
> *I didn't choose this life*
> *I would have stayed in Russia*
> *if I could, with my family*
> *But I followed you, even though I was so afraid*
> *I thought my heart would stop*
> *I followed you and raised our daughters*
> *the best I could*

It wasn't always so
In the early years, she laughed so easily,
her head tilted a little to one side,
pulling her hair back, looking at me . . .
That simple motion filled me with such happiness!
Before we married, her family was all she knew
The world for her, for all of us, was no bigger
than the distance a wagon could travel in a day
I loved her very much and I believe
she loved me . . .
But we grew harder with the times
There was love of children,
love of God, but for us . . . *Zoh*

When the trouble began,
it was our families, people from our village
who made it possible to go
A few young couples sent to find land in Canada,
sponsor others
But there were no others after us

We already had a small baby
when we boarded the train to Petersburg
Martha wept for days over leaving her family
and for the fear that possessed us all,
a cold, icy presence that never left her
There was so much to be afraid of,
the stopping and starting of the train
for weeks, the gunfire
in the forests around us . . .
Our first winter in Canada,
it seemed we had fallen
over the edge of the earth
Two families in a two-room sod house,
six children

The wind blew through the chinks in the walls
and the children were sick and hungry
Our baby cried all winter,
diapers hung around the stove
There were arguments and hard words
We were not wanted,
but who could blame them?
Everyone was so poor
At night, Martha would weep and whisper
that we should not have come,
even that God had abandoned us
Such was her sickness

I was a mouse, burrowed under the snow
I nibbled my bread, suckled my young
Outside, the wind swept over the snow,
a Bolshevik horseman with no pity,
cutting the breath out of me

So I burrowed
in my corner by the stove
and never went out,
dirt from the roof in my hair,
my garland of soil
I burrowed
and let the days pass through me,
one by one,
like the shadows
of the dead

You cannot know the loneliness I felt
along those flat, dusty miles
        the stepping of the horses,
        the turning of the axles . . .
as I consigned each page, each German cipher
to ash

How I swallowed that ash at the supper table each day,
soup and bread, everything I tasted was ash,
bitter,
the ash of our poverty, our great loss
My wife and I, strangers to each other in our own house,
in the presence of our children

88

You speak of your loneliness
but what about me?
Most of my life spent in a cold, grey dream
You have no idea what I saw
in my worst times
You speak of those letters
but do you imagine I did not live through as much
in my sickness?
Terrible images that drove me crying from the table
night after night?
I knew they were dying,
I felt us dying with them
The deception at our table, my own daughters
lying to me, afraid of me,
my own husband!
I did not want to know of those letters,
I did not want to know!
Still, I felt their suffering
   and could not reach out

Everywhere I looked along that road
were the tiny houses and blown fields
of others like us,
the countless, scattered children of other continents,
struggling for their lives,
for the lives of those who would come later,
for you, *mien Grottsehn*
What could I do, but hide my tears
from the little girl beside me
and carry on?

  You could not have imagined
  I would live for another thirty years
  after all we had come through
  A crazed, old woman talking nonsense
  to the doctors . . . Shame!

  I didn't ask for this, Peter
  I didn't . . .
    ask . . .

Remember, husband
You brought me here
and then left me to grow old
alone

Grottsehn, do not ask for the grief I left
along that road
You remember a grandfather who built you
a wooden stool, who spoke softly to you in your bed
in a language you could not understand
An old man who died
before you even started to school

Be content, and don't ask
for the sorrow of others, the unhappiness and misfortune
of people you never knew
Let them rest
You can see them if you must,
in the lines and shape of your face,
your mother's easy laugh

Be content with that, *mien Grottsehn,*
> *sie toufrehd*
and look no farther

ANNE SZUMIGALSKI

Deadwood

My father was born in a distant country where every person is a tree—every adult that is.

Children are fieldflowers, they are grass, they are lilies and poppies and small blue lupines. Until puberty they are any plants they choose. More than that, they may change their minds as many times as they wish. A child may wake as a gillyflower and go to sleep as eglantine. Is it any wonder that in that country no one is in a hurry to grow up?

At the age of twelve or so each must name a tree and is stuck with this choice until the tree falls from age or is struck down by the axe of the woodcutter. This last is their way of explaining the death of the young in battle, for, in spite of their worship of the peaceable plant, they are a warlike lot.

All this my father told me, but though I bothered and cajoled him he would never say which tree he had chose nor whether, in this new country, he still felt bound by the customs of his birthplace.

He always seemed just a man to me and very like other people's fathers: that is strong and infallible in my childhood and, as I advanced into adolescence, more and more clumsy and over-bearing.

There was one difference though. Unlike other men he was never seen without a shirt or a sweater. Not that he was particularly modest in other ways. Several times I caught him pulling on his trousers in a hurry. I had a good look. Nothing strange there. But what was he hiding beneath his T-shirts and button up cardigans? Was he afraid of woodpeckers? Was there a hole there beneath his heart where a squirrel had made her nest?

I was almost a grown woman when he took me for a holiday in a warmer part of the country. It was May and already early summer in that gentle climate. He pointed out a tree I had never seen on the Prairies and acknowledged it as his own. *Hippocastanum* he explained proudly. Its leaves were huge green hands and be-tween them sprung tall racemes of bloom like white and yellow candles. This then was my father's tree, generous in its spread, amazing in its summer complacency.

We stood there hand in hand as he told me about its various phases, of how in fall it would bear inedible brown nuts in leathery green cases, nuts that are the weapons of little boys in their battles.

All this was years ago, and my father is dead now, hollowed and fallen like every tree before him. I was with him when he died.

No sooner had he taken his last breath than I leaned over him and began to unbutton his pyjama jacket. What did I expect to find? Simply the chest of an old tired man, the tangles of coarse grey hair intricate as twigs, the nipples hard and resinous as winter buds.

And the Children Shall Rise

He watches her small thin fingers, quick like animals, scrabbling. They crouch together on the side of the road.

"Help me," she says.

He obeys and runs his hand along the curb base until he strikes a pebble.

"Here." He smiles.

She takes the pebble and puts it in its place, her only acknowledgement acceptance, although he waits for a word.

"Give me that one." She points at a rock nearby. He needs two hands to lift it. He is only four.

"More little ones," she says.

Soon the circle of stones is closed. He places his palm in the centre, but she grabs his wrist and yanks him away. She leans forward so her hair brushes the ground, then spits where his hand was. From her blouse pocket she takes a matchbox and holds it out to him. She shakes it; the sound is not matches.

"What's in there?" he asks.

Carefully, solemnly, she opens the little drawer.

"Caterpillars," he says.

She nods.

"Caterpillars! Caterpillars! Where did you find them?"

"Watch," she says.

She takes a caterpillar from the box and puts it in the centre of the circle, on the dark mark of her saliva. The caterpillar is a beautiful thing, peacock, iridescent, starred, fringed with fine hairs. It crawls away. With her finger she guides it back to the centre. He reaches out to play too, but she stops his hand again. Then, quickly, so quickly he sees only the fleeting blur of her arm, the arc of a movement, she slams the rock down.

He stares at her. After a moment she turns her face, squinting at him as if the sun is in her eyes, and lifts the rock. In the circle of stones is a jellied mass, green and yellow, glistening.

"Is it dead?" he asks.

"Yes. Do you want to do it?"

"No."

"Then you pick one."

He selects a caterpillar, then watches the stone crush it.

"What are you doing Carol?"

They look up and his mother is standing over them.

"Nothing," Carol says.

"It's not nothing," his mother says. "You're killing things." She crouches too. "Look, poor caterpillars. How do you think they feel?"

"Dead," says the boy.

"How do you think they feel?" she asks Carol.

"How do you think I feel?" Carol replies.

He watches his friend go away down the road. She has long black hair past her waist and a walk that is smooth and careless. Barefooted, she moves as if she has her whole life to get where she is going. She stops and bends, scratches her ankle, then walks on with her arms out from her sides like wings.

"It's not that I don't like Carol Bell," his mother says later.

"I like Carol Bell," he says.

"I like her too. But she's seven, you know."

"I'm four," he says.

"I know. That's what I'm saying, Philip. You are four and she is seven."

"And you are a hundred," he says.

She laughs and kisses him. "I'm sorry there aren't other children your age here. Do you miss your friends?"

"I miss Daddy."

"Yes," she says. "Sometimes I do too, though I shouldn't."

They have left his father behind and come to this little house in this summer town, where the roads are always dusty and no one wears shoes. His mother is painting again now, on large papers the boy helped her make.

"I like Carol Bell," he says.

"Yes, she has beautiful hair."

He is playing on the swings with Carol Bell. She swings high, then leans back so her hair sweeps the grass. He tries to do the same but falls.

She asks, "Do you want a push?"

"No."

Carol Bell has pushed him before, slammed her hands against his back and sent him to dizzy, terrifying heights. He called for her to stop, pleaded for her to stop and, when she finally did, she ran away. He does not want her to run away now.

"Let's sit sideways then," she says.

He gets up and they straddle the swings, facing each other. Carol sways back and forth and looks up at the sky. Her eyes are dark and deep-set, ringed with a faint blueness like smoke. Still without looking at him, she glides forward and knocks her swing against his.

"Don't," he says.

Her face does not change and she knocks him again.

"Please don't."

Then she smiles, just slightly, turning up the corners of her mouth and making her lips look smooth like fruit skin. She smashes into his swing with such force that between his legs there is only a sharp, singing pain. His face crumples. He is going to cry.

"I'm hungry," she says quickly. "Go get us something to eat." She takes his arm and shakes it. "Get something to eat."

By the time he is in the kitchen, he no longer needs to cry. He comes back with his mother. She wears her painting shirt.

"She'll only give us carrot sticks," he tells Carol, who takes one.

"Don't you get breakfast, Carol?" his mother asks.

"Yes."

"What did you have for breakfast this morning?"

"Pancakes with blueberries and strawberries," Carol says. "And coffee."

"Coffee?"

"Yes. I always drink coffee. I like it."

"Do you want to have lunch here?" his mother asks.

"Yes." Carol takes another carrot stick.

At lunch his mother asks after Carol's mother. Carol says her mother is dead.

"What?" his mother exclaims. "When?"

"Four years ago," Carol says.

"You're not telling the truth. I met your mother. And just the other day I saw her drive by."

"It wasn't my mother."

"Yes, it was. She waved to me."

"Anyway," Carol Bell says, "my brother is always screaming because of it."

The boy stares at her with his mouth hanging open, showing his half-chewed sandwich.

"Carol," says his mother, "I don't think you're telling the truth."

"I am," she says. "He sounds like this." She throws back her head and screams.

The boy looks at his mother unhappily.

"Well, we hope your brother will be all right," she says. Then, slyly, "Here's a cup of coffee for you. What do you take in it, Carol?"

"Nothing. I drink it black."

And she does. She drinks it down black as if it were chocolate. His mother puts her hand over her mouth. She knows better than to test Carol Bell, or the boy's father, or anyone.

There is just the boy and his mother living together, in the small house, warm and close.

"Two buns in a basket," she tells him, beginning their game.

"Two bugs in a rug," he says.

"Two birds in a nest."

"Two pigs in a pen."

They fall down laughing and snorting like pigs. There is a love in this laughter that clings like burrs. But the boy wets his bed at night and sometimes cries for no reason.

In the evening when he bathes, she sits on the edge of the tub and sings all the songs he asks for —"Froggie Went A'Courting," "Little White Duck," "Suzanna's a Funny Old Man." She takes up the washcloth but he always escapes from her embrace.

"Dirty thing," she teases.

When he is in bed, she reads to him, not more than three, four, stories. Then he must brush her hair the hundred strokes. He falls asleep before forty.

"One. Some people lie," she tells him while he draws the brush through her hair. It is shoulder-length and greying.

"I don't lie," he says.

"Two. Of course not. You would never lie. Ouch. Daddy lied."

"No."

"Three. Yes, and sometimes Carol Bell lies. I want you to know that. Four."

"Okay."

"And don't play with Carol Bell except in our yard. Five. All right, Philip?"

"Okay."

They are almost in the yard, just at the end of the driveway, on the road. They have collected sticks, handfuls of dried leaves and grasses, bits of paper, and put it all in the circle of stones. Carol takes out the matchbox. She shakes it and the sound is matches.

At first there is just smoke, a brown veil that catches on his face, makes his eyes tear. He shifts over, but the smoke follows, so he gets up and stands behind Carol. She arranges and rearranges the debris, blows on it, mumbles quietly in sing-song. The pile ignites in a sudden burst of flame. She pulls her hand away and he sees that her finger is burnt. He wonders if she will cry and leans around to look at her face.

"You got hurt," he tells her.

"What?"

"You got burnt."

"No, I didn't," she says.

"You did. Look."

"I didn't."

She pulls a stick out of the little fire and waves it around in the air. The flaming end makes a glowing baton. The boy can see the circles and figure eights she is drawing and he laughs.

"Watch," she says.

She takes the end of her own hair, as she would a rope, then touches the fire stick to it. He hears the sizzle, smells the stench.

"That's awful," he says and she laughs.

Other days they build other fires, in the yard now, under the willow where they are hidden by the curtain of leaves, next to the swing set, on the walk. His mother catches them when the fire spreads to a dry patch on the lawn. She rushes out of the house with a doormat and beats the fire into the ground, but a star-shaped singe remains, a reminder. The mat is ruined. The boy stands by with his finger in his mouth and Carol Bell is gone.

His father is an artist too. The boy did not see him often because he worked at night, slept days. Their city house was large with windows even in the ceiling, fireplaces, a spiral stair. The boy played in the studio most afternoons. His father's paintings were huge, almost the size of the studio wall, bright as balloons and puzzling. In some smaller paintings the boy could recognize a subject, usually a person, but only because his mother pointed it out to him, saying, "Look. Who do you think she is?" and never answering when he said, "I don't know."

Now in this new town, this small house, his mother works all day. Sometimes she paints him as he plays and later he laughs at the border of gold she draws around his body. She bought him a bamboo cage and two finches, then painted the birds preening a plumage that was not theirs at all, too vivid, shocking. When she does not paint, she cooks and bakes, changes his sour wet sheets in the dark, kisses him. She throws down her brushes.

"I have hardly worked in four years. Now I have all the time I need. So what's wrong with me?" She says this aloud, to no one.

He sits on the front step with Carol Bell. She stretches her thin legs out in the sun. Her feet are astonishingly dirty, the soles black, toes grubby, nails encrusted. He has never seen her wearing shoes. While she speaks, he fidgets nervously. She says everyone in her family has a disease; her sister was sent to where they put crazy people.

"Where do they put crazy people?" he asks.

"Far away. Another country, I think. They tie her to a chair."

Her mother coughs ceaselessly. "Sometimes blood comes out, sometimes green stuff, sometimes spiders."

He cringes. "Spiders!"

The boy does not know what to say about these horrors, so he says nothing. Then she gets up and walks to the middle of the lawn. She raises her arms in the air and lifts one leg so she is posed in a crude arabesque. The sun is on her back. He watches and waits for her next movement.

She does not stir for a long time and he is just about to call to her when her arms suddenly stretch and her hair comes alive, fanning and spreading into a wheel. He watches her, open-mouthed, watches and is dizzied. Minutes before she frightened him; now she mystifies, turns and turns, a bit of paper trapped in a wind eddy, and he is sure she will rise up from the lawn and spin away. Seeing her prepare for flight, he leaves the step and his sandals, runs onto the lawn.

The moment he joins her, she stops. He is embarrassed and goes back to the step. Carol Bell walks carefully along the edge of the flower bed, then crouches while the boy struggles to buckle his sandals. When he looks up, she is just disappearing beyond the hedge.

"Gone home," he says unhappily.

He shuffles over to the flower bed to look for the print of her bare feet. He sees instead that Carol Bell has pulled the heads off the flowers.

"Did Carol Bell do this?" his mother asks.

"No," he answers.

"No? Who did it then? Philip, who did it?"

"Me," he tells her.

"You? Oh, Philip, don't say that. I know it's not true." He looks at her and notices a streak of paint across her cheek. "Did Carol do it?"

"No. Me."

She sighs and takes his hand. "Now what am I supposed to do with you? Why can't I just decide? Okay, listen Philip, if I catch Carol Bell at this sort of thing again, I'll go to her mother."

"Her mother has a disease," he says.

"Nonsense. Carol Bell tells stories. Carol Bell lies."

He says, "I like Carol Bell."

She covers the paint streak on her face with her hand, as if it pains her.

The boy brings a tumbler of water from the house and takes it to Carol Bell at the end of the driveway. He is conscious of his mother standing in the front window and watching him, the way she used to watch his father. Carol grips a stick between her knees and works at fraying the end, but her fingernails are too bitten down; finally she uses her teeth.

They have made a volcano, swept the dust off the road to shape a hill, then pushed a finger down through the top. Carol carefully pours water into the hole. He smiles at her ingenuity.

Now she stirs with the frayed stick, adds more water, and a thin batter is formed. "Paint," she tells him. He claps his hands.

She bites her lip, showing small teeth, and her face twists up with the strain of concentration. She begins painting with the mud on the driveway.

"Do a boat!" he says, but she is not listening.

Soon her strokes steady. With each line he tries to guess her picture and hopes it will be a boat. He thinks that she, seven years old, must be a fine artist and capable of drawing a fine boat. Then his face falls. She is not drawing but writing. He cannot read.

He sits in silent disappointment. She appears to be writing a painfully long word. Bored, he looks up and waves to his mother at the window. She disappears and a moment later is walking toward them, arms crossed, frowning. Carol continues writing.

In one motion his mother swoops down, tears the stick out of Carol Bell's hand and hoists her up by the arm. She shouts, "You wash that! Do you hear me? Wash it and never do it again!"

"What does it say?" the boy asks.

"Another thing. I'm going to talk to your mother. I'm tired of your pranks."

Carol Bell stands stiffly and allows herself to be shaken. She stares at his mother with wide eyes. He has never seen the girl frightened before. Then his mother's expression softens and reddens to a fluster.

"I have to tell your mother."

Carol's face stretches into a grimace. He thinks she will cry, but she just stands there with her terrible twisted face, then jerks her arm free. He watches her walk away down the road slowly, rubbing her arm.

"Get the hose please, Philip."

"What does it say?"

"Nothing."

He is brushing her hair. A finch died that afternoon and they are both saddened though he could not accept her comfort. They forget to count his strokes. She tells him the bird was good and will certainly go to heaven. He asks if Carol Bell will go to heaven.

"Oh, Philip. I feel sorry for the girl, poor pretty thing. That lovely hair, those filthy feet. But with her lying, her mischief, she's a bad influence on you. I should have talked to Mrs. Bell and not gone back on my word. But the look on her face! How could I?"

"Will you go to heaven?" he asks.

She turns to him. "What do you think?"

He is not sure, so he shrugs. Then he says, "If Daddy goes with you."

She breathes deeply, makes a noise like wind to clear away his blame.

Carol Bell is gone for several days and the boy misses her. He lingers at the front of the house, on the lawn where she once did her dance, down at the end of the driveway where they had their circle of stones. When at last he resigns himself to her absence, she appears, beckoning to him from behind the hedge. He goes to her delighted, stays the morning but, when he comes back to the house for lunch, he is distraught.

He has trouble with his meal. He keeps his right hand under the table.

His mother laughs. "Is it a game?"

"What?"

"Eating like that. Are you playing a game?"

"Yes," he says and looks away. When he looks back, she is frowning.

"What's wrong, Philip?"

He begins to cry.

"Give me your hand. Oh, Philip!"

Carol Bell has carved a little figure across the back of his hand. It is not deep, and it did not hurt too much. He likes it, in fact: a strange mark, rather like a flower or a star, coloured rust with his dried blood.

"Come with me," she says. "We're going over there."

"No!" he cries.

"We must show Carol's mother what Carol did."

"I'm scared," he says.

His mother goes alone. She is gone not fifteen minutes and when she returns she forbids him to play with Carol Bell.

"Carol Bell is on the swings!"

"What?" She comes and looks out the window. "You stay here. I'll go and talk to her."

This is the very next day. He can just see her form through the trees. Last night he dreamt of Carol Bell walking away with her arms out from her sides like wings. She spun once around and took to the air. He believed he would never see her again.

"Carol Bell is on the swings!" He follows his mother out the door.

His mother says, "Carol, what happened?"

"Nothing," Carol answers.

"What happened to your hair?"

"Nothing."

"Who cut your hair?"

"Nobody."

Carol's hair is hacked raggedly, shorter on one side of her head than the other. She swings slowly and smiles at them.

"Did you cut your hair or did your mother cut your hair?"

"No one cut my hair."

"But it's gone!" the boy cries.

His mother takes him by the hand and leads him into the house again. She sits down on the sofa and stares at the floor.

"Did I make a mistake?" she asks. "Did I do the wrong thing? What would anyone do?" Then she looks at him. "Did you know?"

He does not have any answers for her. She holds out her arms and he comes to her, falls forward and touches her cheek. Then he takes her soft skin between his fingers, takes it and twists, pinches with all his strength. She cries out in pain, pushes him away and slaps his face. They look at each other, stunned, stunned by the hate there. Finally he comes again into the circle of her arms and they weep.

DOUGLAS NEPINAK

Psychopaths Shouldn't Be Allowed to Have Children

conversation in class is difficult
words are chalky   few
the discussion never comes my way anyhow
all the good kiddies reporting what they did
what they got during christmas holidays

well I dodged hate bullets
tiptoed through broken glass
screamed harmonies to the top ten party tunes
prayed
prayed

now this teacher would like to have a frank chit-chat on life
and possibly discover why I put cigarettes out on my body

oh yes   I do hate this world
when it's not smashing down the walls
it's a vaccuum

a bus is barreling at you
don't analyse it
get out of the way

and surviving once again
in your bed at night
you wrap the pillow around your face
and pray

DOUGLAS NEPINAK

Grandmother

in her dreams there is no television
speaking incessantly in a foreign language
of grand magnificent things
beyond her means

in her dreams everyone speaks Anishinabe
there is no confusion
no lapses into english
her grandchildren are not silent to her

the world is whole to her again
she walks through the bush collecting berries   roots
and stories off the great tree with a firm shake
the wind smells of seasons to come
they are good   full

SHELLEY A. LEEDAHL

Two Kids in a Picture

Whenever I think of them, I think of the night. The
doorbell. Mother's soft voice, me waking to find two
new brothers.

It was always like that. Cops, social workers and more
kids on the doorstep. *Priscilla's going to stay with us
for awhile. Let's make up a bed for Brad.* Bawling
newborns. Reticent two year olds. The teens never
stayed very long. I thought we had the biggest family
in the world.

The two kids in this picture, squinting out sun. I've
long since lost their names. I heard the older one shot
his head off in Edmonton. The other one just disappeared.

LALA HEINE-KOEHN

The Cameo

Mother, why do you ask me again to mend the small
drawstring bag where you kept the jewellery
you treasured most? It is gone, long ago,
and the bag is so threadbare
I can see through it

The amethyst ring that once held
the family crest studded with precious stones—
you lost those stones sealing a letter closed
with wax, sent you never knew to whom.
(The other ring, you told us, Father was wearing
when they killed him. *Was he buried with it?* we asked,
but you didn't even know where his grave was.)

The cameo earrings you always wore, a part of a set
Father gave you in St. Petersburg, the city
where you met and married.
There was no time to take them with you
when we had to leave our home. Not even time
to answer us: *Mother, why do we have to go?*
When will we come back?

Later, the three of us among other terrified
women and children, driven like a herd of cattle
from one place to another, Hydra's ugly heads rising
around us, not to be cauterized by guns, bombs or prayers.
You gave the cameo ring to a guard for a loaf of bread.
We ate it, huddled under a blossoming raspberry bush.
It was spring, 1945.

Only the cameo brooch remained in your small drawstring bag.
You brought it with you to your new home, Canada.
You wore it again, as you used to in Poland, pinned
to the white silk turban wound around your head,
the ivory cameo face carved the same as yours.

Perhaps you wore it to tell Father
that it didn't matter whether this was
Russia, Poland or Canada, he was beside you.

You gave the brooch to me when your first grandchild,
my daughter, was born. Mother, your drawstring bag
needs no mending. Your face is carved in all
of us, your children, our children
and all their children to come.

SHELDON OBERMAN

This Business with Elijah

I asked him what he wanted behind my parents' store and he sang out he was the Prophet Elijah. He shook his sidelocks and he danced among the garbage cans. And as I watched his hands coiling above his head and watched his fingers kissing his thumbs I wanted to dance as well, to close my eyes and sway and let my voice bleed with his into the endless sky.

Instead, I ran.

I ran skiddering over the gravel and crashing up the back stairs to our apartment over the store. My mind was burning with his eyes and with his hair sparking blue and green and with his thin body spinning on a fence post faster, faster and his crooked back splitting wider and wider, billowing out fiery wings.

I slammed the door and pressed myself against the wood. A long moment passed and then I began to breathe. The inner hall was hot and airless and the exhaust of traffic fogged the window.

"It just gets worse and worse and worse." My father's voice from the kitchen. "We'll never get out of this hole."

"We just have to talk to the bank." My mother's voice low and strained. "If the bank lets us buy more merchandise—"

"And what'll we tell my ma? That we need to borrow to pay the bank so we can borrow more?"

"If we don't have new stock who's going to come? Who's going to want to shop?"

I looked up at the painting on the wall: a dime store reproduction of Millet's "Prayers." It showed a peasant farmer and his wife in their field lowering their heads to pray at the day's end, the Lord's land golden with the setting sun. At times I had imagined the church bells ringing in the distance, or the words of their prayer, or how the man and the woman had been digging and planting in the earth but, this time, I followed the trail of my father's deep sigh. It seemed to have emerged from behind the picture, from a thin crack in the wall which ran along the hallway back into the living-room. Then the crack disappeared under the wallpaper's pattern of flowers and grains swirling out of a cornucopia. Beyond was my father in the cramped kitchenette. He sighed again, then spoke.

"Ma says we should sell out before we end up worse."

"And what?" my mother answered. "Go back to the factory? Is that what you want? Or maybe go back home to her? Did your ma say that, too?" She leaned over the bills and receipts piled on the table. My father stared down at the ledger beside his plate.

I said nothing. My parents were working. The store was with them from the moment they woke up to the moment they lay down, and this night they were especially busy for it was the eve of Bankday, their day of reckonings. Also, it was Passover. They had closed the store early, dressed me up and sent me out. To toss stones at the garage, to chase the one-eyed Siamese until it spit, to follow one old Main Street lady to the drugstore and then the next old lady back again. To do anything; just stay clean and stay clear and wait to go to Baba's for the family meal. But not to see Elijah. And not to return with any news of miracles.

So I left again and went to the back stairs, with its rickety porch overlooking the parking lot. What I found was quietness. Not silence; the air was full enough with screen doors and clothes lines, restless dogs and hammers, and the service trucks rattling down the lane behind the stores, but these were separate and ordered sounds like the patchwork quilt of the backyards. They spread upon a stillness.

It was the mystery of stillness that drew me out the window, to seek Elijah in the clouds. That was where I imagined him, shaping and reshaping, ready to swoop through the net of telephone wires back to the garbage can lids that were shining in the sun.

I hovered on the window-sill and I gripped the fire escape and climbed onto the roof. I braced myself against the chimney while the grey nubble of the shingles tumbled to the eaves-trough, and I scanned the farthest reaches of the lanes and streets.

I could not see Elijah anywhere, though I felt him close at hand. His voice was spiralling in the song of a knife-and-scissors man hawking down the lane. Then I saw a shadow scraping in the cartons behind the drugstore. I raced down the ladder rungs, the flights of stairs, the spread of gravel, concrete, broken glass across a field to reach the shadow and finally found it, dragging from behind a bloated woman who had bagged her life into a shopping cart. She was as dusty and layered as the bags she pushed like punishment. Even her eyes were layered. She could never be Elijah. She would have had to moult for a hundred springs even to see Elijah.

Across the lane, beside a crate of fruit, a delivery man was laughing to the grocer: "That crazy old bugger. He was behind the bakery juggling three hard loaves of pumpernickle. I tell you

108

I wish I'd had a camera! I could have sold a picture like that to some magazine. He had these kids jumping all around and he was singing one of those crazy D P songs . . . "

I hurried past.

Only later, returning dry and tired to the apartment block, did the delivery man's words echo back to me. I realized he had seen Elijah; that Elijah was moving through other back lanes trailed by other children, ones who did not run away. I curled against the topmost stair and my chest ached with emptiness.

Then came the whispering sing-song. "Lenny, Lenny." The slippered steps of Old Man Werner. "Lenny. I'm all dressed up. It's something new for me." He was climbing up from his basement workshop where he kept his bed, climbing up to the Passover, God's days of redemption. "I'm telling you, Lenny. I am doing this just for you." Standing three stairs below me, he reached out to my shoulder and I uncurled to his touch. "Lenny, you got to tell me the truth because I don't know. Am I looking good enough for your family?" He wore a loose and faded suit. His tie displayed three swallows flying over a sunset. His skullcap was balding velvet.

"You look terrific, Mr. Werner. You should be a model or an actor in the movies."

"Yah, yah. I know which one. 'The Curse of the Mummy.' I know the movies you like to watch."

"No, Mr. Werner. You're great. You're like the wise old guy in Charlie Chan."

"Okay, so now we're both wise guys. So help me with this collar." He smelled of shaving soap and talcum powder, though his face still bristled with patches of raccoon grey. I found myself bending to him, not from the knees but from the heart, wanting to kiss his cheek. And I wanted to tell him about Elijah but I hesitated, because I was ashamed that I had run away. Then I heard my parents behind the door shuffling on their coats. They were restless and worried about the time. They were coming out to look for us.

I patted down his collar and said, "It looks real good, Mr. Werner. I'm glad you're coming." For we were all going to Baba's my parents and I and Mr. Werner, whom I had begged to come and then had begged my parents to invite and finally had begged my baba to accept by making him out to be a lonely Jew who would be even more alone on the holy nights. Somehow I had managed it. My first miracle of Passover.

I had never thought of our Passover suppers as giving honour to the will of God. They were ceremonies of submission to the will of the family. My parents prepared me for days beforehand—not in the meaning of the ritual meal or in the prayers or the four questions that I, as the youngest male, was supposed to ask but in how to avoid the snares of my uncles and aunts, the comparisons to my cousins, and in how to please and to comply with Baba.

Baba above all. Baba dominating everything. The very approach to the apartment proved her power. Smell her herring, her bubbling corned beef, her chicken stewing through the dim hallway even to the outer entrance. These were Baba smells. Climb the stairs. Knock on the greasy brown door. Listen for Baba sounds.

"Rena!" Her voice was a high, strained gargle from the kitchen. Then a clatter of pots. "Rena, somebody's at the door! You deaf?"

"I'm going, right away. I'm going." Bent and brooding, Rena opened the door. She was always the first to the Passover meal: setting plates and taking coats; catching what she could of everyone's words and looks; being extra hands, extra ears and eyes for Baba. Baba who was so large, especially when I could not see her. Who became a huge woman on the telephone, her voice loud and shocking. And who grew larger still in my parents' telling and retelling of her demands, her judgments, her displeasures until she seemed to be a giant.

Baba stomped down her hallway. She swallowed me in a fatty hug, laughing that she had me. My parents searched the floor to find their smiles and meanwhile Mr. Werner watched and watched. "This here is my Lenny!" Baba told us all. "He's my favourite grandson." She turned to Mr. Werner. "And you? Are you Murray's landlord?"

"I am Yossel Werner. A good holy day to you."

"Where you from?" Baba momentarily suspicious. "You come from the Ukraine? Or you got some other kind of accent?"

"First I came from Lenitov near Kiev and then later from Berlin."

"From Berlin? From Hitler's hell?" Baba made the ritual of spitting out the evil of the word.

"But now we're all Canadians," Mr. Werner said. He was a nobleman in my eyes. "Than God, we all are here alive."

"It's good you brought two prayer books," Baba said. "We only got a couple. Next year, someone has to bring more books."

"Mr. Werner knows all the prayers, " I said. "He can make it so we'll have a real good sedar."

110

Baba said, "Good, so he can do the reading. None of the boys ever want to. And Lenny, you can come to the kitchen." I was pulled away, into her soup ladle kitchen with its paint and linoleum curling in the steam of a thirty-year soup. She pinched my flesh and sat me at the table, where I was to wait and watch her stir her pot. Her skin was loose, bleached and boiled as a chicken's, soft as gefilte fish. I wondered if it had ever been firm. She had lifted weights, real weights. The family ran a steam bath where the sons pushed barbells, sons who were themselves pressed down by poverty and prejudice. It was a place where they could steam and beat themselves with hot swatches of oak leaves and then groan under a pummelling massage. Three of her sons had become champions and she worked out beside them all, mastering both steam and weight to make them her allies.

My zaida, though, could not take either the weight or the heat, at least not directly. The depression which kept him poor had also offered him an escape. He travelled to far-off cities where he worked for years sending back whatever he could, like a man trying to buy his time.

So Baba ran the family. She met all problems with a rudeness, a dirt-floor peasant rudeness which had dismayed her gentle husband. She had been the victim of hunger and hate and discreet abandonment, so she used the only powers she understood to keep her children close. She set one child against the next with petty jealousies, resentments, hidden fears and this kept them all clinging to her for support. It was not clear how well she understood these methods or whether the others knew their roles, but such things work even without understanding.

Eventually my zaida returned to sit and sigh by the radiator and try his best to rescue the family from their layers of plots and alliances. They described him as a saint, which simply means he was dead. He had offered them reason and compassion when they had wanted praise and power. Finally exhausted, Zaida had found his final, quiet way out.

Saul, the first son, preferred distraction. Family folklore had it he had barely escaped being crushed by a falling safe. It taught him everything he wished to know about burdens. He chose God instead. He was so alarmed by his own frailty, he had his god send him criss-crossing the world in search of health and revelations.

When Saul needed money, he would collect for one of the many Jewish charities. Wise in the manufacturing of miracles, he made his rounds on two shaking canes and within a week or two he was springing, full of God's blessings, into an overseas travel office. The only proof I ever found of his existence were exotically stamped letters crammed into Baba's kitchen drawer. They offered cures for heart disease, cancer and depression. They decoded prophecies and begged support.

Rena poked into the kitchen. "Ma, they're all here now. You coming out, or what?"

"How can I come? You see the work I got to do?"

"Okay, I'm going to help. Get Lenny out. There's no room in here."

Rena never had words for me; only glares. I was a kid, another potential demand. Her husband had also removed himself to sainthood and left her a widow brooding over five dark and craving children. I acted afraid of her but I was merely going through the motions. She simply could not raise Baba's forceful smells. Rena's were merely a mustiness and a trace of something burnt.

The wives, armoured in hairdos and black lace, chattered nervously and empty-handed in the hallway. The brothers greeted and grunted with thumps and iron handshakes. They shoved each other with hard laughter until chairs scraped and voices rose:

"Murray! Be careful of the lamp!"

"It's enough already."

"Steve, not here, for God's sake!"

It was Passover, a time to recall our history.

The family settled at the table and flipped through the prayer books. This was a grudging recognition of Mr. Werner, who was a guest and might report on us to a larger world.

Mr. Werner lifted his cup for the blessing of the wine. His eyes were dark with memory; he chanted in the way of his father and his father's father. All dead. All dead.

Other eyes glazed with boredom, sharpened with suspicion, wandered along the frill of a blouse, fixed on the jewel of a ring. This table had its own history.

Then Samuel, Rena's son, shied out the first ritual question, the question that was mine to ask since I was the youngest male. But I did not know the Hebrew.

"Ma neesh tanah ha lilah hazeh, meen kol ha laylot?"

Why is this night different from all other nights?

"Because," sang Mr. Werner, "we were slaves of Pharaoh in Egypt and the Eternal One, our God, brought us out with a strong hand and an outstretched arm."

He uncovered the matzoh, our bread of hasty departure. But Baba was already pushing it back along with the ceremonial herbs

112

and the salt water to make room for the food. So Mr. Werner had to rush through the questions and the commentaries, to skip over the tale of the four sons and the story of Jacob. Still, Steve yawned and his mind shuffled playing cards. Mort slipped away to the bedroom phone to make his own contacts and, before Mr. Werner could sing of the writhing rod of Moses and the pharaoh's broken will, Baba burst through with a flood of soup and roast, sweet chicken and steaming barley, cutting off the Exodus entirely.

We grabbed at the plates and heaped one serving onto another. We tore and chewed without tasting as if the food would be snatched away. We were not hungry as much as aroused. It did not matter that we were decades from the poverty which shaped these habits or that there was more food than we could eat. We grunted with desire for these plagues of meats and fishes. We called for more.

Only Baba did not eat. How could she? This was our communion with her, proof of our needy love. We ate of her. Later, she would eat the eaters.

We tired. I ached and could only suck and savour. I lifted a fragment of matzoh which Mr. Werner had broken and passed ritually to each of us. It was as brittle as parchment. I chewed it to sweetness and watched him mourn into the prayer book while the radiators hissed of murder and persecution. I mused about ghosts. I wondered if my zaida could be a ghost trapped behind the wallpaper. I pretended my Aunt Rena's dead husband was a tiny soul hovering over a wine stain on the tablecloth. Another plate boomed down and the spirit fled like a frightened insect.

Steve studied the braised beef drowned in gravy. He rubbed his lips with the napkin.

"So, Murray. How's the store? You making big bucks?"

My father flinched from behind his mound of salad and Jello. He tried to remember the plan to use when Steve began to dig for cuts of his heart and liver.

"Well, you know how it is in the clothing business. Lots of potential but lots of overhead."

"Aw, come on, Murray! You're making a pile! Sarah's got you in there day and night. When you letting go of some of it? Hey, Ma, how about some more cream soda?" Steve looked pleased at drawing first blood, being Big Steve at the poker club rolling in the dough, the dough he rolled into his front pocket where it hung and bulged, dough he peeled off in tens and twenties to throw at shaky boosters or flattering street kids or to toss in a lump at his Montreal wife who laughed it all away. But here Big Steve was still Little Stevey and he gave away nothing. Here he scraped and scrambled for his mother's soup pot love.

Baba set down a half dozen pop bottles. "What kind of money can Murray make? Every time I go there, nobody's buying. Who's going to buy at such prices? I tell Sarah, what makes you think my Murray is a fancy businessman? He had a good job as a packer. Now, you make him lose everything."

My father tensed. Business success. Business failure. He would lose either way. They were different cuts of the same knife.

Baba poured the drinks into heavy tumblers. "And Murray, that blouse you gave me. It's no good. It got torn under the arm. Maybe you'll bring me another blouse?"

Rena burst out at small Shaini. "You stop spitting food, Shaini. Stop it or I'll get mad!" Even angrier because she was missing Baba and Murray's words, words she could keep to cook in her own oven, words she could serve at their next dinner. She poked Shaini's lips with a spoon of grey barley. "Now you eat! Look at her. Four years old and she won't listen to nobody!"

"Ma, never mind the blouse. I got a deal." It was Mort smiling over his connections. "Tomorrow, I'll bring you a whole box of ladies hoses." Sharp Mort who never needed any sucker job because he had so many friends. He promoted. He "made arrangements." "Hey, Murray. I can get you a couple of gross. Dirt cheap. How about it, kid?"

But what if they were hot? My father didn't deal in heisted goods. "I got plenty of hose, Mort. The whole summer stock. Where would I put them?"

Mort stiffened. He would sulk for Ma. "Fine! Go try to help a brother. Not even a thank-you."

"What's the matter, Murray?" Baba leaned over the clutter of plates. "You can't return the other hose? Jacky Winestock won't take back some hose? I used to feed him right here at this table!"

My father lowered his head. His hands groped for words. Then my mother spoke out. "It's a business situation, Mother. It's great that Mort wants to help. We appreciate it, don't we Murray? Only, right now we have to keep up a line of credit with the wholesale. It doesn't look good to return stock. It hurts your reputation."

Baba drew in her resentment. Mort tapped it out on his plate. Steve was smiling, pleased with this new rift. He knew now they could not ask for any loan. "Hey, let's forget about it, already!" He laughed. "Murray must be sick of women's hose. Selling them all day long. It would drive me crazy. Tonight's a holiday and we got all this wine. Let's have a toast to my Ma!" Steve lifted the silver goblet, full to the brim. "Ma, you made one hell of a meal! Many happy returns!"

"No! You don't drink!" It was Mr. Werner, glimmering with anger. "What's the matter with you? That's Elijah's cup. Don't you know anything?" It was the prophet's goblet, set at the empty seat. It awaited his invisible visit to the holy meal.

"I saw him," I said without thinking. "I saw the Prophet Elijah." Mr. Werner, Steve, the whole table turned to look at me. "He was behind the store. He was dancing and singing and he was going to fly. He was going to fly!"

Even my cousins were still. Then, carefully, Mr. Werner asked, "What did this Elijah look like?"

"He had long black curly hair and a long black coat and a beard. And he had a funny bent back. I wasn't the only one. Max, he drives for the bakery, he saw him too."

What if Elijah would come? Could Mr. Werner and I draw him back? What if he would sit beside me even here?

Uncle Steve's laughter broke over me. "I'll bet it's that crazy Dukhobor! They call him Castro. He sleeps out by the river wrapped in newspapers. You're lucky he didn't get you."

More voices clattered overhead.

"Naw, it's that rag collector, Zaivi. The one who mooches wine and cake at the synagogue."

"A shame! Jewish welfare should do something."

"Some prophet. He collects bottles in back alleys. What you got there is a nickel and dime profit! Ha! Ha! You get it? It's a joke. Ma, did you hear?"

Their laughter stung until I broke away, pushing against the chairs. "Let me go! Let me go!"

Against their swollen backs, which rumbled and twisted with fists of hair, and creasing necks. Past Uncle Steve's smells of cigars and sweat, past his wife's perfume and bites of hair spray. "Damn! Damn! Hell! Crap!"

I was coughing out the only swears I knew even as I tangled in the straps of my mother's purse. The bag ruptured Kleenex smeared with lips, compacts of powder, a gaping mirror.

She reached towards me with painted fingernails but I slapped them away. "Leave me alone!"

Across the no man's land of shouts and laughter. Until I was stopped by Mr. Werner's mild voice threading through it all:

"Who knows what the boy saw? Do you know? You don't know."

The other voices dropped into mutterings.

Mr. Werner's voice grew deep and strong. "My grandfather, Isaac Werner, may his name be blessed, when he was twelve years old he saw an angel. It was the day the peasants came with axes, to make a pogrom against the Jews. They murdered his whole family. An angel appeared and showed him where to hide in the bushes. And all the time the angel was shining down on him protecting him like a great fire. But what did the peasants see when they looked? Maybe bushes. Maybe a pile of dirt. But my grandfather, he saw the angel."

The tablecloth rustled. A chair creaked and then was silent. A knife was quietly laid upon a plate. Mr. Werner raised his finger. "So you want to drink wine? That's good. You should drink wine. And with the wine you should make the prayer. Lenny, you open that door for Elijah."

It was the prayer of Shvoch Chamatcha and the door was to be opened to welcome the spirit of the holy prophet.

I felt a cool rush of wind: Elijah's wind tinkling and laughing, flying over stains and bones, dancing on the silver rim of the wine cup, sweeping out the heat and smell. It pushed me too back into the room, back to Mr. Werner who rocked over his leather prayer book, one finger crooked over the page, motioning. "Come, Lenny. Come. Come."

Then his hands were under my armpit, scratchy against my shirt and finally, with the prayer ended, I was turned from the table and lifted onto his bony knees. And he was all around me.

"Lenny, this is Hebrew. Do you read this?" They were black twisted letters. There were no cartoons of the long-haired men with whips or the bent people in towels and sheets.

"I don't know how, Mr. Werner."

"That's okay. Do you know what Egypt is, eh? What's Egypt?"

"It's a place in Africa."

"Is that right? Good! And what else? What else do you know about Egypt?"

"We used to live there once, a long time ago."

"Yah. So was it a good place or a bad place?"

"Everybody was mean. And they made us work way too hard. We had to build pyramids."

"So you know a lot about Egypt. So did we stay there? Did God make us stay in that bad place forever?"

"No. He sent the man with the stick."

"Moishe. He sent Moishe."

"Yah, Moses. And Moses made them let us go."

Then Mr. Werner sang his weaving love prayer, rocking me dry and dangling on his knee. Finally, he sighed and opened his eyes. "Lenny, you know what *'Ma neesh tanah'* means? It means 'what's different.'"

"Ma neesh tanah."

"And *'ha lilah hazeh'* means 'this night.'"

"Ma neesh tanah ha lilah hazeh."

"Yah, just like you said. You're a smart boy. *'Meen kol ha laylot.'* This means 'from all the other nights.' So, Lenny, what's the answer? What makes this night different from all the other nights?"

"Because we're not in Egypt?"

"Yes. And because tonight we learn about how God can take us from all the bad places. Because He loves us."

So Mr. Werner cradled me in his arms and under his chin as if he would carry me as light as smoke, as light as tears up to the clouds. And we swayed with his book full of stains, full of twisting black letters singing, "Ma neesh tanah ha lilah hazeh, meen kol ha laylot?" Our voices rising, entwining, we swirled above the table and out the window in a tiny thin song, a shy strong song while he creased me and folded me, rubbed me and swayed me. "Ma neesh tanah ha lilah hazeh, meen kol ha laylot."

BARBARA RENDALL

Coming to China

Halfway through the year I come to it—it comes—
Not in the travelling, but in the biding,
Like the ultimate moment of tipping over into love,
When, with amazement, one discovers what one has always held.

Crossing from the island to the city on the ferry,
Jammed to the rail, the skyline of Xiamen exquisitely ugly,
The channel rough, I find an equilibrium
Remembering the flowers of Gulangyu half an hour ago
As they poured, a wash of purple, over courtyard walls,
And thinking ahead: another twenty minutes endured,
And there will be the temple roofs,
Red, green, and gold, climbing the side of the mountain,
Their sudden configuration, for an instant,
The very shape of prayer.

But between two points of beauty here, there are rude roads
To be negotiated, the boat, the bus, the long trudge home.
Now the disreputable old boat
Rams the dock as usual, bouncing off the tattered tires
Hanging there: Thud! China! Yet no one ever falls—
A sense of balance here is second nature.

I've had trouble finding this, myself,
Always fretting over which is truer in this maddening place:
Beauty, or indifferent neglect?
Bureaucracy, or constant thoughtfulness?
Ancient wisdom, or modern single-mindedness?
At last, I learn to live with both,
With the pendulum rhythm of the Orient,
To move to meet it, even,
Managing such opposites like familiar furnishings,
Or relatives, enduring one for the other.
One comes to expect it as the only sure thing in the East,
And finally, the central adventure, and the prize.

BARBARA RENDALL

Letter Home from the Far East

So, did you think I'd gone around
The other side and fallen off?
I will admit—to you alone—there was a slip,
But I'm healed and whole again,
Whole as the world.

I write that with authority, like Columbus from the bridge,
For I've seen it now, that curving of the earth—
Seen how the way that leads so unimaginably far
Is yet the same way back, one long and mounting road
That joins itself again. So, fact: to send back to the court:

Leaving you, I've never had you clearer,
And in a new-found light, the Chinese double brightness
That's written sun-in-moon-in-one:
You hold the moon, and half a world away, I hold the sun—
Between us we own all the light there is;
And every dusk and dawn
As each yields to the other
This passes into perfect clarity.

This is my discovery, then, the prize I claim,
The world I've gained—
Surpassing all the distances
And the pages gasping to describe,
Beyond all the gifts that I've gathered,
Silks and jades and jasmines,
All mere riches to measure my richness by,
None near to touching that treasure
Half-known before, in my sure keeping now:
A love that holds the world in both its hands,
Happiness strong as a vision,
And our shape and sum.

BARBARA RENDALL

Chinese Garden

It's exactly what you wanted as a child
But forgot,
A place where every detail meets a need
You never knew you had,
Until by chance in this undreamed-of country, now,
You come upon the language to define it.

Entering by the moon-gate,
Round as a welcome, whole as what you'll find,
Paths draw you on; steep humpbacked bridges aid
And slow your progress; steps wind;
Flowers like birds or paper lanterns rise like fountains;
And finally the nine-curve bridge skims a wealth of water
Toward the floating pavilion: room on room of light,
The only furnishings a branch of apricot or jasmine,
A scroll of poetry,
And all the rest is space and thought.

"A place to nourish the heart," the poet-gardener says;
And all day long they come; at dawn,
Old men at their ritual dance
Wave their wings like cranes and seek their balance;
At noon, children swarm the giant rocks;
And at dusk, monks and lovers go by twos
Beside the pond, murmuring, marking the lotus buds
Newly sprung from the water that day,
Upright and luminous as flames.

Everything is jewel-like, neat,
But proportion is never sure or steady:
A rock by the path can be an entire mountain,
A miniature plant is a giant tree as well,
With a whole village spreading out about is roots,
Meaning every Chinese village,
Made for the palm of the hand.

It's a world to enter
With all senses open,
But never studiously: easily,
A painting to live within, to learn,
A poem to touch, to breathe, to use—
Every loveliness we need, selected and arranged,
Exalted and brought back again,
And rooted in the earth.

TAIEN NG

Shun-Wai

My mother's a strong woman, and she's also Christian. The two aren't synonymous, but they both describe her. I admire my mother a great deal, but this isn't something I'd readily admit. She'd only say, "You see? Mothers know best!" Then she'd move on to her speech about the inadequacies of my vegetarian diet.

When she came to Canada with my father some twenty-five years ago, she didn't have an inkling of the English language. Then my father left her. Now she's got an accounting business, and a house with a garden, and Jesus. And me, of course, which is probably why she turned to Jesus.

My mother and I aren't often on speaking terms any more. She says I'm like a gwua-mui—a white girl—never listen to the parents. I know I ought to be more patient with her, but we're both stubborn people. Anyway, I think it's good she has Jesus. Ever since I left home, she really has no one else.

Shun-Wai translates literally into "Spirit Place," a shrine for ancestral spirits. It can sometimes be quite large and take up a whole corner of a room with red lights, red and gold banners, and offerings. More often, though, it's very minimal like the one my grandparents, Poh Poh and Yeh Yeh, had. Theirs was tucked away in a space on the bookshelf and consisted of incense, a plate of oranges, and pictures of my great-grandparents.

When my mother saw the Shun-Wai, she tried to take it apart in the name of Christianity.

This is what I remember of Hong Kong: the stink of garbage and rotting food and sweat; narrow alleys crowded with beggars and people trying to sell their wares; chickens running loose; mosquitoes, flies, cockroaches. I went there with my mother for a week and a half, in the summer of my thirteenth birthday. It was Hong Kong, and not my mother, that made me realize I was Chinese.

We stayed with my grandparents, who lived in an apartment about the size of your average living-room. This included the kitchen, bathroom and bedroom—all squished into one living space. They were considered lucky to have so much room, since many families with twice the people lived in apartments half that size.

One night, all the relatives came over for dinner. In this small space were Poh Poh (Grandma) and Yeh Yeh (Grandpa), two uncles, one aunt, three cousins aged three to eight, my mother, and me. With everyone crowded around the table, Poh Poh began spooning out the soup.

My mother cleared her throat. "Put the soup down," she said to Poh Poh in Chinese. "We have to say grace."

Poh Poh hesitated, then put the soup down. My aunt, uncles and cousins looked bewildered. My mother held out her hand to me and told everyone to join hands. She closed her eyes.

"Thank you, Lord," she began, "for what we are about to receive, and thank you for this opportunity to have the family together."

I looked up. Poh Poh was staring at the soup. Yeh Yeh was looking at the rice. My aunt was looking at my uncle.

"Please, Lord," my mother continued, her eyes still tightly closed. "Please bless Poh Poh, Yeh Yeh, and my daughter, and . . ."

The electric fan whirred loudly. My five-year-old cousin kicked my three-year-old cousin under the table.

"Shhh!" my aunt hissed.

My eight-year-old cousin giggled.

"And forgive those who have turned their backs to you, Lord," my mother was saying. "Please help them find the way. Amen."

"Amen," I said when she opened her eyes and glared at me.

"Amen," murmured my aunt and my uncles, who were not sure what to say. Poh Poh picked up the pot of soup, and Yeh Yeh continued looking at the rice. My cousins kept giggling.

After dinner, Yeh Yeh left to see our relatives to the bus stop. It was then that my mother took notice of the Shun-Wai.

I also remember this about Hong Kong: it so hot I could barely breathe. I sweated so much everything I touched felt sticky. Even after a shower, I would still feel grimy, as if there was a film over my skin. The big shopping centres were air-conditioned, but overly so, and when we went inside to escape the heat, I could always pass the time by counting the goosebumps on my skin.

There was nothing much to do but shop and visit relatives, which is not that exciting for a thirteen-year-old. All I wanted was a pizza, but every relative we saw took us out for Chinese food. I did not like Hong Kong.

Now that I'm older, I figure I'd been too young to fully appreciate the experience of another culture—which it was, after all. I understand Chinese well enough, but if you asked me to say anything in it, I'd probably stare at you dumbfounded. It's not that I don't know my own background. I know damn well I'm Chinese. My mother keeps reminding me of the fact. As if I would ever forget.

"What are you doing?" Poh Poh said as my mother bent to pick up the oranges. "Don't eat those, there are more oranges in the kitchen."

"How come you have a Shun-Wai?" my mother demanded.

"We've always had one . . . it's for your grandparents."

"You shouldn't have one," my mother said, raising her voice. "It's ancestral worship. These things aren't good. You shouldn't worship anything but God."

"Don't you want to remember your grandparents?"

"If you want to remember someone, then remember them here," my mother said loudly, tapping her head. "You don't need these sort of things."

"Tell your mother not to yell at me," Poh Poh said to me sadly.

"Mom," I said. "Stop yelling at your mother."

My mother ignored me and continued talking loudly for a while. Poh Poh just went into the kitchen. Yeh Yeh came back from the bus stop and then my mother talked at him, too. Finally they let her take the Shun-Wai apart, just to get some peace.

But what I really remember was the look on my grandparents' faces. I wanted to say something to them, but for the life of me, I didn't know how.

Sometimes on the weekends now, I like to take the bus into Chinatown and wander around. I'll go into a bakery and try to order pineapple buns in Chinese, although usually I just point to what I want. Or I'll sit in a wonton house with the smell of barbecued pork and Shanghai noodles, and listen in on the conversations around me. I don't know why, but the waitresses always greet me in English. I guess they can tell.

KAREN CONNELLY

Learning Colour and Demons
Northern Thailand

I.

They tell me it is dangerous
to walk into the fields at night.
The moon may be bright,
    but its clear face
    is not innocent.
It does not matter
    that you can see the stars better, they say.
Are you mad?

Where do you come from,
Fool, child, idiot.
You are white, not invisible.
They can see you, too,
Even better in the dark.

II.

In daylight the rice is greener than anyone's eyes,
Stands slender in sun-silvered water.
The sky is huge, deep, spills bright clouds
                just above your body.
Its blue edges touch you.
You stand on a red clay road, amazed,
    holding your breath to hear
    the snakes whisper away from you.

In the wagon ruts,
        the crushed shells of scorpions sleep black,
                five inches long.
But the land is safe,
The people smile at you
        with the faces of cats,
        clean-boned, beautiful,
                alive.
They touch your white arms,
Smile at your hair:
Gold, they say, and laugh.

There is no need for photographs.
All of this will exist forever,
        you could never forget
        the colour of the fields, their faces,
        these lives.
This is no dream.

III.

You don't understand,
Can't you see, they ask.
If only you could read our papers.
Your eyes are not dark enough.
This makes you blind.

If they offer you anything to drink,
Don't take it.
Thirst is easier than the thicker tongue of poison.

In your country, yes,
But here women do not choose freedom.
It is not universal.
Beginnings end at borders.
History is not a subject here, it owns you.
You live in its hand and it holds you still.

There is so much noise in the city, they say,
That no one hears screaming.
There are so many people,
Death-lists are never accurate.
Pieces of paper are lost, burned, or torn
        as easily as hair and skin.
Why do you believe everything?

IV.

They believe everything, the women
        of the fields.
You wash clothes with them,
Explain that machines can do this.
Laughing: What would we do then
                with white boxes thieving our work?

In Canada, they ask you,
Can you ever see the ghosts?
What do they look like?
You cannot answer.
You do have ghosts, though?
Yes, you tell them.

Here each family has a house
        beyond their own, a temple
        in miniature offering small dishes of food,
Ghost-houses, golden and red, hung with jasmine,
                frequented by ants, sparrows,
                        and spirits.
They give their gentle demons a place to live.

At night, under a net thin as shadow,
You lie awake, trying to remember
        the ghosts in Canada:
                the shape of snowdrifts,
                the colour of stone,
                the sound of wind over ice.
Images they could not fathom.

V.

One hundred years ago,
It was law that the women
      who lied or spoke too loudly for too long
      were executed; not murder
            but correction.
Whipped to shreds, roasted, beaten to death
                  with clubs carved of amber-red teak,
            or fed to alligators, or poisoned.
Whatever the methods, the result
            was silence.

It is not like that today.
Though it is possible to know too many words.
You might be learning too quickly.

VI.

You do learn quickly,
You cannot wake without some new knowledge,
            ants on your skin,
            a praying mantis on the bed,
            a frog in your shoe.

The mist slides into the village
            thick as cotton.
There are bells on the people's clothes.
The children teach you games with coins and stones.

You have never seen the grace of beauty
that does not see itself.
Here it is everywhere; it slips
            sun-alive as water
                  from the shoulders of the people.

At night, the lizards talk.
Cicadas ring a song clearer than silence.
Cats dance a stacatto on the thin roof.

128

Before you never knew colours.
The darkness here is bright.
You sleep curled against skylight,
prisms, wind-curved clouds.
Even in your dreams, you sing.

MICHELENE ADAMS

By De Sea

Is de bell bring dem to de beach by Uncle Cyril. Not de beach yuh could call Uncle Cyril front yard dat is go on fuh miles, de clumps a pitch like mistakes in de white san. Is de other beach dey walk to, de tiny one dat de river is open out on. It separate from de big beach by a stretch a rocks so yuh have to take de long way, down de road dat run behin Granderson house an all de other houses dat have a sign on de fence sayin, "Private Property, No Trespassin." Den yuh pass through de pave yard a de Catolic church, den through a gate dat paint green.

Nate walk dere wid his mudder an Auntie Carmen steppin in time to de ringin a de bell, swingin his hans an singin a tune he make up bout wakin up an water, till he hear other voices singin strong agains de crash a de surf. A group a people gadder on de shore. De women in white, dey head wrap up, an de men in black pants an stiff white shirts. Nate surprise at de good shoes, lace up black shoes, strange in de san. Some a dem holin candles. More candles burnin in de san roun dem, yellow flames flutterin in de breeze, but dey ain outin. Flowers in clusters roun de candles, red an orange hibiscus, petals bright an unfurl.

Den, all of a sudden, de clang a de bell stop an everybody quiet. Anudder man headin towards de group, walkin along de river. De minister, wearin a robe over his black pants, readin aloud from a bible as he move towards dem, steerin a boy in front a him. De boy face clench like he frighten an he draw up his shoulders as dey reach de crowd, an a man an a woman walk on eider side a him. De four walk togedder straight into de water. Nate watch up in his mudder face an squeeze her han buh she ain even look down. He watch dem wade out till de water by de boy wais, an as dey stop, a wave rock agains dem an dey sway. Den de man hol one arm an de woman hol de other an, while de minister read from de bible, his open han hoverin over de boy head, dey ease him under de surface. An dey draw him out again, gleamin wet, eyes wide, an de bell start, an singin, an everybody dance in time.

Nate sleepin when he hear de voices comin from de beach. He run by de window, see a group a people gadder in front de house holin torchlights in de darkness. He could make out Uncle Mackie, so he put on his sandals an run outside. Men crouchin

130

down over someting. Fuh a secon Nate tink it might be a fish, buh den in de glare a de torchlights he see a bare foot. "He coulda swim better dan all of us," one a dem say. "He use to swear de sea woulda never take him." Everybody mutter an shake dey head. Den two a dem lif him up, one by his shoulders an de other at his foot, de body saggin in de middle. As dey move pas Nate, he watch in de face, de eyes still open an starin. Den he watch de arms hangin, one han fingers spread open, de other one curl tight as a shell.

LOIS L. ROSS

The Parcel

The prairie is like a great ocean, one that takes you and shapes you and forms you, and in the end never lets you go. No matter how far you wander. I've learned that. Others learned it before me. I spend a lot of time looking out on that ocean from the living-room window of my mobile home. I watch the sparrows weigh on the clothesline, the crows hide in the windbreaks and the partridge scurry, bobbing through the tufts of grass alongside the road. Sometimes I see the dust devils dancing wildly in the fields of fallow.

In the distance, near the river's edge, my grandfather's house still stands erect despite its eighty years. The weathered porch, which faces the groves that wind along the river, has sunk a few inches as though it needs to announce the burden it shouldered with the comings and goings of the heavy-footed.

Inside the fibreboard walls of the mobile home, the ringing begins. I've never liked telephones, but there it was, ringing again. I couldn't leave it unanswered.

"Got a minute?" It was my mother Vivianne. "Is Dad in the yard?"

"Yeh, he's here," I said.

Here was a relatively modern farmstead which, along with its adjoining half-section, had been acquired recently to help fend off the cost-price squeeze. Brown's place we call it, and God only knows who homesteaded it.

"Then . . ." She paused. "Maybe you could tell him that I just received a call from Moose Jaw. You knew Uncle John was sick?"

"No . . . not really . . ." But it didn't strike me as unusual.

"It happened suddenly. He just wouldn't go to the hospital though. He died this morning about two-fifteen. Could you go out and tell your dad?"

The news didn't stun me. I wasn't so sure I wanted to cross the yard with the information, but it seemed senseless to call Émile to the phone just to have the message repeated. "Well. Yeh, okay." I said. "I'll go out and tell him."

I hung up, thoughts scurrying. Should I do it right away? Was it really all that pressing? After all, John had really died years ago, hadn't he? Even if his body was only turning cold now, I thought.

Throughout my childhood I heard snippets, tidbits. I viewed John's life mainly second-hand. Only after I posed several questions would my parents share portions of his life with me, but I always felt there was more. I was a bystander, never completely allowed to understand their comments, perhaps because straight answers were too painful. Perhaps because there weren't any. By the time I was eight, John was reeling from the alcohol. He worked on nearby farms just long enough to make the money he needed to disappear into that cave which, for one reason or another, harboured escape for him. Escape from what? I often wondered. He wasn't a great farm worker and, toward the end, even money wasn't enough to move him. He didn't own any land; just a few animals, which he kept in the barn and pasture down by the river. The cows were John's insurance against a dry spell.

My father would sometimes take me for a mid-morning ride out to the old homestead. John still lived there with my grandfather Dieudonné. My father walked through the small front porch, and I ventured in behind him. The old screen door hung off the top hinge and slapped shut behind me. He made me wait there among the pails and half-used bags of fertilizer and called me in later as though he had to check to make sure the coast was clear for his girl-child. Then I sat waiting in the kitchen. He headed up to the second-floor bedrooms.

Sometimes I inspected the old cupboards and wood stove. This had been my grand-mère Adéline's kitchen. I could still see traces of her. The rusted cookie jar was no doubt glossy and clean when she had died, years before I was born. On the top shelf of a cupboard lay odd pieces of china trimmed with dainty pink roses or a single thin line of gold. I could never imagine my grandmother putting up those calendars, some with pictures of Cockshutt equipment, others of women. Calendars given by a local car dealer at Christmas. Years later I would recognize the kitchen's distinctive odour as a blend of cooking oil, dust, machinery grease, ashes and empty liquor bottles. Those bottles always stood stacked against the kitchen doorway and begged for attention.

I heard muffled voices trickling through the upstairs floorboards. The voices rose and fell, sped up and slowed down. Sometimes, I caught snippets.

"Bein, voyons Jean," my father said. During those years, he always said John in French. "Get up, you've got work to do. It's not good for you. Move around a bit. You've got to feed the cows. Have they had water today?"

My grandfather must have been up there too, but I rarely heard his low, gruff voice. The springs on the bed eventually creaked and, before long, I heard steps in the stairwell. My father emerged alone, and the clomping of work boots upstairs ushered us out.

"What's the matter with Uncle John?" I asked.

"Oh nothing," my father said. "He's just not feeling too well today."

"Where's Grandpa?"

"Sleeping."

Often, I never saw them when we visited the homestead. Sometimes, while we drove the old Ford truck into the yard with dust trailing, I saw Uncle John carry pails to the wind-blown barns to care for the few milk cows crowded inside. On those days he used a quick, curt, even stride while he rushed to the barns in his dark green work clothes, both arms loaded down. On other days he gave a quick full wave followed with a nod of the head and sometimes came over to chat. He smiled at me and said a few words with the awkwardness people have when they are rarely around children.

Sometimes my grandfather, Dieudonné, stood on the outside porch steps, acknowledged our presence by staring, and then went back inside.

Once in a while we all went back into the kitchen and sat around the table. There were never enough chairs, so I stood. Or I sat on my father's lap and sometimes, reluctantly, on my grandfather's.

"Want a shot?" Uncle John said.

"Go ahead," Dieudonné said to my father.

He hesitated before saying, "Non merci, I've got lots of work to do. Just wanted to ask if I might use the swather. Need a man to run it though," he said, looking over at Uncle John. "Want to make a few extra rounds if I can. Time's running out."

They chatted a bit more and some agreement emerged, or they silently disagreed. Those times, my father seemed tired and frustrated. We climbed into the dusty cab of the Ford and his large hands would be in control once again. They rotated the wheel in long, confident strokes, and his left foot pumped a clutch that comforted me when it thudded on release.

"It's okay to have a drink once in a while," he said, "but you have to learn how to use it. Otherwise you don't want to work. Nobody wants to work, but you have to. You have to try to get ahead a bit. They don't want to even." His voice trailed off as he sensed the need to be careful. "I do things for them. It's okay to ask for help when you need it. They won't even do things for themselves."

The dirt road created swirls of dust. When we turned onto the highway, there was always a race to roll up windows; to make sure the clouds didn't billow into the cab.

Then my father looked over and flashed a big smile. His eyes crinkled. "Oh, well, it's okay. I have my family and we'll always be a family, that's the most important thing. We help each other. You're helping me. You're keeping me company. It doesn't matter if we don't have everything we like to have. When you don't have any money left, you can't spend it. Right?"

I remember wondering, as a child, what the big deal was about being a family.

As the old homestead faded from my mind, I opened the door of the mobile home and stared out. Émile was fixing the swather. Exactly what part of it, I wasn't sure. When I was a kid, I'd held a lot of different tools and pieces while he'd repaired equipment, but I hadn't graduated to naming the parts. Although I'm sure he was more than willing to teach, he was busy trying to keep the farm together. From one thing to the next, time passed. I suppose my being his girl-child also made it less pressing for him to make a farmer out of me. These days, his knees seemed to have a slight, permanent bend. He moved around the swather and gently swaggered from time to time as though one of his feet had accidentally caught a tuft of grass.

John was Émile's brother. It was important to let Émile know what had happened. I knew he'd managed to cushion himself against the pain John had always caused him. And yet, Émile could remember John when he was whole and innocent, before he lost his soul. Émile could remember John the way he was and the way he turned out to be. Which way, which eulogy, would Émile choose now?

I walked across the yard quickly at first, then more slowly. Don't blurt it out, I cautioned myself. Even though I felt nothing, it was up to me to make this as easy as possible. This'll be the last time John causes pain, I thought. It ends here.

Émile looked up from his work.

"Hi," I said, pretending the usual. "How are things?"

"Oh, not bad," he said. He continued to remove a piece from the front-end of the swather. "Always so many things to do, but I guess what you can't get done today you leave for tomorrow."

"Is it a big job?" I asked.

"Just a few broken guards on the knife." He turned the wrench. "At the end of last year's harvest, we hit a few rocks. Should have fixed it then, but time goes."

"Vivianne just called," I said. "I asked her if she wanted to talk with you, but she said I should come over and tell you, give you the message. She just received a call from Moose Jaw. I'm not sure what time she got the call, but it mustn't have been long ago."

He looked up and stopped working.

This is taking too long, I thought. "Well," I continued, "she told me to tell you John died last night, probably around two or so. She didn't give me any other details. She probably knows more." By now I felt I should have had more information; that I should have listened more carefully; that I should feel more for John.

Émile took up the conversation while he put down his tools. "He didn't want to go to the hospital, you know," Émile said. "It wasn't that serious an illness, but he didn't want to go. I guess he wanted to pick his time."

"Sometimes people just figure that it's time to give up," I said.

"Maybe."

By now Émile was sitting on the swather tire and mustering strength by scanning the horizon. He pin-pointed the old homestead. Perhaps he was giving John a few respectful minutes before continuing on. I could see the memories flipping by.

From the porch of my grandfather Dieudonné Charrette's house, you can see my great-grandfather's simple white house, less than a mile east, downriver. It's a two-storied structure that became a happy meeting place for those who gathered to cross the narrow river. The house and homestead were lost in a poker game because Great-grandfather Adélard didn't know the X scrawled for the pay-off would forever sign away his family's dream. The players in that game have been forgotten. The land has been bought and sold so often the original winner is no longer blamed for having forever erased the future of "Charrette's Crossing." Émile still remembers the story, though. He would like to have that land again, someday. Since after the war he has wanted the original homestead, Adélard's homestead, to be back in the hands of those who first worked it. But at sixty-six he'll likely have to be content without it. He has Brown's place and the half-section along the river he began to work after the war. And he has Dieudonné's. I know he feels comfortable having the river on his land and only being a mile west of the old homestead. He can almost see it. They say the walls of those old homesteads are insulated with dirt—the same rich, clay soil the pioneers broke to plant their first crops.

"P'tit-Jean, y'en avait dans," Émile said at last. "He was real mischievous. In the thirties p'tit-Jean and I would chase down gophers—no poison then—we'd run like the devil and catch them on the head with a hammer. The tails were proof of who had gotten the most. We'd even skip school once in a while to chase those gophers or pick chokecherries down by the river." He smiled. "He was the youngest of the seven, you know, and he always wanted his way. I remember that I had gotten a bicycle from Maman. She had made clothes to earn a bit of extra money, pauvre Maman. Boy, I was proud of that bike, but John would always grab it and since he was the youngest Dieudonné stuck up for him. Well, that was the end of my bike." Émile chuckled and shifted position on the swather tire. "He should have fought for his life."

"Some people don't know how to fight," I said.

"I guess so, but I was ready to try and help him. He just couldn't make up his mind. He always seemed to be that way. You can only push so much. Ol' Dieudonné kept promising him a piece of land. You know that parcel south of the river before the six-mile road? And I think Jean always believed he would get it. So he stayed on. I signed up for the war, but he waited to be called. We'd joke with him and say he'd better not go because he was so tall the enemy would pick him off first. Maybe we shouldn't have teased that way. I guess we scared him. He hid in the countryside, worked from farm to farm, and they never did find him. Then he came back to the homestead, but nothing had changed for him."

"Well, what about you? You managed it," I said.

"The old man didn't really feel he had to help anybody start farming. John wanted to farm—he really did and for a while worked really hard—but Dieudonné never made room for him. Or anybody else. He figured it was okay for his sons to always work for him. He would play one of us off the other. Letting us think that eventually we would get land. And for a while the work got done." Émile's eyes trailed the horizon again, then came to rest on the dust devil in a nearby plot.

"After the war they wouldn't release me. They wanted me to stay on in Europe as part of the peacekeeping forces. But Maman was sick, pauvre Maman. She sure suffered. I had to come back. I hadn't seen her in two years, so when she was dying they were forced to find a place on a boat for me with the returning soldiers. They didn't want to, but they had to. It was my right. I got here, and two weeks later she was dead. She was so sick, but I think she hung on, waiting for me."

Pauvre Grand-mère, I thought; perhaps she died knowing that sometimes a long life is not worth the pain.

There wasn't anything on my grandfather's farm for Émile either. By that time John was already out of hiding and sitting around the kitchen table with Dieudonné. Every once in a while John grabbed the old mare and headed for town. He rode home hours later, his body folding, the mare leading the way. He lost his index finger, I'm sure on one of those winter trips, although he always maintained it was a farming accident.

At other times, when there was a quota open on wheat, he drove to town with a load. If there was a line-up at the elevator, as there often was, John put the vehicle in the queue, left it, and headed to the local bar for a "quick" beer. Hours later he hitched a ride back to the farm. He forgot about the truck while a disgruntled elevator agent waited and eventually called my father to help unload.

Émile began crushing a head of Durum and picking out the seed. We've all searched for the reasons in John's life, I thought. "Vivianne wanted to stay in the city," he said. "Your Maman had been waiting for me and working at William's. So I got work in the stockroom of the department store. But I started getting sick. It was the four walls. I wasn't feeling well, nobody knew what was the matter, just pale and weak. I lost thirty pounds. Then one of the doctors asked me where I was from. He told me that I had to get out, I had to work outside, or else I would just get sicker. So I got the half-section by the river. That river, you know not many people have water running through their land. Others didn't want that piece because of the groves and the bridge that separates the parcel. It's not quite a full half-section. They wanted every acre in crop. I rented it for years from the VLA. The government had land for returning soldiers. Paid it off bit by bit, took me twenty years, but the rates were good. Boy, it was hard. But Jean couldn't do that. I was alone and we had no money, but he helped out when he was around. I let him keep some cows in the pasture, but you have to pick a trail."

Émile blew the chaff from his hand, popped the cleansed seed into his mouth, and slowly worked it into a gum.

I remember as a child finally making it to the stairwell—when the coast was clear and the men were all in the yard talking business. At the base of the stairs was an old cabinet, ruined by layers of chipping paint. Opening it, I found an old Coleman clothes iron. Fuelled by oil, it was a model from the early forties. It had hardly been used, but I knew it had been Grand-mère Adéline's. I couldn't quite comprehend why, as if by magic, it had appeared there after all these years. I replaced it and walked slowly up the steep stairs. Off to the right was a dingy room with a bed at its centre. A woman's chenille blue bathrobe was draped carelessly, a sagging, makeshift window curtain. I'd seen that bathrobe in the only photos my father had of his mother, those taken shortly before she died. On the chair was an old suitcase with locks open but lid down. I opened it and found it empty except for a lone ace of spades. Rummaging through a pocket, I felt paper and pulled out an old black and white photo. There was Uncle John, a much younger Uncle John, an almost honest one, in a suit beside a well-dressed, dark-haired woman. There was nothing written on the back.

Émile chuckled. "Boy it was hard starting out," he said. "Vivianne says that she still remembers me talking in my sleep. Sometimes I would dream when I was overtired. I'd be fixing up old pieces of machinery. I had to make things stretch and I'd ask John to pass me another little piece of rag and a splinter of wood."
Life is full of Band-aids, I thought.
"Did he ever have a girlfriend, a serious girlfriend?" I asked.
"Once."
I waited before asking why he hadn't married her.
"I guess he might have, but she said it was her or the bottle. Maybe if he'd had a piece of land, someplace where things could have been different, maybe if there had been some kind of a government program to help farmers' sons get started. Maybe, I should have worked with him more, I tried." Émile ran the thick fingers of his left hand over the callouses of its mate and worked at massaging the palm. "I asked him to work with me. We could have farmed together. Maybe if we could have farmed together."

I could see myself sitting around the kitchen table and smelling the freshly baked oatmeal cookies my mother had just pulled from the oven. She always wore an apron, and it was clean even after the baking was done. Dieudonné had visited the night before and my mother was swearing politely, but still swearing, that he wouldn't come back into this house again. It was one of the three times he had accepted an invitation to our supper table, but he had shown up after spending the afternoon sitting around his own.

"Il viendra plus me chanter des louanges," she muttered. "C'est la dernière fois. He didn't even eat his meal."

My grandfather had sat there picking at his food and telling my mother what a great woman she was, what a good wife and cook. The liquor had robbed him again, and he had sat crying in front of all of us while he had pulled out his wallet and offered us each twenty-dollar bills.

"Dieudonné put that away, the time is past for all of that," she had told him. "You're welcome to a meal in this house any-time, I've always told you that. But not in this shape."

The cookies were cooling on the face of the arborite table. I took one and it left a ring of fresh crumbs.

"Dieudonné and John would show up to work with your father and bring along bottles," my mother was telling me. "You can't drink and work, not around machinery. But I'd swear that old man was doing it on purpose, to divide. He was jealous, and for a while Émile wouldn't see it. He would fall for it because he liked the stuff too much himself. I told your father that he'd have to decide."

When my grandfather finally died, Uncle John was left alone. I was approaching my teen years and no longer felt I should go into my grandfather's house without being invited. I never seemed to know if the coast was clear. There had only been a few items of real worth but everyone seemed to be waiting before they divided up the leftovers, wiped the dust from my great-grandparents' oval wedding portraits, and scraped away the layers of paint which covered the odd piece of period furniture. My grandfather's estate had to be settled first.

But one day my father came home tired and dusty from working on the cableless tractor. He'd stopped to check on John. "Vivianne, tu sais qu'est-ce-qui s'passe? The old cabinet that Maman had," my father said. "It's gone. That should stay in the family. That belongs to the family. If Maman knew! John says he doesn't know what happened to it, maudit."

"Oh, sure, well it couldn't have gone too far," my mother said. "Jean was probably loaded and he gave it away."

"I'll have to get it back. I bet that old Ben Lacoste, he knows antiques, and I saw him over there last week. But he wouldn't do that?"

"Fie-toi pas, c't'vieux diable là, he probably saw it and went over with a bottle one afternoon and tried to poison Jean. That Lacoste has always been an old horse-trader."

"Well, it can't go on. I'll have to talk to John about it. Those things are not his to give."

My father did eventually get the cabinet back from Lacoste but, before the estate was settled, other items slowly went astray. Uncle John would come over once in a while, sheepish when sober, foul-mouthed when drunk. No matter his condition, he never stayed for supper.

Even in death Dieudonné held his grasp. The will stated the homestead had to be sold as a single parcel of land at a price agreed on by the seven brothers. With John's lifelong investments amounting to only a herd of twenty cows and five brothers waiting anxiously for inheritance money, the lawyers, commission in mind, were pushing to sell to the highest bidder. My father managed, over the years, to bring the price down a bit.

"La terre, that belongs in the family," he said. "It should be sold inside the family first. A member of the family should have first option to buy at a fair price. Nobody wants to give it away. Okay, so the price is a bit lower than on the open market, a family member should still have a chance. We had two Charrette homesteads and we lost the first one. We can't sign this one away. If it goes, that's it. What about the groves around the river? They'll clear them for another couple of bushels."

John, who knew he didn't have a chance to buy the land, didn't care. Nor did the five brothers living in faraway cities. The river, the groves, the homestead were all part of the past. After all, it was only land and land was for buying and selling, wasn't it?

But my father wouldn't let go. I would overhear my parents going over the figures and the possibilities. He did eventually buy it—for more than he wanted to pay.

John continued living in the old house for a while. One weekend, I came home from university and went out to the old farmstead. There was no wind; the barns were empty. The path leading from the sunken porch seemed narrower, knobbed with tufts of prairie wool. The screen door was still off its top hinge. I walked into the house and passed the kitchen to the cabinet at the foot of the stairwell. Opening the cabinet, I wondered if it was proper to remove pieces of the homestead. Is it wise to carry portions of history with you? I wondered. Later that afternoon, I told my father, "I took something from the old house, today. I think it must have been Grand-mère Adéline's." Hoping to be entrusted with it, I showed him the Coleman iron.

"Where did you find that?" he asked. "It must have been Maman's, pauvre Maman. I've never seen it before. She must have gotten it during the war. You might as well have it. It's not much. Most everything else has disappeared over the years. There've never been many family gifts . . . never much to give . . ."

Émile was up and moving around the swather to where the tools lay. He didn't seem to want to know more about John, or the rooming house where he had spent the last several years, or even the exact time of his death. When Émile bent over to replace the tools in their box, he braced himself against the swather for support. He straightened, then walked over to the scratched box of the old Ford, opened the rear gate, and slid the tool box in. He closed the gate and leaned back against it.

"You know," he said, "when Dieudonné died I told John that he could stay. That there would always be a place here for him. But he didn't seem to care, anymore. He never cared about the harvest, maybe because he felt the land wasn't his. The house was so old and he never fixed it up. He could have. He had his cows and I didn't charge him anything to keep them in the pasture. But he wouldn't quit drinking. He wouldn't even take care of his cows. He only had a few left but you can't treat animals that way, you can't let them suffer. That little pasture was so overgrazed the cows would get into the groves and break the trees." His glassy eyes fixed on a point down the road. "Well, I asked him often, then I warned him. But you can only push so much. I had to tell him to sell them. Then there was really nothing for him to do, I don't know, maybe if he'd had a piece of land all his own . . . We could have farmed together. We could have shared equipment so he could get a little place going. Something to start with and then maybe bit by bit . . . Nobody likes to borrow or ask for a hand, but sometimes you have to. What's a family for? He just wouldn't . . ."

Damn John, I thought, for hanging around.

"A family can only do so much, Dad," I said. "A person has to have the will to ask for help—to live—right?"

"Yeh, but some people are dealt a bad hand."

Nobody is ever dealt a perfect one, I thought. "You have to know how to make the best of the cards," I said.

"I guess." Émile paused. "We'll have to think about getting the funeral together. It'll be small . . . just family . . . maybe the chapel will be big enough. Should we have a eulogy? I don't even know if he has a plot."

"Probably not," I said.

"Maybe there's space in Dieudonné's . . . There's always cremation," Émile said, looking out at a nearby fallow field. A lone dust devil raced toward us, ran into a light crosswind, and quickly dissipated into thin air.

"We'll iron it out, Dad." An urn doesn't take up much space, I thought, even in an already crowded plot.

Émile walked around the truck and climbed into the driver's seat. "Well," he said. I followed behind him and stood by while he slammed the stiff door closed and started her up. "Needs grease," he reminded himself.

"Dad, if there's anything—"

"Non, non. I'll be okay. I've just got to keep moving, you have to keep moving. We'll be harvesting that quarter . . . You know the parcel south of the river before the six-mile road in about three days."

While Émile drove off, I could see the truck's rear gate sag slightly to one side from the years of use. I watched him round the corner onto the main road. He quickly rolled up the window so the swirls of dust wouldn't get into the cab. I watched long enough to see the billows settle back onto the road.

GLEN SORESTAD

Beer at Cochin

The lazy August fire
                wanted quenching.
Even the slightest breeze
                  from the lake
could not suppress the knowledge
that Cochin pub was near
and cool
      and wet.

Entering the dim-cool
               (alive
with beer promises) room is
so good
       you want to stop
                 forever
the moment
       to hang suspended.

      The Indians and Metis have their own
      section in the pub at Cochin—
      no cordons
            no signs
                no markers
      of any kind
      no, nothing so blatant.
      But in Cochin
      they know
            where to sit.
      Everyone in the room knows
                    even you
    total stranger
            even you know too.

But you ignore it and sit down
next to a table of Indians
               and wait
and it doesn't take long
             no
not long at all.

Someone flips a switch
                    and conversation
in the room is silenced—
and even the table next to you
is frozen.

And the bartender comes over
                    his face pained
and he asks
            if you wouldn't like to
            move closer to the bar

and you are well aware
that it isn't really a question
                    now
or ever.

GLEN SORESTAD

Number One Guide
(for John Seewup)

1.

Fifty-six years he has beaten
a life from these dark woods
with a Harper's Island trapline.
And fifty-six summers here
on Jan as boy and man,
                fisherman and guide.

"I'm number one guide,"
                        John shouts.
And who can question this?
He has forgotten more about this lake
than any *moonie-ass* can dream
or ever hope to learn.

But years of booze have bent John
like a rough wind. Lodge owners
hire him now only
                as a last resort.

2.

Forest fires have swept
the camp of all Indian guides, all
but John, here, with the women
and children. His age and condition
a comfortable reprieve
from days and nights of smoke
and heat, and endless shovels.

So John is Jan's sole guide:
transformed from last year's pariah
to this year's saviour, besieged
with requests and promises.
American twenties and bottles
of Old Crow swirl around him
like the dangerous drift of smoke.

146

3.

In the morning the camp rises
on Seewup time and John heads
his flotilla of American boats
strung behind like empty promises
to Deschambault River.
                              We decline
his offer to follow him,
                              prefer
to map-read our own route
alone to Grassy Narrows where
we will find our walleyes.
John throws us a jaunty wave
and captains his armada away.

4.

Early afternoon. We have returned
with our limits of walleyes.
John returns with seven boats,
all babbling about *grayet nathren piehk*.

John has been liberally plied with booze.
He has little desire to fillet fish,
looks instead for a beer or whiskey.

He tells us of last winter. Falling
through the ice. His narrow escape.
How his son caught him by the hair,
somehow managed to pull him out.

"By the hair!" he roars, running
his hand through his dark hair.
"John was THAT close!" he shouts.

5.

We show John our map. Where
we have fished. The spot at the Narrows.
Mark it as closely as possible,
indicate where we caught our limits.
John grins. Nods his approval.
But our black **X** seems to stir something.
He grabs the pen.
                    "Look. I show you!
Best walleye spot.
P.P. Walleye. Look here.
This one right here . . ."

He **X**'s a point on our map.
". . . my favourite. P.P. Walleye."
The **X** is just off Harper's Island.
His winter grounds.
                    "Here's another.
And this one too."

There are now four **X**'s.

His excitement dies. He stares,
seems embarrassed at his marks.
Finally, *"Don't tell nobody."*
A sadness has taken over.
"You go there. But don't tell
nobody I showed you."
                    Subdued,
he wanders away to his camp,
away from something he understands
and would rather forget. Somehow.

RICHARD STEVENSON

Shooting Pigeons

Bang! Clatter, clatter, clatter . . . thunk:
the third stone rolls down the corru-
gated zinc roof of my castle,
rousting me, a sweaty, angry Goliath,
from sleep. I sit bolt upright on my
terry towel stretched beneath the fan.

Neighbourhood kids after pigeons again,
only in the moments of half-sleep I think
of seagulls circling the high-tide stones,
dropping clams to crack their shells perhaps,
or of breaking glass, consciousness
a piece of paper wrapped around a rock.

I stumble in confusion, pull on my pants,
unlock the door, remove the padlock from its loops.
Storm the gates to rant about the windows,
snatch their slingshots from their hands.
This way, I point, away from the house.
Ba English, they say, ba English.

My syllables bounce off
the tin roofs of their eyes and ears.
The pigeons turn their iridescent feathers
to the sun, the grapeshot of their red eyes
spraying out from the obnoxious
blunderbus of my booming voice.

Ba Hausa, I say, ba Hausa.
The words, flung out in a slow arc
against the gold feathers of sun that
rustle, flap, settle themselves again
in the gnarled branches of the thorn trees,
the thin crotch of my only tongue.

ROBBIE NEWTON DRUMMOND

Pineapple

It's Hawaiian night this New Year's Eve.
Inuvik's whites and displaced souls jam
into the apartment block on stilts
off Bootlake's frozen blank where the spring
Muskrat furrows a wake and the summer
Loon lands in a flute of laughs.
It's black-out black
out; cold as a stropped razor.

Fat Sandy the Newfie hairdresser
in a beach brown grass skirt
sips Kiwi Daiquiris laced with rum
eyes the pilots and new doctors
through shades, pie-eyed.

A whiff of easy love percolates
like the smell of fresh spilt beer.
The ritual tete-a-tete of couples
coupling agitates . . . easy as a two-step,
the music cranked high.
A glass or two breaks.
A blonde kid limboes under a pole
for kisses.

No one
will ever go
native here.
No one knows
any natives here.

The host in the kitchen
with a souvenir samurai sword
hacks a pineapple into pieces.

—Inuvik, NWT

150

MARLIS WESSELER

The Wall

Barbara and Hans walked through the ancient archway leading from the bar to the cobblestone street. They strolled along various sidestreets until they came to Königstrasse. Barbara felt glamorous and European—Marlene Dietrich or Greta Garbo—and wished she could see Berlin the way it had been before the war, before everything old was bombed. She wanted to see real cabarets; she wanted to dance in the Grand Hotel. She looked down at the supple leather of her high-heeled boots, pleased at how she, with her narrow feet, had found boots here that fit perfectly with no trouble at all.

She stopped. Brown mush was oozing out from under the heel of her left boot. Self-satisfied Berliners, none of them noticing anything on their own boots, hurried around her. Why did things like this always happen to her?

Hans looked at her and grinned his good-naturedly evil smile. That was why she had married him, she thought sometimes; because of his smile. She scraped her boots on the sidewalk in disgust. "Berlin must be the dog shit capital of the world. It's unbelievable."

"My grandmother says Paris is vorse," Hans said. He leaned lazily against a *currywurst* stand.

The first time Barbara met Hans's family, they had all gathered together to meet her. The hearty handshakes, enthusiastic guttural speech accompanied by touches to kneecaps, wrists, shoulders, the laughter—Barbara found it exhausting and bewildering. The grandmother sat gazing silently at her own thoughts, ignoring everyone, and finally Barbara sat down on the couch beside her and made hesitant conversation: two quiet foreigners in exuberant territory.

The old woman reminisced about her girlhood, conjuring up stories of dances and fairy-tale evenings of frosted drinks at summer spas, *gluwein* around the fireplace at winter resorts in the Alps. When she was a girl her hair was so long, she said, she could sit on it. She used to play the piano at friends' houses, her back straight, as she had been taught, white hands held delicately above the keys, wrists flexible and dainty, her long chocolate-brown hair almost touching the carpet. She remembered herself wearing a white dress with a red sash, and a red ribbon in her hair. "Ach, but now I am an old woman," she had said to Barbara, patted her hand and smiled.

151

They continued their walk, Barbara watching the sidewalk until she realized where they were. There it was again. They kept running into it. A perfectly normal street, pavement over cobblestone, would suddenly lead to thick cement looming over them. A dead end. Wooden-faced soldiers at attention watched from tall stands that resembled lifeguard towers. Death guards, she had thought on first seeing them. Most sections of the wall were a dirty cement grey sprayed with graffiti, fluorescent greens or oranges looking like Phentex wool strewn over a basement floor. In the no-man's land between East and West was the odd Doberman or German shepherd, which could only be seen from tourist stands or hills overlooking the wall.

She had gone sightseeing with Hans's relatives and, each time, the wall was pointed out to her: *"Da. Da ist die Mauer."* It was said with a certain pride, she thought, intermingled with a satisfied sense of communal self-pity. Berliners had long ceased to feel horror or sorrow whenever they passed the wall, simply because it had been there so long. It had become ordinary, an inconvenience that couldn't be helped, rather like bad weather. In fact, she realized, Berliners pointed out the wall in much the same way people from Saskatchewan spoke about the winters.

"Sometimes it's forty below," she'd found herself saying to one of Hans's friends.

"Mein Gott, das ist vie Siberia!" he'd exclaimed, and she'd nodded smugly, pleased.

"There's ze wall," Hans said.

"I know," she said abruptly. "Let's get out of here for a while. Let's take a drive to the forest." There were islands of parkland, part of the city's property, in and surrounding Berlin. After a twenty minute drive, they left the car near the woods and started to walk, shuffling through the thick mat of fallen leaves.

"Forest." Barbara looked around at the ancient oak trees, brown-gold carpet, vines out of Grimm's fairy tales. "We don't even use that word at home, we say 'bush.'" They stopped beside a huge oak tree, split almost in two. "How on earth did that happen? Lightning? I think it's still alive, look at the colour of the wood."

"Zat," Hans said, looking seriously at her with wide grey eyes, "is the famous Berliner Baumgartnerschnitzenschmatzen, one of the great vonders of the vorld. It's been like that for five hundred years and was a great tourist attraction even then. Why, I remember coming here as a youngster . . ." He started his atrocious imitation of an American accent.

Barbara poked him. "Great vonders of ze vorld," she imitated. "You're really too much."

They began to wrestle. Hans chased her around vine-covered trees: huge, centuries old, the bark rough and friendly beneath their hands. He caught her, and they fell together onto the soft golden carpet. When they discovered the mushy underlay of rotted vegetation, they got up immediately.

They started to walk again, arm in arm. "I expect to find a house made of gingerbread any minute now," she said.

There it was. They stopped. White, she thought. Only Germans would bother to whitewash something like the wall. It seemed to loom larger, even more incongruous in this deserted forest like a giant prop for a science fiction movie.

"I wonder if it will still be here in 2001," she said.

Hans shrugged and walked along the wall to higher ground, to see into no-man's land. "Come here," he shouted. "Look at these dogs."

She ran to him and saw two Doberman pinschers. They raced silently intent along the inside of the wall, their ears razor flat. They swiftly became small dots in the distance, closing in on another, somewhat taller dot.

Barbara's stomach knotted. She shivered as if someone had touched her spine with something cold. "Did you hear a shot?"

"I'm not sure."

They watched. The dots were like those in a video game: search and destroy, the two finally descending on the one, the one disappearing, all three becoming one mass, a larger dot. Finally more dots appeared.

"Let's go." Hans's face was white.

Barbara, unable to move her legs, continued to stare.

"Let's go!" he shouted and grabbed her arm.

They ran through the decaying leaves, dodged tree trunks with bare, witch-armed branches, and tripped on vines. Feathered branches from juniper trees brushed their faces.

During the drive back, she finally broke the silence. "Do you think," she said, "do you think they were chasing some *guy*? Someone trying to get to West Berlin?"

"No, it was probably an exercise, zey were training the dogs."

"But—"

"Ya, it was only a training exercise."

She wondered it the soldiers were Russians or East Germans. They were probably Russian. Surely they couldn't count on an East German to shoot? "Have they ever posted East German soldiers on the wall?" she asked.

"They're all East German," Hans said in careful English. "All the guards."

She looked at him and said nothing. It must have been a training exercise.

They spent the rest of the day quietly reading and writing breezy, everything's fine postcards. That evening they went to a movie, an American comedy with German subtitles. By the last half of the show, Barbara's laughter became almost spontaneous.

The next day they went to the zoo. At least we can't run into the wall here, she thought, watching an elephant. He scratched himself against the cement of his enclosure. Clean striped tigers, looking artificial somehow, paced back and forth in their cage. "Let's go and see the monkeys," she said. "They're all inside."

The primates were behind glass rather than bars, so a person could walk right up and stand nose to nose with any of them. The faces were what interested her: the shrivelled yet babyish chimps; the flat-faced, reserved baboons; the enthusiastic, bearded orangoutangs; the great variety of chittering, surprised-looking monkeys.

The walls of each cage had loops and ladders of rope attached to them. A variety of apes and monkeys clambered from the walls to the floors and back again, each species housed in a separate cage. The orangoutangs and chimpanzees made a game of putting sacks over their heads and snatching them off again, much to the amusement of the onlookers. A few, however, refused to play. They put the sacks over their heads and sat like lumpy potato bags in corners or swung, like hanging lampshades, from the walls. A giant ape suddenly squatted and put his hand under himself.

"Good God," Barbara said. "He's catching his own shit in his hand."

A dark man standing beside them smiled, his gold fillings catching the light. "Ya," he said, "he used to amuse himself by throwing his *dreck* at the people, when these were cages with bars."

The ape had a calculating, sly expression. He pretended to be about to throw, and waited for a reaction from the people he was observing. Instead of the mass panic he seemed to expect, the reaction was one of condescending amusement. He looked perplexed, faked a throw once or twice and, finally, there it was, splattered on the glass in front of Barbara.

"What else?" she said.

The ape looked bewildered.

Hans nudged her and said, "Vat's that saying about people in glass houses?"

The ape swung unsteadily across the cage to the glass. He stood swaying back and forth like a crazy metronome, gazing stupidly, his eyes rolling.

"Something's wrong with him," Barbara said softly, uncomfortable.

The ape continued to rock from side to side until, with concentrated fury, he attacked the glass. He kicked, made it ring loud, hollow bongs, then punched it until he finally sat, exhausted, on the floor. He began his insane rhythm again: the back and forth cradle rock. Hans and Barbara walked out.

It was beginning to rain when they left the zoo. The sidestreets were grey and shiny under the *Kneiper* signs.

"We have to be at your grandmother's by six-thirty," she said, as they got into his father's tiny Fiat.

Hans's grandmother rented an apartment in a modern building in which other elderly people lived. She managed to keep it all spotless: her beige carpet, the flowered couch, the china cabinet, and all the other furniture and knick-knacks. Barbara remembered, when she first met her at the family get-together, noticing her skin. She had the smoothest skin Barbara had ever seen on someone so old. Not that she looked young; it was just that her face hadn't wrinkled. It was round and smooth, with slightly sagging cheeks and a few broken veins creating faint blotches.

She greeted them at the door with energy and enthusiasm and fed them a huge supper. After dessert, she sat down comfortably with her brandy and started reminiscing. Hans's parents never discussed the war seriously, although his mother had once said, about the concentration camps with their high walls and barbed wire, "We didn't know what went on. We had no idea." Barbara had believed her. But late in the evening, Hans's grandmother spoke in slow direct German while looking straight at Barbara. "When I was a girl we were a rich family. Then came the depression and the inflation and we were ruined by Jewish speculators. Others as well as us. By Jews. Jews were not popular, we called them pigs. Then Hitler came and they all disappeared."

Barbara felt ice on her spine, the same ice she had felt watching the "training exercise." She watched Hans's expression change from that of shock to apology (she's only an old lady) to belligerence (she's here and she's my grandmother, whether it suits you or not). He stood up and thanked the old woman for supper and said they had to get back. She only nodded and looked closely at Barbara's face before kissing her goodbye. Hans, Barbara realized, had inherited his smile from his grandmother.

"Most of us say we didn't know what was happening back then," she said. "But we knew enough. We knew what to turn our backs to."

On the way to his parents' apartment, Hans said, "She's had a hard life. Her parents lost everysing and died in poverty when she was young and the Russians killed her husband in a work camp after the war. Then she lost her house in East Germany. She calls the Russians pigs too."

"And that's supposed to make everything fine? That she calls the Russians pigs *too?*"

They drove on in silence for a while. Then Barbara asked, "Did I understand everything? Did—"

"Remember, she's eighty years old," he interrupted. "Who knows what goes on in her mind. Anyway I didn't hear all she said." His voice was harsh and resentful. Against her, Barbara realized; not his grandmother.

She leaned her head back on the headrest and closed her eyes. They hadn't talked about the incident at the wall, and now they weren't going to talk about this. Fine, she thought; this is the end of it. A newscaster on the car radio was speaking German too quickly for her to follow. She wanted to go home. She wanted to be able to turn on the radio and hear Peter Gzowski's mellow but earnestly Canadian voice. Thinking of that voice made her want to cry. She glanced at Hans's grim face and reached over to touch his knee. This is only a holiday, she thought; in a few days we'll leave it all behind.

NIGEL DARBASIE

Pan Man

Ravi Mohansingh is a Trinidad boy
come to make good in Canada
now dat is one indian
who could beat steelpan like a lord.
One time
bout three o'clock in de mornin
he was leavin a dance hall
on de east end after playin in a fete
when some bad white boys take in he ass.
Dey close in like shark
sayin how dey go sen he back to India
like a mummy
wit only he eye showin
from de bandage.

He tell dem he eh from India
but dat eh make no difference
dey callin he paki
an intend to sen he dong
de North Saskatchewan River.
What runnin in Ravi mind
is what move to make
a good few yards to he car
an dem boys tightenin up
have he in a bad way: heart beatin fas, fas
he sweatin profuse although it cold
mouth dry
he feelin sick like he want to shit.
Jes den sombody call out
"Wudds happenin, bro?"
Is Eddoes and Chanel 59
comin up de road.

Ravi smile broad
at de sight a dem two gigantic creole
movin quick an smooth under de streetlight
like two panther when dey huntin.
An dey have plenty experience too
dem boy used to ramble an ting back home
all kinda bottle an razor scar on dey body.
Since dey come Canada
dey livin respectable
wuckin as pipefitter an makin good wage.
An dem doh see no kinda trouble wit de police
not even a speedin ticket self.
But dis time anyting could happen.

Well tings turn out fuh de best.
Jes as Eddoes an Chanel 59 move in
de white boys slide out
so nuttin heavy go dong
no blood fall
only sweat
an all was Ravi own.

De nex day
Eddoes take Ravi by Deloris
de hairdresser.
She cut he hair an put in a perm
have Ravi lookin cool an funky.
Well yuh know
de white boys stop callin he paki
dey might call he nigger
but not too loud.

MICHELENE ADAMS

To Livinston Lettin Go

Is only when Miss Lurvy dead dat Livinston Lurvy start carryin on. When she alive he come home straight from diggin trench fuh Water Works, no dominoes or whappy wid de boys in de evenin. An on sundays he in his grey jacket an pants, shirt collar starch an cheeks smood, an he walkin wid Miss Lurvy an de three girls to de service, a prayerbook under his arm. Every sunday after service, he drive pas Samlal rumshop, Miss Lurvy an two a de girls in de back seat, de tird chile in front wid him. Dey goin to visit Miss Lurvy mudder who livin in Palo Grande. All de boys limin in de doorway a de rumshop shake dey head an snort an chuckle. Rock say like Livinston is look in sideways when he pass an Ralph say he have a feelin if Miss Lurvy ever leave, even fuh a three days, Livinston go leh go. So all de boys raise dey glass an toas to Livinston lettin go.

An he leh go. After dey bury Miss Lurvy, her mudder take de three girls an leave Livinston in de house by himself. Wasn a week before he turn up by Samlal, say he could use a brandy, he finin it hard to cope. Buh one brandy turn out to be two, an a rum, an de beers some a de boys buy fuh him, an Livinston en up weavin his way home after midnight wid work de nex mornin. Now Livinston dere regular, an when he ain dere, he playin dominoes, even on sunday, wid Banfiel an Rock, bettin a dollar a game, a white towel roun his neck an his shirt unbutton.

De firs time dey see her was de night Livinston lose bad. As he pull out his wallet to han over de money, she come in from Banfiel kitchen an clout her husban in de back a his head. She ain stop to say nuttin, she jus trow him a look over her shoulder as she walk off dat have all de boys dumb. Livinston button his shirt, get up an say he gawn.

One afternoon she come in de rumshop an lick down de half bottle dat sittin on de table in front a him. De bottle roll, an rum pour out onto Livinston work pants, de floor. He watch in his lap, watch up at her. She fol her arms an stare back, den she turn roun an head fuh de door.

De night Livinston trow a party she walk bout scheupsin at everybody, gawn over by de D.J. an turn down de volume. Livinston in de kitchen bennin over a styrotex cooler wid ice. She lean over him an shove his head down inside. He swing back at her buh she dodge his han an she gawn. Once she even follow him to de races in town. He in line to bet forty on a horse name Toco Toco, but as he reach de wicket, she push in front a him, drag de money out his han an fling it away.

Still Livinston ain give up. Until one night when he an Gloria Braithwaite decide to drive to de lookout. De two a dem leanin up on de front a de car, Livinston wid his arm roun Gloria, Gloria wid her head on his shoulder, her han under his jersey. Den Miss Lurvy appear, draggin her foot over de gravel. Before he have time to tink, she open de door, turn on de engine an leh go de hanbrake. She stan up an watch de car roll backwards as he pelt pas her behin it. Lucky fuh him, it roll into a ditch on de side a de road an stick dere—back tires wedge in, front tires up off de groun an spinnin.

Nex day, Livinston gawn by his mudder-in-law an bring de three girls home. Monday to saturday, he diggin trench fuh Water Works, comin home in time to eat wid de family. Sunday he walkin to de service wid dem, hair trim, collar starch, sayin, "Mornin," as if no sunday was ever not like dis one. After de service he drive pas de rumshop, all three girls in de back seat, an when de boys raise dey glass at him as he pass, Livinston nod.

RICHARD STEVENSON

A Photo for Daheru

His white baba riga, fresh
from the bathtub, is clean
and pressed for the occasion—
thanks to the gods that fire
your electric iron and stay
his hand along the creases
of that hour, that perfect day.

His young Kilba wife seems
happy too, decked out in her
prettiest wrapper and scarf;
sits prim as a cat beside him,
the three tribal lines scored
on each side of her parted lips
exquisite as a cat's whiskers.

And yet they fidget as you
focus, open the aperture
that one extra stop that will
insure you capture the rich,
dark patina of their skin,
and not over or underexpose
the true radiance that is theirs.

And when the picture doesn't
pop out like the quick baby
Jack-in-the-box that it is,
he does not understand, you
must explain the slow birth
process, the white negative that
requires midwifery and trust.

It is not the juju of the thing,
the idea that you would steal
his soul, but that he is used
to polaroid systems, the quick
catch-as-catch-can kind of life
that has as its dark correlative
the visible gestation of light.

S. PADMANAB

Pastoral

cleft feet
and bit grass
in a puff of flies:

bleating goats,
droop-teated,
dropping black beads
like chiselled gems,

pulling down
the pleated hay
of heat-hardened huts.

i dont know
what bliss there is
in a memory
such as this,

or of sun-burnt,
bone-thin children,

but there is,
dammit,
there is.

S. PADMANAB

At Fifty-Three

Give me the grace of words.

In a small house
give me a girl of twenty-one,
hid away and grown in hills and fields,
knowing no speech
but the whispers of birds
and the anger of the sun.

O how I will dance around the room,
painting the walls in red,
singing my incantations
in a quivering, hoarse voice
in a strange language.

I will be her teacher
and make her understand
how telephones work and stars roam the skies.
She will be initiated
into the three waves of the pulse
and the intricacies of the stock-market.
Yes, I will be her teacher
and teach her all I know.

Then I will turn lover.
Gathering her small breasts
in my plump wet hands
like flowers of gold, raising her oval face to mine,
I will teach her what people can do
with their lips, their hands and thighs.

When at sixty-three I am tired of games
and this giving away,
she will tuck me in bed
like a fallen bird,
find a young lover
with his beard hardly grown,
and teach him things.

ELIZABETH ALLEN

from the gateway between us

a gravel path, a difficult
descent to grey sand
the ocean's edge
and a white wooden dinghy
waiting

on the bay dipping oars
& pulling smoothly out to the heads
I look up, see you on the clifftop
a figure sinking
into the land's curve
in a moment
you will disappear altogether.

JOAN GIVNER

Jump Sunday

When I get letters from home, they seem to come not merely from another country, but from another planet, peopled by beings with different mentalities, different physiognomies, different speech patterns. Sometimes I feel I'm being zapped by rays that drain off my psychic energy.

My mother writes mainly about funerals which, as she grows older, seem to have preempted all other forms of social life. You might think this would be morbid for her and for me. It isn't because of a strange quirk whereby she seems not to register that the guest of honour has really died. Phrases like "passed on" and "gone to a better place" are not used euphemistically. She tells me that Herbert Greengrass has had a lovely funeral and he would have loved it, as if another commitment had kept him from attending. She writes that Fred Parry died, had an open coffin and looked so wonderful that several people remarked his recent holiday in the Isle of Man had done him a world of good.

And, of course, she writes to me about Nigel. Because she writes letters on Sunday afternoon and because she hates to waste any of the airmail letter, he gets at least two paragraphs. Nigel is now the first and only doctor in the village, the church organist and choirmaster and, as always, everybody's favourite person. He's the son every mother wants—attentive, dutiful, and never straying too far from home. He hasn't changed much from our childhood, when old crones we met patted him on the head and murmured that he was a gradely little lad. And then they let their eyes slide insolently sideways to where I stood, insulting me by their silence, or their perfunctory "and Frances, too."

I try to respond in kind. Although I am a fair typist and now use a word processor, I wouldn't dream of typing letters home. I keep in my left-hand desk drawer an assembly of articles like the trappings of some shameful fetish. These are an inkwell, a pen with removable nibs, a package of pink blotting paper and a box of tinted paper, which I mentally call "stationery." I write letters that express concern for the dying, dead and recently interred. I say, "I was grieved to hear about Herbert passing. How fitting that he's buried by the church wall, since he never did like going inside the church." I say, "I was dismayed to hear that Rover Riddlesdale had to be put down, but seventeen is a great age. I hope Maude can come to terms with the loss."

And, of course, I speak of Nigel. I write, "Tell Nigel I have several new hymns for him." I have a plot under way to Americanize the church service with "The Battle Hymn of the Republic," "Amazing Grace" and "There's an Old Rugged Cross on the Hill." I add, "Tell Nigel I'll be home in three months and am counting on him for a good pub crawl."

Nigel and I go back a long way. As children we were inseparable. I used to seek him out when the scale of my mother's cleaning operations made the home front unbearable, which was most of the time, but especially on washing days. The houses in the village were like fortresses defended against all comers. If you went collecting for the church or the RSPCA, people would keep you standing on the doorstep for hours in the worst weather rather than invite you inside. It was part, I suppose, of the small town effort to maintain privacy in a place where every move comes under public scrutiny. But I was always welcome at Nigel's house, partly because our mothers were friendly and partly because his mother Connie was a breezy, friendly person who never put on the dog. In fact, my mother disapproved of her for that very reason. She thought her unmindful of her position as the wife of someone who, in peace time, was a bank manager and who now, in war time, was a naval officer. I loved standing in her kitchen looking around at everything they had on the shelves and watching her feed garments into the squeezers and bring them out flat as boards on the other side. She would chat with me in a friendly way and, between remarks like "How's your mother's head?" she would yell, "NI-gel, NI-gel, look lively, lad." And eventually he would put away his book or whatever he was doing and come downstairs ready to join me in my search for amusement.

This could have been a fruitless search in our village, except that our expectations were minimal. On washing days we were happy to stroll about or sit on a wall and look at the washing. We liked seeing the intimate garments of our school teachers and the vicar displayed to public view. We watched voluminous bloomers, nightshirts, patched pyjamas and darned long underwears blowing in the wind. Our surveillance bore fruit on Sundays, when the owners marched down the aisle in church and we looked at each other and laughed at our shared knowledge of those concealed patches and darns. I was with my parents in our pew and Nigel was in the front row of the choir stalls, neat and cherubic in his white surplice.

Now, well into his thirties, he was still there in the same outfit more or less, only leading the choirboys instead of being a boy soprano warbling as melodiously as a little song thrush. Sitting a continent away in some rented apartment, wondering about the next posting of my serviceman husband and our transient life, it gave me a sense of security to think of Nigel still there—a permanent fixture every Sunday to the end of time.

And so, when my mother wrote, "The church was lovely for Easter and Nigel played beautifully," I received the news gratefully. If she wrote, "Nice service this morning, but it isn't the same when Roy Unsworth plays the organ. Nigel was out on the Moss somewhere delivering a baby," I suffered a slight pang. For one thing I thought of Nigel's butterfingers, his absolute inability to catch or hold anything. I could still see him in a game of rounders, standing with his hands cupped, making a nest as if he expected the ball to fly into it.

At first, when he graduated from Medical School, a lot of people shared my feeling. But it changed rapidly and soon they were disarmed by his pleasant manner, swearing by him and getting agitated when he took a two week holiday. My mother said her head had been a lot better since Nigel took her off codeine and put her on something new. I imagined him seeing her out of his surgery and saying in the jocular Lancashire accent he had affected for so long that it was his only way of speaking, "How's the lass? How's the old married woman?"

My mother was always hinting that he would make someone a nice husband as if I was remiss for not snapping him up myself. Indeed, he was not only eligible but very handsome with his smooth black hair, big brown eyes, tip-tilted nose, and his Tyrone Power air of sweetness. I think my mother was sure that I refused to marry him because he was younger than I. He strengthened this belief by announcing regularly that he remained a bachelor because Frances wouldn't have him. I got so irritated one time that I had a stab at explaining to my mother why he wouldn't marry me or any other woman. After that, whenever she was seeing him out of our house, she looked nervously at the hall closet as if she feared he might dash inside and hold our gum boots and wellies hostage.

Not that Nigel and I ever discussed the matter. Though recently I thought he almost did. I said to him, "You know, I think you're going to make a very plausible middle-aged man with that accent of yours. Sort of like James Mason in *Georgie Girl*." And without hesitation, he said, "More like Peter Finch in *Sunday, Bloody Sunday*." "Well," I thought. But then we went on talking about accents. I grumbled about all the neighbours who feared I would contract an American accent, like coming down

167

with a deadly disease. "Doan get an Amurricun accent, luv."
"The great national myth of perfect speech," I said, "remains
intact despite all evidence to the contrary. Like the Queen's
Christmas address."

Actually, it didn't seem surprising to me that Nigel should
have been as unfitted for married life as he was for military ser-
vice since he had been adrift from birth, more or less, in a world
of women. The three older children were girls, and the household
had early fallen into the clutches of an old dragon called Mrs.
Percy Heap who came to help out and established complete
domination over the family. I remember the children filing into
the community air raid shelter. Most of us got hurriedly wrapped
in blankets and old coats with nightdresses underneath when the
sirens went off. But Mrs. Percy marched Nigel and his sisters in,
all completely dressed as if for school.

I can almost fix the date when Mrs. Percy took over. I
remember going over one washing day and finding the house
strangely silent. Instead of Connie, Mrs. Percy loomed in the
doorway. I said, "Can Nigel come out and play?" She said in her
genteel, bossy, schoolteacher's voice, "Yes he can but no he may
not." Then Connie's voice called out that he might as well go
outside and Mrs. Percy said, "Nay-gel will be out directly," and
shut the door rudely in my face. I went round to the front of the
house and sat on the doorstep until Nigel came out looking green
and sick.

Later in the day, my mother said to me, "Did you play with
Nigel and how was he?" She said to my father, "Those poor
children. I can't think what Connie will do. She won't be so
happy-go-lucky now." My father said, "Well, she's still young,"
and my mother said angrily, "But four children under twelve.
Who would want to take that lot on?" And my father said, "He's
only missing, remember."

Then Connie started to give music lessons. Mrs. Percy was at
the house all the time and, when I went for Nigel, I heard
children playing scales in the sitting room. I thought it must be
awful for Nigel to hear that racket from morning till night. People
kept saying how brave Connie was, and I think some of the
bravery splashed over onto Nigel because he became everyone's
little pet. I was with him most of the time because he liked to get
out of the house, but none of the bravery ever washed over
on me.

Now, when I came back to visit my parents, Nigel came
rushing to our house to find me and take me out. The last time he
came my mother said, "Frances, give Nigel a sherry." I went to

the sideboard and poured a tumbler half full of whiskey and waved the soda siphon over it. My father raised his eyebrows at the colour but Nigel only grinned. He said, "Tomorrow's Jump Sunday. Let's go to Aintree and walk round the racecourse."

"Don't you have church? I said. And he said we could leave immediately after morning service because it wasn't all that far on the new road.

"Would you like me to make you a picnic?" my mother asked and Nigel said, "Ee, we would that." I walked him to the car and he looked down at my stiletto heels and said, "A pair o' clogs'd be better for t'racecourse."

"Do your patients mind that you smell of whiskey?" I asked.

"They expect it," he said. "They think it's a kind of disinfectant. Like formaldehyde."

"I see," I said. "You can do no wrong. What about your housekeeper?"

"Ah well, that's another matter," he said, sighing I thought rather heavily. I remembered the last time I'd been home it was summer and we had spent a hot afternoon in his garden, sprawled in deck chairs, drinking and laughing under the disapproving eye of the old woman. I thought at the time that Mrs. Percy had established a pattern in his life so that he had to place himself in the custody of a female guardian for protection. But from what? From some Bad Influence like myself?

"If you came to church, we could leave from there," he said. "I'd play all your favourite hymns. They'd like it," he said, nodding at the house, where my mother was watching us from behind the lace curtains in the front window."

"That's just the point," I said.

"Always determined to thwart them," he said and I took offence at his putting my actions in the light of kind of adolescent rebellion.

"A point conceded," I explained, "would be the thin end of the wedge. Then they would go on to what I should wear—hat, gloves, shoes and dress—and after that how much I should put on the plate and whether I should offer to read the lesson or take offense because I wasn't asked to. . ."

"Alreet, alreet," he said, "I'll come and get you. I usually run your mother home anyway."

"I'll be ready," I said. "Sensible shoes, walking stick, picnic—the works."

I should have known better than to concede the picnic. My mother stayed home from church to make it, not out of a sense of martyrdom so much as out of her sheer genius for making a production out of everything domestic. She mithered all morning about the most opportune time for making the sandwiches so that they wouldn't go soggy and whether the thermos of tea should have sugar in it.

When Nigel arrived she said, "I made tongue sandwiches."

"Mmm my favourite," he said, making a Bisto-kid face.

"Oh good," she said, "because some don't like it and I wondered if I should have popped in some ham as well. I've got an old mackintosh here too that you can sit on. Put it under the rug because it's damp at this time of year. It's an old one and you don't have to worry about what happens to it. Put it waterproof side down . . ."

"Mother!!!!!" I shrieked, ready to call off the whole expedition.

"Silence, young woman," Nigel said, grabbing the picnic and the mac and bowing. "I don't want you getting poorly and having to be treated for lumbago before you return to America."

"Lumbago!" I said. I could see why all his patients loved him so.

When we finally got away, it was with the heady sense of having escaped, the being let out for good behaviour that we always had as children, especially when we were doing something that was marginally forbidden.

"You'll find a small flask in the glove compartment, if you'd like a pre-luncheon drink," he told me. "I usually reward myself after morning service." I opened the glove compartment and saw two large leather thermoses with silver lids for drinking out of. I opened one and sniffed Scotch but didn't take a drink. It occurred to me that he must be rewarding himself for this and that much of the time.

"Why not a bar in the car?" I asked.

"Wouldn't create the correct impression," he said.

When we went for drives we did a lot of lighthearted do-you-remembering. It was a harmless revisiting of our childhood stripped of all the unpleasant times. Once it amused him to take me to Barton Bridge because we had thought it was one of the seven wonders of the world, alongside the pyramids and the Taj Mahal. Then we'd adjourn to a pub and get very giggly and silly.

This time I said, "Nige, I'm going to leave my husband and get a divorce."

"Oh my God," he said. "Have you told them?"

"No," I said, "I haven't told them and I haven't told him. I thought I'd practise on you as my oldest friend and get used to the reaction." For some reason, we had a convention, the two of us, of never calling my husband by his name. It was always "my husband" and "your husband." I was self-conscious because of the English inclination to think names like Dwight and Duane somewhat uncivilized and comical.

"It'll kill them," he said simply.

"Well, Nigel," I said, "thanks a whole lot. Here I am trying to screw up the courage to break the news before I go back and that's all the moral support you give me."

"I'm just being realistic, Frances," he said, dropping the Lancashire accent for once.

"Hey," I said, "you can talk like a gentleman when you really try."

"Remember Mother Perk?" he said. "Lancashire people are the hardest workers and the laziest talkers!"

"That was before the era of structural linguistics," I said.

"That was before the era of everything," he replied. "Before the wireless, before the flush toilet, before the wheel..."

And so we were off on our usual patter like a couple of not-so-funny vaudeville comedians.

After that neither of us said anything for a while. Then he said in a somewhat strangled voice, "Frances, I'm thinking of making some changes in my own way of life too."

"Oh, hello," I thought, "here it comes." I had heard a rumour that he was courting a woman on the Cheshire side of Manchester and I thought perhaps the rumour was half true. "Coming out of the closet, are you?" I said boldly, and he gave another of those heavy sighs.

For two people who had been closest friends since childhood it seemed we were very inhibited with each other. Then I thought that our entire conversation had always been a careful avoidance of anything that ever concerned us. It was all innuendo and veiled comments and, of course, jokes. What I wanted to say was, "Is there someone in particular?" And I thought that perhaps he wanted to ask me the same thing. I definitely didn't want to go into the details of my disreputable life at that moment.

"You know," I said, "you could do anything you wanted to in this place and get away with it. They eat out of your hand." I envisioned him having a friend move into his home and it seemed a perfectly acceptable arrangement all round. Consenting adults and all that.

"It isn't quite that simple," he said, and the thought flashed through my mind that it wasn't a question of consenting adults. I thought of him in the church vestry surrounded by the little choirboys and everyone saying he was so patient with them.

Then I thought that this was going to be a terrible afternoon. It would be all fragmented conversations, blind alleys and cross-purposes. And that's exactly what it was, only it took place through a haze of whiskey.

"Will you come back here to live, after this divorce?" he asked.

"God, no," I said. "This'd be the last place. I'll stay in the U.S. and look for a job in a library. Let's run away together," I added. "To Greece and pick up sailors."

He didn't laugh and I thought he was something of a stick after all. Or perhaps he was just terribly cast down.

We walked round the racecourse and looked at all the jumps. There were crowds of people, women with patrician faces, loud county voices and shooting sticks. Most of them were serious about inspecting the course and would be coming to the steeple-chase next week and placing substantial bets. Of course, we wouldn't be. It was clear that we were among the non-aficionados. We would be nonattenders of the main event where the big prizes were to be won, the honours awarded. We were the fugitive and cloistered ones who would inspect the course, register awe, and then slink away never to return. After a while, we spread a rug (with the mac under it) beneath some trees and sat down. I nibbled some of the sandwiches. Nigel didn't eat much because it turned out he couldn't abide tongue, but he smoked a lot and drank some.

We were half way home before I realized we had left the mac under the trees.

"Well, she said it was an old one and didn't matter," he said.

"That's all you know," I said.

"I'll take full responsibility," he said, the old confidence in his irreproachability having returned.

As it happened, he had forgotten all about the mac again by the time we reached home and, when he dropped me off, he said, "I won't come in, Frances. Tell them I have to make a house call."

"Whose house?" I wondered, and I had the feeling that he did whatever he wished and had the perfect excuse for everything. Only he was now involved in something that he couldn't quite control. I wondered if he regretted confiding in me. He had come near to naming something and, therefore, called it into existence. Maybe I'd trapped him by confiding in him and now he held me responsible for his discomfort.

My speculations were confirmed when I saw very little of him

172

for the rest of my stay. Once, he brought my mother home from church and asked me quietly, "Have you told them yet?"

I hadn't and I didn't. All the rest of the holiday I heard about the mac. If it was raining and my mother had to fill the coal shuttle, she said, "I wish I had that old mac, I always used it for dirty jobs like this. I'm lost without it when I take rubbish out to the dust bin." This was just one of the minor irritants that accumulated and made me so damn mad that I not only went off without telling them, but resolved never to come back home again.

For the next few months my mother and I lobbed shocks like hand grenades at each other through the mail. I wrote and told her that I was getting a divorce. She wrote back and said that they weren't going to tell anyone until after the festive season. I wrote that I was living with a chap I'd known for the past few years. Unfortunately, I'd mentioned him once before and they'd remembered that he was married and had three children. After that, I didn't hear a thing from them for several months. Then my mother wrote and said that Nigel had been killed. His car had gone out of control one night on the East Lancashire road and collided with an oncoming lorry. He had been killed instantaneously. So had the driver of the lorry and the passenger in Nigel's car.

My mother sounded more sorry for herself than concerned about the effect of the news on me. She said her nerves had been very much better since Nigel had put her on a new prescription and she didn't know how she would manage without him. That reaction was widespread. He was mourned by all, and his funeral was one of the grandest the village had ever seen. Also, a memorial tablet was to be put up in the church in his memory. Mother cut the notices of the funeral and the eulogies out of the paper. There was a lot about the untimeliness of his death and about how he gave his time and energies so selflessly and contributed so much to the life of the parish. It sounded to me as if a lot of people in the parish had him mixed up with the Son of God.

I got the details only when I broke down and went home a few years later for another visit. My mother said, "You really should go and see Connie." I went because I liked Connie, because I wanted to ask for a photograph of Nigel and because Sundays still seemed consecrated to his memory. Connie was living with Nigel's sister. I had never liked Anthea, with her Brownies and Girl Guides and her athletics. She was a gym teacher before she married, and she had always acted as if Nigel and I were both foolish and silly but that I, at least, was old enough to know better.

I found I disliked her just as much as ever, with her conventional house and her brood of youngsters. It jolted me when I went into the house to see Connie aged so much and with a plagued look about her. And to see the large framed photograph on the sideboard of Nigel in a cap and gown. I couldn't stop looking at it. Anthea made tea and offered a profusion of nasty-looking things—bread rolls with fish paste on them, plates of iced cakes and chocolate penguin biscuits wrapped in silver paper. I realized that this was her main meal of the day, and she murmured that her husband was off on a business trip in the Midlands. Seemed odd on a Sunday evening, but I thought he could have a game on in all the neighbouring counties, for all Anthea cared, as long as it didn't disturb the placid surface of her life. I remembered a rumour that her father had been quite the ladies' man. But after he died and became a hero and Connie became the courageous widow, all that was forgotten.

After tea, Connie took the children out to some nearby swings. It was my chance to ask about Nigel. I asked if he had really died instantaneously after the crash. Anthea said yes and that he was speeding pretty recklessly. Fishing for information, I said that didn't sound like Nigel because he was always so cautious. She said that he was drinking a lot that last year and generally cracking up. She said he had one of the choirboys in the car and that the little lad was killed instantaneously as well. There was no inflection in her voice as she said that, and I couldn't tell what she was thinking. My mother thought Nigel had been giving someone a lift home. I said, "I'd so much like a photograph of Nigel, Anthea, as he was in recent years. A snapshot would do or, if you have a negative, I'll get a print made and return it to you."

"I'll see what I have," she said, in that noncommittal tone that in Lancashire means just plain "no." I could tell she didn't like me any more than I liked her and that, in some obscure way, she resented me, perhaps blamed me for what happened to Nigel. But I thought that was a bit far-fetched and I was getting paranoid. All the same, I felt sick about the whole thing and saddened at being denied a photograph. All I had was a newspaper clipping with a crease down the middle.

When I got home my parents asked me how Connie was. "She took it very hard," my father said. "When you think about it, she's had a hard life."

174

"No more than most," said my mother with an edge to her voice. "After all she has three daughters living nearby and all those grandchildren."

"Now then . . ." my father said warily. He got nervous when my mother's resentment started coming to the boiling point and she made digs at me.

It was an overcast Sunday evening and the smell of roast beef from lunch still lingered in the house. I could see that my mother had one of her headaches coming on and would be going to bed soon. It was all drearily familiar. So I thought I would get my coat on and go out for a breath of air, maybe walk over to look at Nigel's grave.

My mind went back to that second Sunday in November the year the war ended. There was a great church service in the village cemetery where the war memorial was. Crowds of people were there—the town councillors with golden chains around their necks, the home guard in uniform, a regiment of the Lancashire fusiliers, a ragged assortment of veterans of other wars, all with medals on their coats. The church choir was led by the vicar with Nigel, who had just recently become an altar boy, beside him. My father said that if we kept well to the back, he would hoist me onto the cemetery wall and I could see everything from there.

It was a cold drizzling day and the crowd was quiet. Everything was still except for the rooks in the tall elms, and there seemed to be a suppressed excitement about the grey, silent day. The choir sang and the old vicar said solemn beautiful lines:

"A nation mourns for her dead across the sea."

I liked the hymns and poems and listened with a concentrated attention. Sometimes the vicar would use long words in his sermon that even my father couldn't understand, but today he was speaking simply and even I could understand.

He told of all those who had fought for their country, had gone away and lost limbs, and of those who had given their lives and would never return and be seen again by their loved ones. The phrases, intoned so carefully, ran along and repeated themselves in my head like lines of poetry. At the same time, a dull little ache, which grew stronger as the voice droned on, attached itself to the words. The same words seemed to ring over and over again like chimes, and then they separated and took on a life of their own and existed apart from the speaker and the listener. Floating on the air, they attached themselves to certain images. "Some lost limbs . . ." and I saw the ghastly sleeves of the veterans, pinned back and empty of arms. "Some gave their lives . . ." and I saw Connie's face pale and taut. And suddenly, with perfect clarity, everything that had happened was illuminated—war, death, loss and the hatred stamped on all the faces of the people I met. I knew in that moment that all the fathers of all the children in our village had gone to war. Some had returned and some were missing and some would never return. But they were all heroes. And my own father had stayed safely at home and had not gone to war and I was disgraced.

The message I had been reading in the eyes of the old women and had not understood was, "You don't belong here, stranger, daughter of cowards and pretenders. Why don't you go find your own kind." As I interpreted this message, suddenly an old woman who was standing in front of us turned. She hawked and spat a great gob of phlegm onto the front of my father's coat. I was so astonished that I nearly fell off my perch on the wall.

And I looked over at Nigel, standing with the vicar's hand resting ever so lightly and caressingly on his shoulder. His small face was pale and sober and he looked the perfect picture of sweetness and innocence.

Later, after it was all over, I sat indoors by the fire recovering my senses and trying not to listen to what my parents said. I no longer needed to watch out for hints and pick up clues in stray remarks, for now every word assumed a meaning the minute it was spoken.

"Well, it could have been worse," said my father in a trying-to-be-cheerful voice.

"Mrs. Heathcote said there should be a monument to those that didn't go," my mother said.

"Take no notice," my father said. "Their Harold, remember. It will all blow over."

"Sometimes I think we shall never hear the last of it," my mother said. She went to lie down because the next day was washing day, and she could feel a bad head coming on.

ANNE CAMPBELL

In the Whole of Yugoslavia the Older Women Dress in Black

In Canada in the last few years
I've come to dress in black. This inclination,
mixed from time to time with white, seems right

In Yugoslavia, in parts of Croatia: Lika and Dalmatia,
I see women of a certain age also wear black, they match
this inclination with a certain bent for outdoor work

The exact time they do this eludes me and though
on the street I try I am not able to determine age.

ANNE CAMPBELL

The Itinerary

Takes us to the Vatican prepared for Easter splendour

but this is an Italian holiday: the family from Naples
at our pension is barely in control.

The Polish Pope's voice, when we get to the Vatican by bus,
is deep; his trappings take me back to the Croatian church in
Canada when I was small: mystery was complete.

On the road later going south each tiny olive tree is
my Croatian grandmother grown small each season and ripe.
I've come to the Adriatic to see her place, also Diocletian,
Croatian and the Emperor of Rome but on this road at every turn

men who look like my uncle, all the men look like my son

LALA HEINE-KOEHN

The Blue Candle

Because it is hard to be
without, because I am in need
of it, I address this to you, love.

I have watched the seasons here
change the lemon from green
to yellow, fill the apricot,
nespola, peach, the fig with honey,
my drinking glass with flowers.
The blackberries peer now through
the leaves along the road,
shiny and moist, like the eyes
of the village children.
Early mist muffles the tinkling
bells of sheep and goats
pealing from the high hills
down the fluted clay brick roofs,
waking the hooded chimneys,
the pergolas laden with grapes.
Erica has ignited the hillocks
with crimson: it will be
an early winter.

I look out to sea, its blue
that brought tears to my eyes,
it seems like only yesterday,
now subdued, the waves washing
the yellowed leaves to shore.
In my hand the stone I picked up
last year in Dodóni, adding to it
ones I have collected
the past three seasons here.
Stones from a volcano on far-away
Santorini Island, Delphi, Gouviá.
Stones I was to use as foundation
for building my new home.

They do not fit into my palm.
The blue candle you gave me
before I set out on this
journey is almost all gone.
I am bringing it back,
though only a stub now.
It belongs to you still, love.

MYRNA KOSTASH

The Collaborators
(for Brian Fawcett)

They Meet

This took place in Nafplion, on the Peloponnese, in late May of
1981. The woman, a Canadian in her mid-thirties, was vaca-
tioning in Greece, which she had last visited in 1969. In 1969 she
had visited Sounion to see the sun set behind the pillars of the
temple of Poseidon and was now ashamed to realize that, at the
time, beyond the splendid view had lain a little treeless and
waterless prison island on which Greeks were sweating, weeping
and dying under the curse of the Junta.

This kind of oversight is, of course, beyond correcting.

She was a solitary traveller but did not mind being so in
Nafplion, a quiet town in which people seemed content to go
calmly and courteously about their business and leave her to hers.
From her modest hotel room window she had a view of red-tiled
roofs and domes and, beyond them, the blue mountains of the
Argolid. In the late afternoon she would sit on the hotel terrace
and look at these mountains and be amazed to consider that
there, just beyond the first ridge, amid the ruins of the acropolis
of Mycenae, stood the royal hall of the house of Agamemnon and,
somewhere in the rubble, the bath (she supposed of tile or
mosaic) in which Clytemnestra had murdered her consort at the
end of his journey, across the stony plain from Argos, home from
the war at Troy.

She could be seen having yoghurt at a battered table in a milk
shop or lying on the beach or strolling through the narrow streets
glimpsing, between garden gates ajar, tiny courtyards of lemon
and orange trees and bougainvillaea and geraniums. No one took
much notice.

How did you meet him?

I sat down to have supper at an outdoor taverna by the
harbour.

You didn't mind being alone?

Not at all. It was a warm evening. There was almost no one at
this taverna—I had come early—and so I felt relaxed. I wanted
just to keep on sitting there, sipping the wine, looking out at the
water and the boats. But a man came and sat down at the next
table, seating himself so he was looking in my direction.

And this changed everything.

Yes. I knew he was looking at me. Suddenly, I was no longer a woman alone but a woman without a man.

Did you leave?

I asked the waiter for a pen.

Oh, so you would have something to *do*.

You know what I did? I took out the little notebook in which I was keeping track of my expenses and I began converting all the drachmas into dollars. But then the waiter came back for his pen.

And now you would have to leave.

The man at the next table jumped up and offered me his pen. In English.

Did you take it?

I decided I could. The man who was offering it was neither particularly young nor good-looking.

He left you alone?

For several minutes. Then he asked me if I was a writer. Because this seemed an honest question—certainly more interesting than "Where are you from?"—I decided to answer.

What was your answer?

He asks me what I write about. How do I begin? I wave my hands around and speak carefully but I think I make no sense at all. Does he even know the words: prairie, Ukrainian, Indian, counterculture, New Left, sisterhood? This Greek place is like none of that, this place of perpetual mountain ranges and of a people so deeply rooted in their communal past that they share a physiognomy, carry the same body. Here there are emigrants, not immigrants (Greeks running pizzerias in Toronto) and there were no hippies (except those on the road, overland from London, Paris, Munich to Kabul and cheap hashish) and no free-for-alls in campus offices, nor any parades of young women exultant in the sapphic mode. No, here in this place were only dead students (trapped in the searchlights beamed from the tanks that rolled over the iron gates of the Polytechnic and into the forecourt, the machine guns following the beams of light): dead students, and women who bring dowries into their marriage, handing them over to the husband in the kafenion who is playing cards and losing. So I try that other vocabulary, the common currency of my generation and, I suppose, of his: I write, I say, about oppression, exploitation, resistance and struggle. And I wince at their bromidic effect.

"Yes," he says with a burst of enthusiasm, laying his hand on my wrist. "I know what you mean. At the university I was a Communist too. I *am* a Communist."

And he whisks me off to a club where we sit on hard, narrow benches, and order a bottle of wine, and toast each other and our absent friends and our youth and the shades of Che Guevara and Ho Chi Minh and Jimi Hendrix. A man at the front is singing songs of Mikis Theodorakis, the whole club is singing them; the Communist sings too, his eyes shut, a hand on each knee. He tells me these songs are about partisans and squatters and dead students, about the death of Garcia Lorca, about the execution of Communists and the roses that grew up in the craters left behind by the bullets in the wall. I tell him I have never heard such songs before. Who would sing them?

The Affair Begins

In the morning he fetched her in his white Fiat and they drove to the nearest beach, quite deserted. It was a very clear morning, almost still: the only sound that of the pebbles at the shoreline being rolled leisurely in the retreat of the lapping waves. She had her bathing suit on under her clothes. She undressed and walked slowly into the sea, slid into it and swam back and forth in a line parallel with the shore, conscious, from the moment she had unbuttoned her shirt, of the regard of the man who now, leaning on his arm, was watching her. This was not entirely unsettling. Later, curled up into the bend of his body, the sun heating her flesh, she felt she was desirable. He stroked her hair and called her his comrade.

They had lunch at a taverna at the other end of the beach. She was learning to like this kind of meal: cool resinated wine out of the barrel, a slab of white cheese, chopped tomatoes in olive oil, a plate of small fried fish (which she dismembered with her fingers because he had laughed at her plying the knife and fork). Then they drove away to his hotel—she could come with him or not—and, the shutters pulled down against the late afternoon sun, they made love. He fell asleep but she was not used to afternoon naps. She smoked cigarettes and wished she had a book. His back was turned to her and she didn't want to wake him up by leaning over to look into his face.

Who was this man?

Kostas Karapanayiotis. It took me a while to memorize.

What was he doing in Nafplion?

183

He explained he was an organizer for the socialist party, PASOK. It was his job to travel to the villages in the Peloponnese and drum up support. There were going to be national elections soon and everyone was expecting the Left to make a strong showing.

But he said he was a Communist.

A lot of Communists were going to vote for PASOK, just to get the Right out of government. On their own, the Communist Party could only hope for twelve or fourteen per cent of the vote.

Did he have political ambitions of his own?

I don't think so. He struck me simply as someone terribly committed to doing what he could to spread the gospel, so to speak, and very much aroused by the political debate. The second night we were together, we went for supper to a fish taverna where he immediately became embroiled in a furious argument with several old fishermen at the next tables. From the look on their faces, and the emphasis in his voice, I took them to be politically hostile.

You would have expected fishermen to be on the Left?

Yes, and yet in Nafplion I heard about an old fisherman who is a Communist. From time to time he finds his nets cut.

Did Kostas think the socialists would win?

They had a very good chance. But he also expected the Americans would move immediately to destabilize a socialist government. Like all left-wing Greeks, he was paranoid about the Americans.

Paranoid is a strong word.

Listen, he was so convinced of this that he had joined an underground group of Communists in Patras, militants who met regularly but secretly to train for guerrilla warfare.

That seems a little extreme.

The memory of the seven years of the Junta, propped up by the Americans, is still fresh.

Why was he telling you all this?

He called me comrade. But he didn't tell me everything. There were mysterious phone calls.

Ah.

The night of our third day together, he told me he might have to leave early next morning for Patras. An urgent meeting of his cell. While I was still half-asleep, he slipped out to make a call. And in fact he did have to leave. I didn't see him again for a week.

184

We are tearing up the little fried fish and stuffing the flesh into each other's mouth. We take long swills of retsina, leave grease on the rim of the glasses. He laughs and lays his head on my shoulder. But when we talk we are very serious. We slow down as he searches for the words, as I try to fit them into what I know of the history of this too often wretched country: what I have heard or read of a population abandoned to semi-literacy and cowed into political diffidence by generations of tyrants in the schools, the courts, the police stations, the offices of the county clerk (not to mention at home, in the family). A population making its way under the eye of the CIA and breaking away, at least every generation, in furious political violence futile in its consequences: blood-soaked village squares, ghost armies, unmarked graves.

The least I can do is listen.

Later there are songs and more songs. He has a big black case in his car and he pulls one ragged cassette out after another and plays Greek songs. Listen: this one is about a partisan—of that Resistance still unhonoured, still without memorial, in Greece— lined up against a wall, about to be shot by the fascists. Tearing the blindfold from his eyes, the partisan sings out that he wants to see, at the moment of his death, the light of the freedom to come. Kostas rewinds the tape, begins it again, again this song, again and again. I am unbearably aroused.

He has a Bob Dylan tape too but for the first time in fifteen years I do not believe that, at this moment, the words to "Desolation Row" could move me.

I am now frantically in love with him and would be happy to spend the next ten years hurtling along these highways, running the same circle of towns, villages and beaches, hotel rooms and tavernas, around and around the Peloponnese while Kostas fulfills his obligations to the Greek revolution that lies just ahead. In the next town, or the one after that.

The Affair Continues

The next time she saw him, he invited her to join him on a trip to some western Peloponnesan towns and villages. They drove through Corinth and Patras and turned south towards Olympia, his one hand on the steering wheel, the other either pulling out big handfuls of cherries from the bag that lay between them or resting lightly on her thigh (her skirt pulled up to catch the breeze from the window).

In Olympia, he paid in advance for their hotel room, made love to her, then took her to a café where he ordered ouzo and left her. Explained he had to go back to Patras. By now, Patras had become reduced in her mind to a small house on the outskirts of town (she imagined this) where, very late at night, six, ten, fifteen men, all in their thirties, all with moustaches and smoking furiously, shouting and waving their arms in the chopchop Greek manner, plotted their strategies for the defence of the Greek republic. She further imagined, there in the darkened anteroom, heavy wooden boxes holding AK 47s from Bulgaria.

He was back in Olympia the next morning and they drove south again. Near Pylos, in the early evening, he turned off onto a secondary road which went straight up into the mountains. They got out at a village where he said he would be meeting with some farmers. She could come along. For the next three hours she sat, on a wobbly aluminum chair, sipping ouzo and eating a large quantity of peanuts, on the periphery of a group of men, some gnarled and leathered, others young and smooth, who listened and argued as Kostas held forth in the diminishing light. (From time to time he would pull papers out of his briefcase and pass them around, but the expression on the faces of the men looking at these papers was curiously noncommittal.) The only other woman she saw was a middle-aged peasant in black and side-saddle on a donkey ambling across the far end of the square. She wondered, idly, how this woman was going to vote.

It got dark and she began to fret. This was their last night. Tomorrow she would fly to Athens and from there to Toronto. But this also was important, she admitted: this agitation in the village square. At home she knew no men who did such a thing. Whom would they agitate?

Was he married?

He had a fiancée, Fotini. He wore her ring.

When was he going to marry her?

After the election, if at all. He hated the idea of marrying in church. The socialists promised to introduce civil marriage.

He certainly had his principles.

It wasn't just that. He described Fotini as a nice but simple girl.

Didn't you wonder why a man like him would be engaged to a "nice but simple" girl?

Yes, I wondered. The fact was, he didn't like to talk about it. He had serious reservations about marrying, period. Or having children. Considering his commitment to revolutionary politics, more or less clandestine.

Did you feel guilty towards Fotini?

Not at all. I didn't want to marry him. Besides, there were times he spoke of his engagement to her as a kind of propitiation for having slept with her. Or as though she wanted the engagement only to make her parents happy.

It all sounds rather self-serving.

I could sympathize with his frustration at not often being able to find, among Greek women, a companion with whom to share his political and cultural values.

Companion? Is that what you were?

I was his lover.

He's gone again to Patras, into the dark mountains of the Peloponnese, and left me again to fall asleep alone in a narrow bed. Ah these mysterious errands into the night-time, these rehearsals for an uprising, a noisy, clamorous intervention into the silence of a circumspect and frightened people. Kostas: ambassador of my delight and of my loneliness.

We sat in the heat of the mid-afternoon on fragments of tumbled marble columns at Olympia. The earth is grassy there and spongy with pine needles and shaded by ancient pines. There were crickets. And Kostas's soft voice recreating the antique games, the oily bodies straining for the prize. All of them, for these Olympic days at least, *Greeks*. "I am not a nationalist," he said, "but I am a Greek."

I think about this now and feel forlorn. He has gone off into the mountains of the Peloponnese, mountains that have been made almost human by millennia of activity. I picture the shepherd and his goats and hear the bleating and his rough calls echo up and down the hot, narrow valleys, and I see the old woman leading her donkey bearing a bundle of twigs wrested from the mountain scrub, and I see the priest and the bridal party climbing to the shrine of the Panagia while down other paths stumble the gypsy peddlar, the midwife, the schoolteacher, not to mention, under cover of night, the *andarte*, a guerrilla on a clandestine visit to his village at Eastertime, his hand full of red poppies. All are architects of settlement, but *my* mountains, my Rocky cordillera, emptied now of the peoples who trod there centuries ago (their trails now undecipherable), rest unclaimed by the human. Who goes there except in awe of rock?

He has gone off on his project invoking the name of his people, and I am asking myself, alone in this Greek room, who are mine? How far back can I go? Three, four generations back there are not even any names, only "souls" in the inventory of an absentee Polish landlord. Is this a people: serfs without lineage who knew only that they came from Tulova, village on the Pruth, on the road to Sniatyn? Do I have kinfolk today, labouring on the Ukrainian *kolkhoz*, people abandoned to their harrowing and separate fate on the day my grandmother took her place in the wagon that would take her to the train that would take her to the ship that would land in Halifax? Am I related to a people whose tongue in me is broken and who've married into families I have never met? What then of the Canadian shore where *baba* landed? In this grab bag of heritages striving for a coherence called Canada, do I have a people in whose faces (in the bones of their face and the tilt of their eye) and in whose bodies (the set of their shoulders, the span of their hips) I may discern my inheritance? Which land is the mother of me?

The Parting

He drove her out to the airport of Kalamata. It was early evening. The sun was slanting through the windshield of the car and gilding the dashboard. They didn't speak. A cassette was playing again. The song this time was about the students massacred by the guns on the tanks of the Junta at their sit-in of the Poly-technic in 1973; about how their martyred spirits come back to kiss the eyes of the sleeping. It made her cry. He abruptly ejected the cassette and gave it to her. In front of the terminal building they stood leaning against the car and holding hands. Then she picked up her bag and marched inside. He did not immediately drive off but stood, still, at the car's fender. She walked up to a window and looked out at him. They looked at each other. Then he opened the car door, gave her a salute with his clenched fist, got inside and drove away.

Did you think you'd ever see him again?
    I didn't think it was impossible.
    Did he suggest you might?
    What he suggested was that, in the event the socialists lost the election, he would leave Greece. He would come to see me in Canada en route for El Salvador.
    What did he have in mind?
    That he would join the guerrillas there.
    That cell in Patras, then, was guerrillas-in-training?
    It went deeper than that. He'd grown up in Xanthe, in the north-east, had spent hundreds of hours scrambling through the hills in the company of his uncle, both of them with shotguns, out hunting together. From his earliest memory there had been guns

in the house. His uncle had been in the Resistance. From him Kostas learned to hunt and shoot. From him he learned to hate injustice with a revulsion that would make him physically sick. He told me some of his uncle's stories. How the guerrillas dressed themselves in whatever was at hand—old army uniforms, Italian uniforms, village sandals—and most carried Greek army rifles from the First World War, or no weapon at all. How starving children, rooting about in garbage, were recruited by German intelligence. How, near the end, neither side took prisoners. How in the main square of the town of Trikkala, strung up on a gibbet, swung the head of the fiercest guerrilla of them all: Aris, betrayed, some say, by his own comrades.

Did he want you with him in Salvador?

No. He talked instead about how I could help the struggle of the *Greek* people for national self-determination. By writing. By writing about the truth of their history, the justice of their ideals—arguments to that effect.

Did you feel up to the task?

Oh it was the least I could do. This man had given me many things—songs, stories, names—and the least I could do, if I was not prepared to die for their bitter territory, was to offer to write a magazine article!

So you wanted to keep in touch.

He told me to write him. Poste restante. Patras.

His back rigid so he seems taller than he is. His dark face, the once-broken nose, the clear brown eyes, the moustache. Already under the skin I can see the face of the Old Man of the Village, although he tells me he expects to die violently before he is forty. In the shady square of Pylos, under the large, flat, fluttering leaves, two small white cups of sludgy coffee. He has left his to dash off across the street to the offices of PASOK. On the road to Kalamata he tells me the story of the Polytechnic. He was there, behind the barricaded, slogan-strewn gates when the tanks, manned by soldiers the students called brothers and topped by the pitiless searchlights, crashed through the gates at 3 A.M. and crumpled them like matchsticks, the rest of the city asleep. And I am ashamed. I did not know this story. Where the hell was I, and all my friends, on November 16, 1973, that this story should not be known? I feel cheated as though, in a photo album, between the sequences from Paris in 1968 and Saigon in 1975, there was a blank page waiting for us to assemble the pictures: Greek students pressed against the gates of the Polytechnic and holding up a sign, WE WANT BOOKS!; dying in ambulances staffed by the secret police; buried in unmarked graves. Listen, tell me the story! (My datebook for November 16, 1973: Ceta's birthday party, BYOB.) Down there, below on the highway, Kostas is driving to Patras. He goes somewhere; it's a point on a map, a place on the Gulf of Corinth. Me, I leave, vaguely north-westward.

Interlude

Of course he would not be able to imagine my place. The light is blue at midnight, the shadow is two porcupines eating saskatoon berries, the sounds are of a ticking clock and a moth burning to death in the yellow flame of the kerosene lamp.

If he were here, I would take him to the patch of wild straw-berry, crush the tiny, piquant fruit on his tongue, take him to where the wild tiger lilies grow. Take him down to the river bank and tell him: here, look, this water flows on like this another eight hundred miles, it empties where there is ice. Can you imagine that, Greek? Or look behind us, on the slope, the weathered wood of a small church, topped by a tarnished dome. It's empty and useless. The Galicians built it and then died; see here, under the wild buckwheat, their graves. Can you imagine this, Greek: bones in virgin soil?

I want my revenge on you. On that moment you flipped out the cassette of Theodorakis and his bloody partisans and played instead Bob Dylan and said, "Now you tell me what this song is about." And I began, word by word, "in your brand-new/leopard-skin/pillbox hat," but I could not go on. These very words, these songs which have excoriated my memory like sandpaper for the last fifteen years, suddenly became feeble in that car of yours as we rattled through the Peloponnese. Even the broad May daylight there is spooked by the ghosts of bellicose *klephts* and assassinated politicians and partisans strung from a noose, poets flayed alive and students with broken skulls, all shuffling their chains outside the car window. Confronted with such specific terror and the murders of real people, Dylan's song has become unbearable. I see you smirking and I will concede you their anti-narrative, their anti-story, which is to say their presentation of the American self as a *tabula rasa*, a collective consciousness of a community continually recreating itself in puerile autobiography. No wonder the "I" is the irreducible of awareness among us.

But I am of this continent. If I don't claim it, who the hell will? What do I expect to find, retracing the ancestral webbing between crumbling Byzantine frescoes in a deserted church near

190

Sparta and a wedding dance in a Galician village near the Polish border, except that my people have all left? My *baba* is dead. There are no more Europeans here in the western Canadian woodland. Whoever it is that's dancing in the tavernas of the Argolid and bringing in the harvest near Tulova, I do not know them.

More. Look here, Greek: this language I speak, this English, this "native tongue," is a kind of gift. It is not mine by race or history; it is only mine because my parents learned it. Behind *them* stand a hundred generations of peasants who never spoke a word of it; who spoke instead a language lettered by monks of Byzantium. Of all of these, which one is my mother tongue?

You talk of Turks and Ottomans, bandits and guerrillas, wars of liberation and those betrayed and, do you know, I have heard these stories too, of Huns and Mongols and Cossacks, wars of attrition and betrayal. Can you sort your story out from mine? You tell me of your parents' neighbour, a man the anti-Communists strung up on a lamp-post and left there until he rotted, and I tell you of my Great Uncle Petro, dragged out of his hut at Christmastime and into the barn and shot by Ukrainian nationalist insurgents, and left to die face down in the dung in the village of Tulova for the crime of his Red Army uniform. And what of your brothers and sisters and their youth in the torture cells of the Security Police and of *my* generation, condemned to another death by the boredom of their enemies? Are we not related after all, Greek?

The Affair Resumes

Over a period of six months she sent a flurry of letters to Patras, poste restante. In return, he phoned her from time to time. She could hear the coins dropping in the box and imagined him under the melancholy light of the booth, surrounded by the pitch-black night of the Peloponnese. It was after the election of the socialists that, on hearing his jubilant voice, she decided she would return. "Yes, come," he said. "We need you. You can help us."

He met her at the airport and drove her straight to Nafplion where he helped her find a room. They stood on the balcony and, against the fading light, he suddenly burst into a kind of dance, skipped backward and forward and thrust his right arm about while the left hand rested on his hip. He had been a champion swordsman at the university in Thessaloniki, he explained, and these were the parries and thrusts of the Bavarian style. She imagined a short, stubby blade.

And then he was gone. For the next two months it was like this: he would arrive unannounced at her room having driven like a maniac from (she supposed) Patras; they would make love and then go out to eat. Pulling shrimp apart and licking fingers, he informs her he must go back to Patras because tonight the head of the Communist Party will be speaking on television. She wonders to herself why he can't watch this on television in Nafplion and stay the night with her. But she makes no protest. She understands that in his own good time he will let her know what she's come here for.

It sounds like a disappointing reunion.

He was under tremendous strain. Now that the socialists had been elected, he and his comrades fully expected the Americans to begin their behind-the-scenes manoeuvres.

Was this any reason to treat you so off-handedly?

He apologized but he simply didn't have time. He promised me that in the New Year he would take me with him on his trips again.

What about the fiancée?

When I pressed him about this, he became angry. Said no, Fotini did not know about me. Said I was not to ask about her again.

He sounds very evasive.

But there were also moments of quiet happiness between us. One night of a full moon we went walking along the beach. We were quite alone. We sat on the overturned fishing boat and told each other the names of the planets and constellations and quoted bits of poetry and confessed that neither of us knew much about the sea. A pregnant cat waddled into view and straight under Kostas's hand. As he stroked her, he said he liked cats because they are like women: one minute they are rubbing up against you like you were the only one they cared about in the world; the next minute they are on their way without a backward glance.

Did he mean that as a compliment?

By the way he was stroking the cat, yes.

I am the woman he is hiding away. The lovers under the glare of the sun at the summertime beach have become the furtive couple embracing behind the shutters of hotel rooms as the winter light goes out. He is skin and bones. He is so slight, it's like embracing a child. My own body struggles for its satisfaction under his nonchalant, distracted hand.

God damn the things that estrange us. Our speech, for instance. I speak very carefully; I pick the common words; he curses and slaps his knee as he strains to find a word, and I cannot help. I feel stupid before his language. He is enraged before mine. I show him photographs from home. He stares at them without comprehension. He does not know how the earth can be flat or how black earth smells. I show him photographs of friends and try again to explain the passions that bind us but, even as I speak, of Ukrainian weddings and the crisis in the writers' union, of a picket line and a study group, I can see on his face how risible these are compared to the project of the Greek revolution. I put the photographs away and ask him to explain again the problem of Cyprus. I want heat in our embrace and harmony in our discourse.

I am in a bar. It is cosy and polished and masculine. Am I going to grow up to be one of those middle-aged ladies who sit alone in foreign bars and scribble in a notebook to give them a reason to be there that is not whoring? In one ear, the chatter of a Greek conversation. In the other, a song on the phonograph. "Mack the Knife" by Louis Armstrong. Oh Bertolt, oh Brecht. Oh hell.

The Affair Founders

She saw him one more time. It was a wet and blustery day. He grabbed her by the hand and took her out to the seawalk. As they rounded the bend toward the open sea, a furious wall of wind and wave swept over them. They clung together until it retreated. Now soaked to the skin, they returned to her room and laid his clothes to dry on the radiator. He would have to leave in an hour.

She had many things on her mind and she felt the press of time. She would begin to speak—both of her own loneliness and of recent world events—and he would turn away to look out the window or to light a cigarette and pour out brandy or to ruffle through her newspapers or, finally, to wrap her towel around himself, Roman senator style, and step barefoot into her high-heeled shoes and strut mockingly around the room. His flat, narrow buttocks swayed waggishly within the folds of the cloth. At this moment, his hairy legs knock-kneed as he pivoted coyly at the window, she thought he was disgusting. She yelled at him to sit down and burst into tears.

Why so high-strung?

His hairy legs, one crossed over the other, bargirl style. I couldn't bear it. The stack of newspapers that didn't interest him. It was the end of December 1981. On December 13, the army in Poland had taken over the state and crushed Solidarity. That's what was in those newspapers. And he didn't give a damn. I had been devastated by the news and felt very lonely.

Why lonely?

The foreign newspapers always arrived a day late. Every morning for two weeks, I was in an agony of suspense knowing that whatever I was reading was already superseded by events and that I would not know for another twenty-four hours what were the catastrophes of that morning. Knowing, too, that at that moment in Canada my friends were huddled together, talking, analyzing, strategizing, mourning while I was completely alone. I would sit in the café with the TV set and watch the grainy grey film of snowbound Warsaw; the bulky, shadowy figures flitting to who knows what destination; the clear, bland faces of the Army spokesmen. I would feel immobilized, speechless. I thought I would choke.

So you had hoped you could talk with Kostas.

When we were in my room together, drying off, I tried to tell him what I had gone through. Something of my feelings attached to Solidarity and those terrible events. Just as, before, we had sat close together, almost embracing, and shared our indignation and hurt and gratification in the recital of the events at the Polytechnic, in Vietnam, in El Salvador, so now I wanted us to share the events in Poland, the Silesian coalminers shot to death, the strikers herded into freezing prison camps, the students beaten like dogs.

He let you down?

I was naive enough to have believed that, as a man of the Left, he would champion the Polish workers. Instead, he started yelling at me half in Greek that I was stupid, understood nothing. He shouted that Poland was a captive of the Roman Catholic church, hostage of the CIA and prey of counter-revolutionaries. He barked that the security of the Soviet Union was sacrosanct; that nothing must be permitted to jeopardize it, least of all a so-called workers' movement in a workers' state. Finally, with a look of contempt screwing up his face, he spat out, "You are not a Communist!" And I knew I had failed him.

Let him go. I am not a Communist. I am not a Greek. I am not even a financée. Inside my head run other movies, not those of

194

Kostas, who shuts his eyes and sees ragged bands of desperate Communist guerrillas scrambling on the nude hills for shelter from the pulverizing bombs, sees a friend disappear into the back of a police van in the middle of the afternoon, sees the muzzle of a tank swing in his direction as he yells a slogan, sees a village— squat, stony huts on the slope of a hill bearing dusty olive trees— from which he leads a bride in a white dress to the church of St. Nicholas.

He had promised me his country, he had promised me his stories, he had promised me the comrades I could help. Now this place is depopulated. Lies? Who is to say? His stories brought me here to a window, where I see a red-tiled roof and a hibiscus tree blossoming in the rain. A ragged guerrilla passed by here all the same.

The Affair Ends

On New Year's Eve, she was preparing to go out with friends when she was summoned to the hotel telephone. In musical but apologetic terms, a woman's voice at the end of the line told her, "Excuse me, I am Fotini." Fotini went on to say that she was the wife of Kostas and the mother of his two children and that—she excused herself again—she had found certain letters in her husband's pockets. And that he would like to say something too. After some seconds, Kostas came on the line to say, in flat, uninflected tones, that he had told her many lies and would not see her again.

She hung up the phone before he did.

Who is Kostas? (A Probable Biography)

It is 1950 in Xanthe. Kostas is five years old. Dressed in Sunday best, he sits stiffly on a chair in his parents' modest home and watches the celebrating of the adults. His uncle, who has just been demobilized from the army, is telling stories. He is a big hero and boasts of killing Communists. Noticing Kostas, he pulls the boy into the circle. "And this one," he says, clapping his big hand on the boy's shoulder, "this one will know what to do with those sons-of-whores!"

It is 1960. Kostas is in a movie theatre watching old swashbuckling films. In the hills, by himself, he will pick up a stick and pretend he is Errol Flynn.

It is 1970. The Junta has been in power three years. Kostas's uncle has got him a job in the post office in Thessaloniki. One afternoon, from the window of the room where he works, he sees a man he knows, someone he has gone to school with, being arrested. In broad daylight, the man, who had been walking across from the post office, is suddenly engulfed by two plain-clothesmen and frog-marched into the back of a van pulled up alongside. It is over in seconds. Kostas goes out for coffee.

It is November 1973. Kostas is in Athens to take his mother to a doctor. He has heard there is something going on at the Polytechnic. He walks in that direction. A block from his destination, he sees a crowd running toward him. They are strangely quiet but some have blood on their heads and faces. He walks on. Now come puffs of tear gas and he begins to cough. He stops, looks at his watch, turns around and hurries back to the doctor's.

It is 1980. Kostas lives in Patras in a small apartment with his wife, Fotini, and their two children. The children's squalling drives him to distraction. In the evenings he goes to a nearby café where his buddies always meet. They play cards and watch the soccer games on television.

It is May 1981. Kostas is driving up a road to a mountain village. There is a foreign woman with him. They stop at the village square and get out, Kostas carrying his briefcase. There is a small crowd of men sitting around as if waiting for him. The woman sits on the edge of the group and pulls a book out of her bag and begins reading. Kostas is speaking, arguing with the men who seem unmoved. He opens the briefcase, takes out a handful of papers, distributes them. The men look at him. Kostas begins his pitch again.

The Meaning of It All

He was selling something?

Agricultural chemicals manufactured by an American multi-national corporation.

You knew?

Only after. After, I remembered I had been rummaging for cassettes on the back seat of his car and had seen the advertising flyers quite clearly in his briefcase.

And then you forgot you had seen them.

You don't understand. I might have *seen* them but my brain refused to process the information.

You didn't *want* to see them.

I wanted a lover who was leafletting the Greek countryside with revolutionary pamphlets.

And Kostas?

And Kostas wanted someone who would see him, see him in the blue hills back of Pylos, stride manfully into the village square to challenge his enemies, withdraw his inflammatory leaflets and announce—to her, his lover at the rickety table on the edge of the square, as well as to the toiling Greek masses—the arrival of the next revolution, one of these days.

Nafplion/Edmonton
1984/1988

GEORGE AMABILE

Horizons

The overcast breaks up and sunlight
spills into the street. I'm driving
across town toward the river. Between
backlit tenements the evening explodes, promising
something breathless as Romance, chaotic
but pure, burning beyond the last
wrought iron fence. Well, it's just
the mind of the child surfacing
for a moment before the light retreats
into smoke, and the parkway leads me home.

Exquisite how these highway lights
cancel the sky. Cashmere collar,
calfskin gloves, the smell
of a new car, fingernails trimmed
and growing, everything I dreamed
I could be I am and the glow of power
surrounds me. I've been to Greece. I remember
sunlight tumbling through clouds over broken columns,
retsina in copper cups and sparks
rising from open fires in the Agora at night.

Once, in Rome, I watched a *Tintoretto*
sky collect above the *Piazza di Spagna*.
The fountain gathered overtones
of dusk into gorgeous water. My life
became complete and I was afraid. What
could I hope for if my heart
could melt so easily
into the lift and rush of water?
Light drained from the air and I moved on.

How the great writers understood
the finality of moments like these. And yet
they had to go on with their stories.
Anna Karenina dives under a train. The Roman
Consul bleeds in a stone tub. The hunchback
buries himself alive with the corpse
of Esmerelda. I want to drive all night.
I want to be ragged, unshaven, hungry and lost
in the dawn. I want to believe
that something will happen to change me.

Biographical Notes

We asked our thirty-seven contributors, "What would you like to say about yourself as it relates to this anthology?" Here are their replies (some condensed, others expanded):

MICHELENE ADAMS has lived in Canada for nine years. She is a citizen of Trinidad and Tobago. The Nate pieces are her way of coping with the question that recurs in countless "travelling" dreams: "Have I come too far away from home?"

CAROLINE ADDERSON was born and raised in Alberta but now lives in Vancouver. Her fiction has appeared in several literary magazines; been broadcast on CBC Radio's "Ambience"; and won third prize in the 1987 CBC Literary Competition. Her radio play *Fire of Stone* aired on "Morningside" in 1989, when she also participated in the Canada-Ireland Artist Exchange.

ELIZABETH ALLEN returned to New Zealand in 1985 after spending twelve years in Canada—on a farm in eastern Saskatchewan. It was there she began writing and produced two books of poetry. Since returning to New Zealand, she has been working on a new collection of poems.

GEORGE AMABILE was born in the USA and has been a Canadian since 1974. His work has appeared in seventy-two periodicals including *Harper's*, *The New Yorker*, *Poetry Australia*, *Sur* (Buenos Aires, Argentina), and *Saturday Night*. His five books include *The Presence of Fire* (McClelland & Stewart, 1982), which won a Canadian Authors' Association Award.

BRENDA BAKER is best known as a singer-songwriter, with a self-titled CD (1989) and a children's album (1990). She has performed across Canada and on most CBC national music programs. Her writing has appeared in *The Malahat Review*, *Grain*, *Event*, and the Coteau Books anthology *Jumbo Gumbo*. In the past three years, she has received a Saskatchewan Literary Award and three Saskatchewan Arts Board grants.

MICK BURRS upheld a family tradition when he immigrated to Canada from the USA in 1965: his grandparents had come to North America as refugees from eastern Europe in the early 1900s. He lyrically chronicled his family history in *The Blue Pools of Paradise* (Coteau Books, 1983). His latest poetry chapbook is *Sleeping Among the Pumpkins* (Waking Image Press, 1990). He lives in Yorkton, Saskatchewan.

ANNE CAMPBELL says that for her an exploration of self—out of place or otherwise—begins but moves beyond one's own self to the geography, people and culture of the countries which created the vision given to one by one's parents. In her case, these countries are Croatia and England. The work, keeping open, is worth the enlivening that results.

DONNA CARUSO describes her parents as Italian peasants with strong backs and broad, generous smiles. Her own move to Canada from the USA gave her insight into their emigration from Italy. She grew up in a typical, crowded Italian household: there was Grandma, all the kids, parents and relatives, angels and saints, the Pope, and pizza for everybody. She recalls they spent a lot of time eating and a lot of time praying.

KAREN CONNELLY was born in Calgary in 1969. At seventeen she lived with a traditional family in northern Thailand for a year and wrote a book. In 1988 she began two years in Spain, teaching English and researching a novel, now in progress. Her first book of poetry was *The Small Words in My Body* (Kalamalka Writers Society,

1990). Her second book—poems about Spain and France and the joyous nightmare of returning to Canada—is out in the world searching for its publisher.

ARCHIBALD CRAIL was born in Paarl, South Africa, as the eldest of eleven children. His parents were accomplished storytellers and, as he grew, they increasingly shifted winter-evening storytelling to him. He claims he could never manage the element of suspense his late mother could sustain; nor could he bring an animal alive as his father could. But over the years Archie has tried to become a good teller of stories. More of his stories will be published in his forthcoming collection tentatively titled *The Bonus Deal* (Coteau Books).

NIGEL DARBASIE was born in Trinidad and lives in Edmonton. His book of poetry, *Last Crossing*, was a finalist for a Writers Guild of Alberta award for excellence. His work has been broadcast on radio and TV networks including the CBC. He has also performed at arts festivals and at literary and cultural events.

ROBBIE NEWTON DRUMMOND lives in Crowsnest Pass, Alberta. The poem "Pineapple" is from a forthcoming collection, *Delta Hushpuppies* (Penumbra Press), based on his experiences as a physician in the Mackenzie Delta. He has published widely in journals and anthologies. His most recent chapbook is *Owl in a Cage* (Circle Five Poems, Calgary).

JOAN GIVNER is a professor of English at the University of Regina and the editor of *Wascana Review*. She has written biographies of Katherine Anne Porter and Mazo de la Roche. She has also published two collections of short stories, and a third is forthcoming from Oberon Press.

KRISTJANA GUNNARS is an associate professor of English at the University of Alberta. She has written six books of poetry, one of short stories (*The Axe's Edge*), a novel (*The Prowler*), and a non-fiction work (*Zero Hour*). Her numerous credits include editing an anthology by Icelandic Canadians (*Unexpected Fictions*) and a collection of essays on Margaret Laurence (*Crossing the River*) as well as translating work by poet/essayist Stephan G. Stephansson.

LALA HEINE-KOEHN was born in Poland. Forced to leave, she studied in Munich—international law and voice. After emigrating to Saskatchewan she began to write poetry and to paint, then moved in 1977 to Victoria, BC, where she continues to do both. "Perhaps there are choices in life," she says. "Writing and painting are not one of them. You do it because you must and for me it is still a non-ending battle with the English language alas . . ."

GERALD HILL though more and more placed in Edmonton—in family, studies and, for now, a succession of late winter moments—recognizes that a world out of place is a rich world of difference, language and desire.

SARAH KLASSEN grew up in Manitoba's interlake sensitive to differences between her first language and culture and the predominantly Anglo-Saxon culture of her district. Her mother's stories about uprootings from Russia made Sarah further aware of dislocations. In her teaching she has encountered many students who feel "out of place."

MYRNA KOSTASH was born and raised in Edmonton. After studies at the Universities of Alberta, Washington and Toronto and travels in Europe, she became a full-time freelance writer in Toronto. In 1975 she returned to Edmonton, where she lives in a housing co-op and works as a writer, occasional teacher, and volunteer with several arts organizations. She keeps a farm/retreat in Two Hills, Alberta, and travels frequently across Canada and in eastern/central Europe.

ALICE LEE was born in Saskatchewan and now lives in Calgary. She has been quite involved with the Gabriel Dumont Institute of Native Studies and Applied Research in Regina. Alice's work will appear in over half a dozen anthologies this year alone.

SHELLEY A. LEEDAHL grew up in small towns. She now lives in Saskatoon with Troy, Logan and Taylor. Her short stories and poetry have appeared in numerous journals. Her first book, *A Few Words for January*, is in its second printing from Thistledown Press. She is a copywriter for CKOM and C95 Radio.

RHONA MCADAM is a native of British Columbia and lived in Edmonton for fourteen years before moving to London, England, in 1990. She has published three poetry collections; the most recent, *creating the country*, deals with the sense of displacement underlying an immigrant culture like Canada's.

JIM MCLEAN was born and raised in Saskatchewan and now lives in southern Ontario. He is the author of *The Secret Life of Railroaders* (Coteau Books, 1982).

DAVE MARGOSHES is a fiction writer and poet who worked as a journalist for many years and continues to freelance as well as teach literature. He was raised and educated in the United States but has lived in western Canada—most recently Regina—for twenty years.

NANCY MATTSON is a third-generation Finnish Canadian who spent her childhood summers on her grandparents' homesteads near New Finland, Saskatchewan. Her first book of poetry was *Maria Breaks Her Silence* (Coteau Books, 1989). At present she is a research and information officer at Alberta House in London, England. Her current writing is "poetry dealing with voice and language."

KIM MORRISSEY is the author of a forthcoming book, *Poems for Men Who Dream of Lolita*. Her first book was *Batoche* (Coteau Books, 1989). It received a 1987 Saskatchewan Literary Award, judged by Gwendolyn MacEwen and D.G. Jones; won third prize in the 1987 CBC Literary Competition; was short-listed for the Gerald Lampert Award from the League of Canadian Poets; and is now in its second printing.

DOUGLAS NEPINAK is one of a generation of Natives trying to find a voice within English Canada. Paradoxically, he is also trying to define his Native identity; it was somehow concluded, once, that the two were incompatible. And the silence can only end with stories and with telling.

TAIEN NG has published poetry in *blue buffalo*, *arc*, and *oh baby shrapnel*. She plans to keep writing, wants to change the world, and has ideas of starting a theatre company that focuses on "non-dominant culture." (Make other voices heard!) She is now working on a "multicultural" screenplay.

SHELDON OBERMAN is, among other things, the co-author with Fred Penner of three Juno-award-winning songs. Sheldon's numerous credits include an anthology of Jewish Canadian writing, *A Mirror of a People*; four children's books including the forthcoming *Wannee, King of the Grass* and *The Always Prayer Shawl*; and two works-in-progress: one with Simon Tookoome, an Inuit hunter and printmaker, and one a book of stories set on north-end Winnipeg's Main Street.

S. PADMANAB was born in Bangalore, India, in 1938. His work has appeared in several periodicals and anthologies, and he has read in numerous cities. He was also a sometime editor of *Grain* magazine. He is a member of the League of Canadian Poets. A physician by profession, he lives in Saskatoon.

BARBARA RENDALL has published poetry and short fiction in Canada and the US, where she was born, since the early 1970s. In 1984-85 she and her husband, Thomas, taught at Xiamen University in southern China. How their children fared, she doesn't say, but the initial culture shock and later fascination with place led her to write a sequence of ten poems, "The Other Side of the World," three of which appear here. The Rendalls spent 1990-91 at the University of East Asia in Macau.

LOIS L. ROSS is a journalist and photographer from Gravelbourg, a francophone community in southern Saskatchewan. She writes both short stories and non-fiction. Her books include *Prairie Lives: The Changing Face of Farming* (Between the Lines, 1985) and *Harvest of Opportunity: New Horizons for Farm Women* (Western Producer/ Prairie Books, 1990).

GLEN SORESTAD is a Saskatchewan writer and publisher who lives in Saskatoon. His latest books of poetry are *West into Night* (Thistledown Press, 1991) and *Air Canada Owls* (Harbour Publishing, 1990). He has a book of stories and two more books of poems "on the go."

RICHARD STEVENSON is the author of numerous collections of poetry including *Driving Offensively, Suiting Up, Horizontal Hotel*, and *Whatever It Is Plants Dream* . . .; he has another forthcoming from Cacanadadada Press. The poems which appear here resulted from two years of teaching in Nigeria. He now lives in Lethbridge, Alberta.

ANNE SZUMIGALSKI says of herself that she is devoted to the prairie and to the word. Her next book, a collection of poetic texts, will appear from Coteau in Fall 1991. She is as modest as she is prolific; her latest book was *The Word, The Voice, The Text* (Fifth House Publishers, 1990).

JOE WELSH has at least one goal in life: to write about the Metis and Indian people of Saskatchewan—both historically and contemporar(il)y.

MARLIS WESSELER is a short-story writer living in Regina. Her work has been broadcast on CBC Radio and has been published in various magazines and in anthologies from Coteau Books—which will release her collection, *Life Skills*, in Fall 1992.

ANDREW WREGGITT is a poet and screenwriter from Calgary, Alberta. He is the author of four poetry books—most recently *Making Movies* (Thistledown Press), which won the 1989 Writers Guild of Alberta poetry award. The poem which appears here was produced as a literary feature for the CBC Radio network program "Speaking Volumes."

VEN BEGAMUDRÉ was born in South India and moved to Canada when he was six. He has also lived in Mauritius and the United States. His publications include the fiction collection *A Planet of Eccentrics* (Oolichan Books, 1990) and the novel *Van de Graaff Days* (forthcoming). Though he grew up somewhat High Anglican, he was born a Madhva Brahmin. If he must be reborn, he hopes it will be on the island of Bali as either a woodworker or piano player (classical and jazz).

JUDITH KRAUSE was born in Regina, where she now lives with her daughter. She studied languages and literature at the University of Regina and l'Universite de Caen, France; she also studied and taught in Switzerland. She has been the Literary Arts Consultant for the Saskatchewan Arts Board and now works as an adult educator. Her first poetry collection was *What We Bring Home* (Coteau Books, 1986). She is working on a second collection, tentatively called *Half the Sky*.

ALBERTO MANGUEL is an editor, critic, translator and journalist. In the first three months of 1991, he brought us two more anthologies: *Soho Square III* (Bloomsbury Press/Penguin) and *Canadian Mystery Stories* (Oxford University Press). He also released his first novel, *News from a Foreign Country Came* (Random House). Between leaving his native Argentina and arriving in Canada, he worked in such places as Italy, Tahiti, France and the United Kingdom.

Acknowledgements

Some stories and poems in *Out of Place* have been previously published or broadcast:

"This is Exactly the Kind of Thing Her Parents Have Been Warning Her About Since She Was a Child" on "Ambience" CBC Radio and in *Event* (spring 1991); "The Margin" in Instar (Red Deer College Press, 1985); "The New Man" on "Ambience" CBC Radio (1987); "Playing the Odds" on Auckland Access Radio (1989); "Angela Davis in Regina" in *Northwest Passage* (Oberon Press, 1990); "Palumello" on "Speaking Volumes" CBC Radio (1990); "Basilico" in *Descant* (1991); "Welcome in Edmonton" in *Heading Out: The New Saskatchewan Poets* (Coteau Books, 1986); "Jerusalem" in *Doctrine of Signatures* (Fifth House, 1983); "Kanadalainen" in *Maria Breaks Her Silence* (Coteau Books, 1989); "Geography" in *Contemporary Verse 2* (summer/fall 1990); "Grandmother" (by Kim Morrissey) in *Batoche* (Coteau Books, 1989); "*Praca Jest Najlepszym Lekarstwen*" in *Poetry Canada* (1983); "In Defense of the Burning of Some Letters" in *Making Movies* (Thistle-down Press, 1989) and on "Speaking Volumes" CBC Radio; "Deadwood" will be in a new collection by Anne Szumigalski (Coteau Books, 1991); "And the Children Shall Rise" in *Grain* (vol xvi, no 1 1988); "Two Kids in a Picture" in *A Few Words for January* (Thistledown Press, 1990); "The Cameo" in *Prairie Fire* (winter 1988/89); "This Business with Elijah" in *Event* (January 1991) and the 1991 *Journey Prize Anthology* (McClelland & Stewart); "Coming to China" on "Ambience" CBC Radio; "Beer at Cochin" and "Number One Guide" in *Hold the Rain in Your Hands* (Coteau Books, 1985); "Shooting Pigeons" in *The Greenfield Review* (winter/spring 1983/84) and *Horizontal Hotel: A Nigerian Odyssey* (TSAR Publications, 1989); "Pineapple" will be in *Delta Hushpuppies* (Penumbra Press, 1991); "The Wall" in *Grain* (summer 1987); "A Photo for Daheru" in *Acta Victoriana* (spring 1984) and *Driving Offensively* (Sono Nis Press, 1985); "Pastoral" in *Ages of Birds* (Writers Workshop, 1976); "At Fifty-Three" in *A Separate Life* (Writers Workshop, 1974); "From the Gateway Between Us" on Auckland Access Radio (1990) and in *Mother Tongue* (summer 1990); "Jump Sunday" in *dandelion* (vol 13, no 2); "The Itinerary" in *Event* (vol 18, no 2); "The Collaborators" on "Air Craft" CBC Radio (1989); and "Horizons" in *Poet's Gallery* (1991).